Sir Walter Besant

A Fountain Sealed

A Novel

Sir Walter Besant

A Fountain Sealed
A Novel

ISBN/EAN: 9783337032548

Printed in Europe, USA, Canada, Australia, Japan

Cover: Foto ©Andreas Hilbeck / pixelio.de

More available books at **www.hansebooks.com**

A FOUNTAIN SEALED

A Novel

BY

SIR WALTER BESANT

AUTHOR OF

"The Master Craftsman," "The City of Refuge," "All Sorts and
Conditions of Men," "Armorel of Lyonesse," etc.

New York and London

Frederick A. Stokes Company

PUBLISHERS

CONTENTS.

LIST OF ILLUSTRATIONS

A FOUNTAIN SEALED.

PROLOGUE.

Her Majesty's Own Words.

AT noon, by the shadow of my sundial in the middle
of the grass; by the striking of the clock in the tower
of Hackney Church; by the disappearance of the shadows from the side walls of my garden, which lie
exactly north and south; I was taking the air upon
the lawn. It was, I remember, Saturday morning,
September 16th, in the year of grace 1780. The day,
though the season was already advanced into autumn,
was fair and warm; the orchard was still pleasing to
the eye, those apples not yet gathered showing like
balls of vermilion and gold: the summer flowers were
nearly over, yet there were still some; the sweet peas,
which had been that year more than commonly luxu-
riant, were now piled in a heap of brown seed-pods,
brown leaves, and grey stalks, yet there were blossoms
still among them : there were late roses still in bloom ;
the jessamine on the wall was still dotted with a few
white sweet-smelling blossoms—it is a scent which
makes the senses reel and the heart beat—it recalls old
memories. Wherefore I, who now for twenty years

2   A Fountain Sealed.

live wholly in the past, love that blossom. There were hollyhocks, the flowers finished, all but one or two on the very top of their drooping heads; sunflowers gone to seed weighing down the thick stalk; trailing nas-turtium; flaunting marigolds, which refuse to believe that winter is nigh; mignonette lying all across the path, its stalks breaking at a touch, its little delicate flow'rets without scent yet still beautiful. The soft air breathed a pleasing fragrance; there was no breeze. Such consolations of lingering flowers and perfumed air doth the autumn offer to those who are grow-ing old and have retired from the world. With that strange pride of man, which allows him to regard na-ture as reflecting his own moods, as if the round earth, and all that therein is, had nothing to do but to watch his thoughts and to act in sympathy with them, I chose to take this warm, sweet autumn morning as granted especially to myself, and so sat on the garden bench, or strolled across the lawn, and along the walks, with a mind contented and grateful. The humble-bee who rolled heavily about like some great river barge on the flowing tide, reeling from flower to flower, covered all over with white dust, boomed its monotonous song for me: the honey-bee buzzed louder—a note of accompaniment and solace—for me: the yellow wasp fluttered about among the peaches— for me to see his beauty: a thrush sat on a pear-tree, singing, late as it was in the year—for me. What they said, or sang, I know not, but they filled my mind with peace and such happiness—that of resigna-tion—as can befall a woman such as I am—lonely—

bereaved—with no change before me—and with such a past as mine to look back upon.

It was my own garden, lying at the back of my own house: a large and richly furnished garden behind the house of a gentlewoman. At the end of the garden is a wicket-gate which I sometimes open in order to gaze across the broad valley of the Lea. From the elevation on which my house stands I can see below me the whole expanse of low meadows called the Hackney Flats, intersected with ditches here and there. This morning a light mist rolled over them— not the cold marshy exhalation which all through winter lies upon them by day and night, but a gentle vaporous veil through which I could discern the river winding in the midst; and beyond the river more flats; and beyond the flats the low green hills of Essex, looking upon which, on such a day as this, with the sunshine lying on them, the heart goes up to heaven, and the distant hills remind one of the everlasting rest to come when all tears shall be wiped away and the memory of former sorrows will only show as steps by which the soul hath climbed.

This morning I saw smoke mounting straight to the sky from the bank of the river: 'twas an encampment of the thievish people called gipsies; only a week before they had robbed my poultry-yard. Thus do thoughts and memories of evil always mar the thing most beautiful upon the earth. I shut the wicket and locked it, and turned back to the house.

My own house: my own garden: all that is contained in either is mine. I received them as a gift:

and I have resolved upon telling you why I accepted this gift and from whom it came.

Twenty years and more had I lived in this house alone, save for Molly, my faithful woman. A long time: a peaceful time: a time without pain or disease of the body, without any anxiety of the mind except for the natural sadness which can never leave a mind so full of memories: yet from time to time I am disturbed as I consider the place and remember that I am the owner of all. Mine is the house: mine the books, the furniture, the plate, the wardrobe, the jewels, the garden, the orchard, the greenhouses—everything mine. Yet what kind of price have I paid for these things? Whenever I arrive at this question, my heart beats and my cheek changes colour. If I am in the house I make haste to open a desk and to take from it two miniatures. The one represents him who was once my lover; the other, the fondest, faithfullest friend that ever woman had. These, too, were mine, and they represented the price that I had paid. You shall hear, if you will listen. Good name and reputation I had given; friends and relations I had abandoned; obscurity I had accepted—nay, embraced. No anchoress woman in her cage was more lonely than I, whom no one ever visited except one friend of that undying past and the Rector of Hackney—a good and worthy man who still, against his will, believes the worst that can be whispered of me and waits for the time when I shall make confession. This was a grievous price for a woman, then young, of good repute, well connected, and of pious conversation. I say that this was indeed a heavy price to pay. At the time I counted not the cost. Indeed, I willingly paid the price. Yes, and I would pay it all over again : the loss of name and reputation ; the burden of a shameful story : for nobody in the world who once knew me or has heard tell of me—to be sure, there are not many—but whispers evil things about me and believes the worst. Their whispers do not reach me here : the things that they believe do me no harm. I am dead to scandal : I am dead to the world : I live here, now a woman of forty and more : I hear nothing that is said and know nothing that is done. All my life lies in a brief season of three short months. It is but a little time to make a life, but I live it over and over and over again : I am never tired of letting my memory dwell upon every day of that short time. I desire no other Heaven than to live that brief time over and over again, from the first even- ing when those two, whose miniatures I keep, came to my help, down to the last morning when we parted, never to meet again. Oh! Name, fame, rumour, scandal, reputation—all—all—all would I freely give over and over again and think them of no account for the dear sake of that brief time and of that most god- like lover !

At the thought of that time, house and garden and orchard and lawns, the breath of summer, the blue of the sky, the sunshine, all vanish : they sink and fall and disappear. I am once more in the parlour of the house in St. James's Place, and my heart is beating and my cheek is glowing because I know that he is

coming and because he loves me. Yes—he loves me
—me, the first. To myself I dare to own and to avow
it : I confess it with a front of brass : I glory in the
memory of it : I am so proud of it that I can hardly
contain myself : on Sunday when I walk to church,
Molly—the faithful, fond Molly—who alone knows all
the truth, behind me, I dress myself in my best silk ;
I wear my gold chain ; I draw on my best silk gloves,
and I walk down the aisle to my pew with head erect
and proud bearing. The world knows not why ; but
Molly knows : Molly says to herself, as she carries
Bible and prayer-book, " Madam does well to bear herself proudly. Madam has been loved by——" But
this we never say : we only think it. Some things
there are that must not even be whispered.

Now, as I was meditating this morning, not for the
first time, nor for the hundredth, upon these things,
there came running into the garden Molly herself—
and at the sight of her the past vanished again and the
present returned.

"Madam," she said, quickly, "there is my Lord's
carriage coming up the road : his runners are even
now standing at the door, but the carriage is stuck in
last year's ruts. They are lifting it over. Shall I lay
out your black silk frock? You have time."

There was but one noble Lord who ever came
to see me : there was no occasion to name him.
He was the one friend who remained to me of the
past.

"Molly," I said, "I will put on my grey silk, and,
if there is time, touch my hair before my Lord arrives.

And give the runners, while his carriage stands at the door, a drink of ale and a piece of cheese."

So presently, in my grey silk and my gold chain and lace gloves, I descended the stairs and found his Lordship waiting for me in the best parlour.

Robert, Viscount de Lys, was at this time nearly fifty years of age. Too great a devotion to the bottle in his early manhood had produced in him symptoms which threatened to cut short his earthly pilgrimage. Indeed, he died about three months after this visit, which was the last time that I saw him. The gout flying about him, settled in his stomach, where it killed him after inflicting terrible pains. As befits his rank, he was buried in Westminster Abbey, where, I am told (for I have not seen it) that a marble monument represents him as borne up to Heaven, with the Star of the Bath upon his breast, by two angels. Indeed, I hope that his soul has received the reward of everlasting happiness, though it must be owned that during life, like many other gentlemen of Quality, he lived as if the means of grace were not intended for persons of rank, and as if they had no occasion to regard the next world with either fear or hope. Yet a man of kindly heart and generous, and, except for this vice of drinking, of a cleanly life. To me he was always loyal and true. Wherefore, if the prayers of the living could help the dead, Lord de Lys should have my prayers, night and day.

On this day he hobbled, leaning on his gold-headed cane more than was customary with him. His feet were in soft shoes; his fingers were swollen at the joints; his face was red; his eyes were bloodshot; his voice was husky. He was sitting in the window-seat looking across my front garden planted with box cut into shapes.

"Madam," he said, rising with difficulty, and kissing my hand—he always had the finest manners in the world—"I need not, I am sure, repeat that I am always your most obedient servant to command in anything."

"Your Lordship," I replied, "is, which is much better, always my kindest friend." Compliments mean little, yet show friendliness. For instance, when one gazes upon a man who is the mere pitiful wreck of what he once was; when one remembers what he once was—how tall and gallant and comely; and when one tells that man that he looks well but for the touch of gout in his feet—which, indeed, is a good sign, for gout is better out than in—why, one means nothing but the assurance of friendly interest. Such compliments passed, we sat down, and came at once to the business in hand.

"Madam," he said, "I have in my possession—they have been lent to me by the person to whom they are addressed for the express purpose of showing them to you—certain letters which give me a pretext for making this visit."

"Then am I vastly obliged to the letters. They concern me, I may presume, in some way or other."

"They will certainly interest you. You shall judge for yourself how they concern yourself."

"What letters can they be? You awaken my curiosity, my Lord."

"They are written by a certain Person—whom you once knew—to Lord North."

"Oh! But . . . What has Lord North to do with me? Why does that Person write to Lord North about me?"

"Lord North has nothing to do with you. He does not even know of your existence."

"Then, how can they concern me? My Lord, do not without reason remind me that the world is cruel and censorious and believes the worst."

"I do not seek to do so, Madam, I assure you. Indeed, you have so often informed me of the true relations—I mean, of the true friendship once existing between yourself and a certain Person—that I thought you would like to see these letters, which, in fact, corroborate your information."

"If you wish me to read them I will do so, though I do not desire. I had thought that nothing would ever occur which would bring me back to the world again—or bring the world to me."

"Believe me, dear Madam, I would not willingly disturb your rest, since it is your pleasure to live buried in this solitude. But these letters you must, indeed, read, if only for your own satisfaction."

"But, my Lord, once more: how does Lord North know anything about me?"

"I know not. I am sure that he knows nothing definite about you. I am the only person now living who knows anything about the matter."

"Are you quite sure that you know the story, my Lord?"

"Can any man know more of a woman than she chooses to tell?"

"I am still waiting to know what Lord North thinks or has heard."

"There are rumours—quite uncertain and vague—about the early life of the Person aforesaid: I suppose, because alone among those of his rank he hath led, and still doth lead, an unspotted life. People, as a rule, do not like those in very high places to be virtuous: every Prince must needs commit the common sins in order to win the love of the multitude: his faults, I suppose, bring him down to the common level. Very well, these rumours cling to a certain house in St. James's Place, and to a certain lady who once lived there."

"The rumour is, of course, the worst that can be invented?"

"It varies. The lady ran away with him: the lady married him secretly—it varies according to the imagination or the inventive faculty of the person handing it on: it grows: it becomes embellished: your name is known: your religion is known: nothing else is certain. People turn into St. James's Place when they wish to calumniate that person, and point to the house and tell their story."

"Nothing matters to me now, since I am retired from the world."

"Lord North, therefore, called upon me. He said to me, 'Rumour credits you with knowing something of certain passages which formerly happened in the life of—this Person.' I replied that it was true that accident had placed me in possession of facts which could not be published."

" In a word, my Lord, you allowed Lord North to believe that these disgraceful rumours were true," I replied, but would say no more, thinking of the price I had paid for this house.

" Nothing of the kind, dear Madam, I assure you. He wished me to confess that these rumours were true, but I refused. He then lugged out these letters and asked me to read them. ' If,' he said, ' any other person knows the facts of the case, let that person also read the letters. He, or she, will understand that now, if ever, the most absolute silence must be observed.' "

" But if there is nothing that need be concealed ? "

" So far as I can see, the whole world may read the letters. If," he added, "any money were wanted for the purchase of other letters——"

" Do not insult me, my Lord."

" Pardon me, Madam. I do but repeat what he said."

" The letters, you tell me, come from—a certain Person. Does that Person know of this message of yours ? "

" I believe not. I should say, not. My own existence is probably forgotten by that Person. He desires, apparently, to bury in oblivion a certain passage in his life. Would he, then, be thought more—or less —than Man ? "

" He is more than Man," I replied. " The ordinary man cannot contemplate such virtues as were hers.

Now, my Lord, it is idle to talk about secrecy. I, who might have enjoyed notoriety at least, which is a kind of fame, have accepted obscurity and silence. Is it likely that I am going to attempt notoriety after twenty years and more? As for money—you know why I took certain gifts, once and for all, though I had no need of any gifts, or any help whatever in that way."

"Madam,"—he bowed again—" your conduct has been always full of dignity, and worthy of that passion which was once lavished upon you."

"Then," I said, " without more words, let me see these letters."

He took out of his pocket a book in which lay two letters. "You will, I believe," he said, " recognise the handwriting."

I did. I had one letter—only one—in the same handwriting, which was little changed. He opened and gave me one of the letters. It had reference to the creation of a separate establishment for the writer's eldest son. The following passage halfway down caught my eyes: " I thank Heaven that my morals and course of life have but little resembled those prevalent in the present age : and certainly of all the objects of this life, the one I have most at heart is to form my children that they may become useful examples and worthy of imitation."

"Well," I said, " the sentiment is worthy of the writer."

"And his gratitude is, no doubt, based on a sound and solid foundation."

"Assuredly," I replied. "Is this all you have to show me?"

"There is the other letter," he said, handing it to me with curiosity in his eyes.

It was a letter of a very private character. I felt that I had no right to be reading it: the letter was not meant for the eyes of any one but Lord North. At the end of it was this passage: "I am happy at being able to say that I never was personally engaged in such a transaction, which makes me feel this business the stronger."

"Such a transaction," his Lordship repeated. "He means an amour—a pre-nuptial amour."

"Not at all. It means that his son has become involved in some love affair of a low and disgraceful kind: that he has now, in order to avoid the exposure which the disgraceful woman threatens, to buy back letters. This Person writes that he has no such odious business on his conscience: that he has never written letters which the whole world might not read: that there is no creature living who either could or would threaten him. That is the meaning, my Lord, of this passage."

"It seems to me, rather, as if his memory was playing him false. Such a transaction. Has he, then, forgotten everything?"

"Go on, my Lord." But my cheek burned.

"Nay! All I would say is that at the present juncture it is highly important that the—the—passage I referred to should not be whispered about. The effect might be most mischievous. It must not even be known that the writer of this letter was ever engaged in any love affair at all before his marriage, not even a simple and platonic affair of conversation only, and, you will allow me to observe, the censorious might ask why a mere friendship was rewarded by a comfortable allowance in the country."

"One moment, my Lord," I interrupted him. "This house and the annuity on which I live were not given me by the writer of this letter. Let me assure you quite seriously upon this point. If you have thought otherwise, pray think so no longer."

"Indeed," he said thoughtfully. "Then I know not who——But, dear Madam, why should I give you pain? I have shown you the letters. I have told you what Lord North said. I have nothing to add."

"About secrecy; who is there left to talk about the affair? You, my Lord, will never speak about it to any one. His brother Edward died—alas!—seven years after it. Corporal Bates was killed in action. Molly doesn't talk; my cousin Isabel is dead; Mr. Robert Storey is dead: he died a bankrupt, poor wretch! in the Fleet. The Doctor, old Mr. Mynsterchamber, went abroad, I believe, and must now be dead. Mrs. Bates, the widow, may know something, but very little——"

"Dear Madam, there remain only you and I and Molly. Yet this Mrs. Bates—it may be that through her the rumours have spread. It is strange how rumours arise and grow and are spread around. Well, we cannot help rumours and whispers: we cannot silence the world. It is enough for me to assure

Lord North that there is no danger of anything worse than a whisper; or more dangerous than scandalous gossip. There will be no proof that the son is only treading in the footprints of his father. Let us now, dear Madam, talk of things more pleasant and, to me, more interesting than of rumours which attack your name."

We talked long and earnestly: there was much to recall—the treachery of the Doctor, the good fortune of the Corporal, the evening of the masquerade, and many, many other things of which he knew a little and thought he knew a great deal. We sat talking together in my best parlour for three or four hours.

" Nancy," he said—for, having taken a glass or two while we talked, he had gone back to the past, when it was Fair Nancy, or Cruel Nancy or Conquering Nancy, or Heartless Nancy, or Nancy the Toast, or any other compliment that he might light upon, in a word—his imagination was inflamed to some degree —" Nancy, whenever I remember that happy time when a bottle—nay, three bottles—brought nothing worse in the morning than an aching head, and when I gazed daily upon thy charms—ah! sweet Nancy"— he laid his hand upon mine, but a twinge of the gout caused him to draw it back swiftly—" I say—devil take this gout!—that whenever I think of that time it is your heavenly face that still I see."

" Through the bottles, my Lord ? "

" Perhaps." He sighed. " We could see through half-a-dozen bottles in those days. Thy face, Madam Nancy, was lovely then, and 'tis, I swear, lovely still.

But in those days, for the angelic sweetness and tenderness of it, I say that it had no equal."

"Your Lordship is so good as to pay me compliments."

"They are the truth, not compliments at all. And this being the case, even though you should a thousand times affirm the contrary, out of your constancy and fidelity, I will never believe that a certain Person did not think so as well. Come, Nancy, we are old friends : I am discretion itself : it is an old story : tell me : was this person a stock and a stone ? "

"Certainly he was neither stock nor stone. Yet, my Lord, the words written in these letters are the truth."

"Ta-ra-ra ! Ta-ra-ra ! " said his Lordship. " 'Twas ever the most obstinate piece—as well as the loveliest."

His Lordship, I know very well, always took pleasure in my society. On this occasion—though he kept his horses standing in the road and his people waiting for him—though as to that he paid no heed—he remained talking with me, I say, for nearly four hours. It pleases me now to think with what kindness and remembrance he spoke of the past which he had in a measure shared. Yet, for all I could say, I perceived that he could not believe one word as to my relations with the Person above referred to. By this time I was accustomed to this disbelief which at the outset cut me to the soul. What did I say above? The price was name and fame and reputation—all the things that a woman most highly prizes. And I had

paid that price. Not one word did my Lord believe
—affirm it as I might—as to the truth of those two
letters. He laughed : he put it off with a smile, with
the uplifting of his eyebrows, with a gentle inclination of his head, with the wave of his hand, with a
" Nay, Madam, since you say so," with a pinch of
snuff.

" Well," said I, seized with a sudden thought, " doth
not Heaven itself send some thoughts, while the Devil
if we admit him into the chambers of Imagery, as the
Prophet calls them, sends others ? Advise me, my
Lord. I am now past forty——"

" For most women it is a great age. You are still
young, however. At forty I already hobbled : I am
now nearly fifty, with both feet hanging over the
grave. But for my advice. How can I advise thee,
Nancy ? "

" I know not what length of days may remain to
me. But I think that perhaps some part of the al-
lotted space might be spent in dissipating whispers or
contradicting scandals which may be flying around
concerning this Person."

" For the moment it would, perhaps, be best to observe silence."

" Yet you say that there are whispers——"

" Undoubtedly there are. When a certain Person
is observed, or is rumoured—his face was not absolutely unknown in the neighbourhood of St. James's—
to visit a certain house : when it is ascertained that a
certain lady of that name really lived there——"

" Add, if you please, that the lady was always accompanied by another lady; and the Person was always accompanied by his brother——"

"These, observe, are facts which the world does not know. Let me add that when this lady disappears suddenly: when no one, not even her own friends, know where she is . . . then . . ." He took a pinch of snuff and shrugged his shoulders.

"Granted the whispers: would it not suffice if I wrote down exactly the truth as it happened—for the sake of the reputation of the Person concerned?"

"Why," he replied, "the world would be very much interested: the booksellers would be enriched: the Person concerned would not be grateful: the lady would not be cleared: and the whispers would go on."

"Still—it is surely best always to have the truth told."

"No one, certainly, would tell it so well as you, dear lady. Besides," he laughed, "what woman could desire a more pleasing task than to relate in her own words the history of her own amours?"

The words seemed, at the time, mocking and heartless. Lord de Lys sometimes spoke in this light and satirical voice: he meant, I thought, that a woman could thus hide what she wished, and reveal what would set her in a better light. However, they were wise words as I now understand. No one, sure, knows the heart of a woman so well as herself.

"My Lord," I replied, "pleasing or not, I am resolved"—the resolution was formed at that moment only—"to commit to writing a full and complete history of an affair concerning which the world knows nothing—not for the clearing of my own reputation, of which I care nothing, for in this secluded spot nothing reaches me : but for the reputation of another."

" Well, Nancy, I think the world will like its own version best. Tell the truth, dear woman, by all means ; and the world will fall in love with thee : and, what is more, will remain in love with thee, long after thou art laid in Hackney Churchyard. Tell the truth : nothing could possibly do more to raise the soul of a young man than to love the idea and the presentment of such a woman as thyself."

"Not compliments, my Lord; but as much advice as you please."

"Then, Nancy, my advice is this. If you write about love, talk little of other matters. Let your discourse be always of love. Speak not of affairs of State : keep the lover always before your readers. Let them have the voice of love and see the eyes of love. Do not dwell at length upon your previous history or your later history, or anything except what is necessary to show how he fell in love with you, and why. Tell the world who you were and what you were, and then let the Tragedy—or the Comedy—begin. When the love tale is ended, close the volume : draw a line : write ' Finis ' below—walk off the stage, and do not let your lover lag behind."

This seemed sensible advice. As my story concerns one person mostly, I must write about little but what concerned him.

" I will try to remember your advice. Meantime, my Lord, here is something for your own ears. You spoke about the fact of a certain lady retiring into obscurity in affluence. I know, of course, what was meant; I have known all along that such a thing would be meant. This house is mine, and it was given to me. I have lived in it since November, 1760. It was given to me at my own request. On the evening of the day when we parted—on October the 25th, 1760, his brother Edward came to see me."

"I met him walking across St. James's Place, I remember."

"He came to me. He remained with me alone for some time: he spoke most tenderly and sorrowfully: he took all the blame upon himself: he confessed that he ought to have told me all at the outset : he asked what I proposed to do: he agreed that I could not go home to live with my brother, which would be worse than anything : he promised that his own lawyers should make him give up my fortune : then, with a noble generosity, he offered to give me what I asked of him—a house in the country, so that I could always feel that I belonged still, and all my life should belong, to his brother and to him."

" Madam," said Lord de Lys, "upon my word, you amaze me. For twenty years I have believed that this house, with an annuity, was given to you by that Person."

" This is the literal truth. I knew what would be said and thought by those who knew some of the circumstances of the case. But I have told you the literal truth. More : this most generous of men, this fond and faithful friend, came often to see me until he left the country on his last voyage, from which he was nevermore to return. No one can ever know with what a truly brotherly love he regarded me, and how he lamented with me the bitterness of fate which dashed from my lips the cup which was just prepared for me. My Lord, the world knows not what a heart of gold was lost when Edward—I still must call him by his Christian name—when my brother—yes, my brother—Edward died."

"Nancy, tell me no more. Why should I revive the tears of the past? Well—give me a sailor—should every woman say : 'tis only a sailor who does the truly generous things."

It was then four o'clock. Molly opened the door to tell me that dinner was served.

" My Lord, I have for dinner a simple breast of veal roasted, stuffed. Molly is a plain cook, but I warrant the roast wholesome and good. There will also be some sweet-pudding or fruit-pie : and I can give you a bottle of good wine, I believe, if you will honour me with your company at my humble meal."

He condescended to dine with me. His appetite, as I feared, was not good : indeed, he could eat but little : yet he complimented Molly on her stuffing, and he professed to find the pudding delicious.

After dinner Molly placed a bottle of port on the table. My Lord took it up with affectionate, though swollen fingers.

" I have loved thee too well," he said, addressing the bottle, not Molly. " But for the warmth—nay— the ardour of my passion for this ruby liquid wherein

I found man's chief felicity, I might now be kneeling at sweet Nancy's feet. Thou hast rewarded me, ungrateful divinity, with ten thousand red-hot needles. Nevertheless, as an invalid, a veteran—a discharged soldier—I must still worship." He filled two glasses. "Madam," he said, "I will drink to you. Strange it is—oh! wondrous strange!" he gazed upon me with admiring eyes—"we have been talking over the past —and behold!—it is a miracle!—your former face has come back to you. Memory is a witch. Your face, divine Nancy, is now once more as young: your eyes are as clear: your cheek is as soft—oh! the peach blossom on that cheek: as twenty years ago, when that young—Person—paid to all those charms the adoration of a maiden heart. Nancy—*à vos beaux yeux!* Could he again behold thee—could he get rid——"

"My Lord! you must not, indeed, talk in this strain. It is unbecoming for one of your station, and it afflicts me to hear such discourse. In this house we take one glass of wine a day—Molly and I—and we drink it to the health and safety of that certain Person."

He bowed. He gave me a glass and poured out one for Molly, who stood beside my high-backed armchair.

I stood up, glass in hand. "I drink," I said, "or rather, I pray, for the continued health, happiness, and safety of the noblest man in these three Kingdoms."

Molly fell upon her knees. "By your leave,

"MADAM, I DRINK THE HEALTH OF THAT PERSON." — *Page 22.*

Madam," she said, " I drink to the health and happiness of your friend." These words we exchanged in fact every day after dinner. To me, if I may say so in all respect, they were a kind of daily Sacrament.

His Lordship rose with some difficulty. " Nancy," he said, " your heart is all constancy and fidelity. It moves me. . . . I wonder if any man born of an earthly mother was ever worth a heart so true and tender. Madam, I drink the health of that Person— once your lover—His Majesty the King!"

CHAPTER I.

On the River Darenth.

IF I shut my eyes and let my memory go back to early days I see a substantial square house: in the front stand two goodly cedars sweeping the lawn: a brick wall shuts out the house from the high road: there are two gates with iron railings of fine workmanship: from the gates one can see a large mass of low buildings—they are paper-mills, belonging to a Quaker named Samuel Walden: the river Darenth flows past the mills: about a mile away there stands the town of Dartford.

The house is cold within and gloomy: it seems a house which never gets any sunshine, yet the rooms are lofty and the windows are high and broad; the furniture is massive and costly: yet, for the bareness of the walls and the absence of ornament, the place might pass for a prison.

At the back of the house is a most beautiful garden, broad, well cultivated, full of everything that an English garden can yield. I see a child running about that garden under the shade of trees and across sunny lawns. The place is lonely and silent, save for the birds in the trees. Sometimes there flits across the grass a pale drooping figure in the grey Quaker dress and white cap: sometimes she is sitting in the shade; sometimes she is looking at the child: but mostly she is wrapped in meditation. It is the child's mother, who is like an anchoress of old, inasmuch as she spends most of her life in considering the Divine Scheme of Redemption: she speaks little at any time, even at meeting: in the Roman Church she would be a saint, and work miracles: in the English Communion she would be accounted a holy woman. In my recollection I always see her thus, a silent ghost meditating in the garden. Also in my memory summer and sunshine always remain; rain and cold have vanished. Always I see the fruit turning from green to gold: always I breathe the fragrance of the flowers: always the air is soft and warm: there is always blue sky: there are always shadows on the lawn, and they slowly turn, so that I know the time by their position as well as by the sundial in the middle of the grass. I can always see the honey-bees staggering under the weight of their burdens; the flowers are always in blossom: I can see them still—roses, lilies, sunflowers, hollyhocks, love-lies-bleeding, ragged robin, ivy's love, lavender, pansy, clove, pink, convolvulus, stocks, sweet-william —all that you may find in any garden.

The child has no playmates, no toys or dolls, she knows only such games as her imagination has invented for her. She has never heard any of the foolish stories of fairies, lovely damsels, brave lads, and happy lovers which are told to children of the world, whereby their thoughts are turned to things of the world: she has read no book except portions of the

Bible, because the godly books on the shelf have no attraction for her.

The child has never heard the sound of music: in the house there was no fond tinkling of the guitar, no uplifting of the voice with a love ditty.

The child has never seen a picture or a drawing of any kind. There were no pictures in the house at all—not a single representation of even a tree or a flower, to say nothing of man, woman, or child.

The child has never heard the sound of laughter— no one in that house ever laughed. The Society of Friends, indeed, have for the most part forgotten how to laugh. Nothing to them is ridiculous; certainly not the sight of a man suddenly suffering pain, which always excites mirth in the mind bucolic; nor the sight of a man in bewilderment, consternation, or amazement, which makes the littler sort to laugh. It was a grave household even for one of that Society. The master of the house was always serious and full of thought, divided between his religion and his affairs: the mistress was, as I have said, greatly occupied in religious meditation.

On Sundays in the silent Meeting-house, while the clock ticked and the members sat with closed eyes, meditating and waiting to be moved, the child looked through an open door upon a green enclosure, which was the burial ground. There were no head-stones or altar tombs, or monuments of any kind. The memory of the dead was not preserved: except for two small slabs, each containing initials, there was nothing to tell who slept beneath : they were godly people who lived and died, and went to Heaven. What were they doing in Heaven? the child asked. Sitting apart in a Meeting-house, doubtless, out of sight or hearing of the golden harps. The child wanted no tombstones to know the people who lay in the ground : they were sitting around her in the Meeting-house: the ghosts of the dead—though she knew nothing about ghosts —sat with the living and waited for the Divine prompting of the Word.

Among such people, the child of such people, did this child grow up. Picture to yourself what kind of child she would become!

Often in the winter evenings it pleases me to recall these old days. There were many things which as a child I neither observed nor understood—such, for instance, as the stiffness and wooden carriage of both men and women. To me, after more than twenty years' knowledge of the world, I still contrast the courtesy of a wellbred man ; the graceful movement of a gentlewoman ; the unconscious ease with which young people of the world move and speak ; with the stiffness which I used to consider part of our holy calling. I blush to remember how my own brother moved with the constraint of a wooden image : how he spoke with harsh voice ignorant of music or of modulation : how he said things uncouth because he enjoyed no softening influence of society to teach him civility.

As for knowledge of the outer world I only knew that it was the freehold property of the devil, the men and women in it being merely his tenants. Surely this was a most wicked thing to believe.

Yet let me not be harsh : let me still remember, honour, and obey the Fifth Commandment. There are no people more charitable than the Friends. My father's hand was always extended in charity to the unhappy; my mother was always making and contriving for the poor.

When these two died I, being about fifteen, was left alone save for my brother Joseph, my guardian.

My brother was twelve years older than myself, therefore already a man, and on that account alone, perhaps, not a companion for a young girl. For other reasons, however, he could not become a companion. It would not be enough to say of Joseph that no one ever saw him smile, because no one in the house was expected to smile, not to speak of laughing—how can one laugh when one cannot forget the small number of the Elect? Of Joseph it might be said that he never even pretended to be cheerful. He knew not the meaning of youthful sallies, of youthful gaieties, of youthful longings : indeed, there was not much scope for youthful sallies in our house. On one account his friends were able to be proud of him : he was perfectly and literally acquainted with certain portions of Holy Writ, and that above any of his fellows—namely, those passages in St. Paul's Epistles which support the doctrine to which Joseph clung as to the very small number of the Elect. Out of those passages he sucked abundant matter for the religious controversies in which he delighted. He spoke often at meeting, and if he failed to persuade he succeeded in terrifying. How can mortal presume so to limit and narrow the mercy of the Most High?

There was another point about Joseph which caused him to be respected by, if not endeared to, many of his brethren—namely, that he proved himself from the very outset a most prudent, far-seeing, keen man of business. Of course, if a young man has to enter upon trade it is well that he should make himself an accomplished tradesman. But it is not good for a man to think about nothing except trade and religion.

In appearance Joseph was always stern, gloomy, and forbidding: his hair was black; he had bushy black eyebrows and strong black eyes; he was tall and thin; he carried himself bolt upright and walked with a gold-headed stick. He had no private friends, such as most young men have: nor did he desire the company of any, but if company came he discoursed upon things religious. He showed no inclination towards the other sex, but held that woman must be in all things submissive to man. In the evening he sat apart, with the ledgers and account-books of the mills spread out before him, and he would groan in anguish if he discovered that the profit account was less than he hoped. He read no books; he took no interest in the political situation of his country: he never knew, or cared, whether the State which protected him and allowed him to become rich was at peace or at war, whether it was triumphant or humiliated. He was what is called a gross feeder, sitting down to meat with eagerness; and he drank largely, especially of the wine called Madeira. Yet he was never fuddled or the worse for wine: indeed I now remember that the more Madeira he took the more resolute he became still more to diminish the number of the Elect, insomuch that after the second bottle there would remain nothing but a poor remnant.

Some children there are who are born for happiness, some whose nature cannot bear happiness. If the former do not obtain what they naturally crave after, they become afflicted in some way. I think, nay, I am sure, that I was one of those who were born for happiness: as I grew out of childhood, and found no happiness, but only a perpetual gloom with the necessity of thinking continually about the safety of my soul, there fell upon me a dreadful sickness of the brain. It came to me when I was in my twenty-first year. Even to think of that sickness fills my mind, after more than twenty years, with horror unspeakable. I fall to trembling when I remember that sickness. It was a despondency which attacked me, first, as to things spiritual: I was convinced that my soul was lost. Then a strange heaviness fell upon me. I cared for none of my former amusements or occupations: neither for the flowers in the garden; nor for the singing of the birds; nor for reading in the Bible. I wished not to eat; I could not carry on any housewifery.

In plain words, I suffered from melancholia. Some physicians call it hysteria, I believe. Whatever its name, those were its symptoms.

The further symptoms of my disorder, then, were, first a strange disinclination to undertake anything: the mind refused to follow a simple argument: I wandered about alone, doing nothing: I would burst into tears without a cause: I lay awake at night: I had swoons and beating of the heart. Further, it vexed me that Molly, my maid, would try to divert me with strange gifts—such things as sailors bring from foreign ports: tears would gather in her eyes while she watched me. I would fly to the garden, then in the beauty of spring, yet found no comfort there: I would be alone, but solitude made me still more wretched: I would compose my mind and reduce my wandering thoughts to order, but could not. There is no misery—believe me—so great as to find that you have lost control over the mind.

In the morning I awoke with apprehensions—I knew not why. The day before me became a burden too heavy to be borne: the night behind me was a wilderness of unbidden thoughts and uncalled voices. In one word, I was possessed, I say, with the demon of melancholy, which is to the mind what leprosy is to the body if it be not expelled.

Then terrible thoughts and temptations entered my head—can the soul be destroyed while the mind is in this condition of slavery? I thought that the only way out of this wretchedness was death: and then since it had not pleased the Lord to call me I must take the matter into my own hands.

There was a deep black pond in the field beyond the garden: a willow hung over it: steep banks surrounded it. Whenever the temptation of death was put into my mind—I say put into my mind because of my own will could I never think of such a thing—I remembered this pond.

One morning—the birds were singing and the garden was full of flowers and the orchard was gay with blossoms—I was made to think of this place. I cannot call it my own action: I was dragged—I cannot acknowledge that I walked—I say that I was dragged by invisible hands—in the direction of the pond. My heart beat; I was agitated by the horror of the thing which yet I could not escape. I reached the bank: I stood over the dark waters: a moment more and I should have fallen in—say, rather, I should have been dragged in. Already I felt the bitterness of death: I tried to pray, but could not: I felt the despair of the soul that is lost—when suddenly I was pulled back. 'Twas my maid Molly who pulled me back: and at sight of my face, which was wan and white, she cried out, "Oh! Nancy! Nancy!" and fell on her knees clasping her hands and weeping.

After that she attended upon me day and night: I was not left to myself—but the temptation did not return; the violence of the disorder left me. Yet I was dull and apathetic, taking no interest in what was said or done. My brother sent for a physician, who came with his great wig and his gold-headed cane. He talked much: I know not what he said, but I daresay he discoursed very learnedly. Still, however, I remained in the same condition doing nothing, saying nothing, thinking nothing. And it seemed as if melancholy had indeed seized me, and that no more was to be expected, for the rest of my life, except that incurable distraction of the mind which we call madness.

There was a certain cousin, Isabel by name, a young widow, having been the wife of Mr. Reuben Storey, my mother's nephew. She came to see me: she was greatly shocked at my condition, and after a while she proposed to my brother to take me away to her own lodging, in London, there to give me change of air and of scene.

My brother was, I think, glad to get rid of a girl in such a condition. He put me off upon his cousin with the greatest alacrity. And so I was carried to London.

Now, remember that my cousin was dressed in Quaker garb, the widow of a Quaker, herself, so far as any of us knew, still a Quakeress, though she was not born in the Society: that my brother would never have allowed me to enter any house that did not belong to some member of the Society: that she was always demure and quiet in Joseph's presence: and that she never once before this revealed herself in any other light than that of a consistent Friend.

What, then, was my surprise when, as soon as we were through the garden gates, she began to kiss me and to talk in a most unexpected manner!

"Dear heart!" she cried, "dear child, thou art starving for happiness. I know the symptoms—I am resolved to make thee cheerful. What? A young girl—a lovely girl—ought to be happy and merry and gay. Well, I shall give you something new to think about : I shall teach you to laugh. Nancy—think of that! I do not believe you have ever heard a laugh in that great silent house. It will be strange for you to laugh : strange at first, but you will grow accustomed. We will talk like other Christians—you will find it very easy. I will teach you to sing and to play music : there are many ways of being happy in the part of town where I live. You shall hear music. Fie upon the Quakers that they have banished music from their Society ! Why, it was music which soothed the troubled heart of Saul : it is music which lifts the soul. As for that pretty face "—she kissed that face —" it shall know another kind of look in a day or two : your pale cheek shall be rosy. Your white arm —it is a poor thin arm at present—but it shall fill out. What say you, Molly?" She ran on without waiting for an answer. I listened with speechless wonder. This kind of talk had I never heard before. And my cousin kept laughing while she talked. Why did she laugh ?

"Ah, Madam !" cried Molly. "This is cheerful talk. The dear young lady wants not Meeting-houses and tombstones. Give her cheerful talk, and I warrant she will come round again, and that right soon."

"Her eyes are brighter already, Molly. It is the sight of the wicked world, Nancy, that does you good already. What? You are looking out upon the wicked world for the first time. There go the wicked men working for their wicked wives for the support of their wicked children—you see them all along the streets. And here"—the journey of twenty miles was done—"here is St. James's Place, close to the wicked Park where the wicked ladies walk; and here, my dear, is my humble lodging."

CHAPTER II.

A Miracle.

I HAVE now to relate an event which, I cannot choose but believe was a direct miracle. How can we doubt, I ask, that such miracles of healing are performed every day, when we believe in the miracle of a sinner's conversion?

You shall hear.

I was overcome with the fatigue and the excitement of the journey. When the carriage drew up at the door of the house, instead of following my cousin I fell down in some kind of swoon and was caught by Molly. When I recovered Molly was standing over me with the hartshorn and my cousin with a glass of wine. They took me into a bedroom and put me to bed, as if I was a child. I fell fast asleep, and continued the whole night through without disturbance, without terrors, without once thinking of my soul, and without any dreams.

It was about eight in the morning when I woke up. I was awakened by a sweet and soothing sound. It was music. Remember that I had never before heard any music at all. How should a Quaker living in a country house hear music? Why, I knew not what it meant. I had never to my recollection heard even the ploughboy whistling on his way to work. My cousin was playing on the harpsichord: she played softly and sweetly, having a most skilful and tender touch, so that the air fell upon my ears like a gentle rain of refreshment. I thought of the harps of Heaven and the hymns of the Blessed. My heart beat; tears crowded into my eyes. When a new emotion is experienced, if the words are wanting which should describe it, one speaks of it in terms that belong to other senses. If I were to say, for instance, that my cousin's music was like the fragrance of violets in the hedge, or like the pine-trees in the rare sunshine of March, or like the tender sweetness of the mignonette, you would understand that I could not tell you in other words the delight with which this music filled my willing soul.

Then I remembered where I was—in my cousin's lodging: not at home. I sprang from my bed and pushed back the curtains of the darkened room. Yes, it was a different room indeed. My own room at home had in it nothing but a bed, a cupboard, and a plain chair of cane: the walls were bare: there were no curtains or hangings: a bedroom with us was a place in which to sleep. This room had coloured engravings on the walls; samplers were hanging over the mantelshelf: there was a soft carpet: the bed was in an alcove with costly curtains and hangings: there was a toilette-table with a large mirror and all kinds of things that women are supposed to want, including a pot of rouge and a silver patch-box and powder for the face. There were two low chairs covered with red plush.

I turned, bewildered, to the window. It looked out upon the Green Park. The morning was fair: it was already eight o'clock; nurses or mothers were there with their children, who ran about playing and crying and laughing: soldiers were exercising: there were trees in one place, and through the branches I saw the gleaming of a pond: on the north side there ran a road through fields—it was the road called Piccadilly, horsemen were riding along: and there passed by a stage-coach, laden and piled high with parcels and packages, covered with mud, because it had come all the way from the West Country.

For a while, filled with interest and curiosity, I gazed upon all these things. Then suddenly I made a strange discovery. It was nothing less than this. I felt no longer the oppression that had held me down.

This was the Miracle of which I spoke above.

What had happened, then? My cousin was still playing. I remembered how King Saul, who also suffered from melancholia, was soothed by David's harp. But when David went away his malady returned. Doubtless when my cousin ceased to play my malady would also return.

She did cease to play. Then I sat down and waited. " It will begin again," I said to myself with terror unspeakable. There should be a Prayer in the Litany—" From a disordered brain: and from the terror of a disordered brain, Good Lord deliver us ! "

But it came not. The fresh air from the Park

fanned my cheek : I heard the laughing children down below : I heard the words of command as the Sergeant drilled his men : I found that I could think and reason : the prospects of my immortal soul ceased to loom before me heavy and black. Was not this a miracle? A single night had done this. A single night only had changed me. What is more, I have never since suffered from melancholia.

Then, with hesitation and doubt, I dressed, and opened the door of the parlour. My cousin ran and caught me by both hands, and kissed me on both cheeks.

"Why," she cried, laughing—why did she laugh? but she laughed at everything—" the medicine works! Thine eyes are bright—tell me, dear, was thy sleep sound? Thy cheek hath already a touch of the summer rose—was thy sleep peaceful? Was it without bad dreams? And thy poor head—it is better? and thy brain—it is clearer? and thy heart—it is stout again?" She made no pause for my replies. "Oh, I rejoice, my dear! To be sure, I expected nothing less "—I had answered not one word—"sit down, now: we will take our dish of chocolate." Molly brought it that moment, foaming, in two bowls. "Here are toast and buttered cakes. Eat, my dear, and drink, and then we will talk. You must long to talk, after so long a silence." Indeed, I was not burning to talk. It was enough to sit and listen while my cousin talked.

I listened, and looked round the room. It needed not the eye of a plain Quakeress to discover that this

room and its tenant were clearly followers of the
world's fashions and pleasures. There was the harpsichord with its books of music : on the walls pictures
hung, as many pictures as could be hung : some were
oil paintings ; some were coloured drawings. I was
never tired of looking at these pictures : for the most
part they presented rural scenes—is it not pleasant to
see, and to recall, the village green, the pond with the
flock of ducks, and all the country sights? They
presented heads—studies, my cousin called them—
groups of people, interiors of churches, men in taverns
drinking—everything that you can think of. What
harm can there be in studying such pictures? Why
did our founder prohibit the practice of Art? Then
there were books on shelves—not serious books, but
plays and poetry. My cousin afterwards encouraged
me to read them.

While I listened and looked about me, my cousin
continued with the utmost volubility, talking of two
or three subjects at the same time. And she looked
into my face with a kind of exultant satisfaction because her prophecy had proved correct, and the
change was already apparent. When melancholia,
which is a disease of the imagination, leaves the patient, the recovery is instantaneous. But the terror—
yes—the terror of it remains until the dying day.

"You are astonished, my dear," she said. "I do
not use the Quaker manner of speech, nor do I dress
after their fashion, nor do I obey their rules about
music and pictures. Know then, sweet Nancy, that I
joined the Friends to please my husband ; and that I

left them, after his death, to please myself. I do but
assume the dress when I go to visit thy brother's
house." She wore a very fine night-gown of pink
sarsnet, with a pink ribbon in her laced cap. Rings
were on her fingers, certainly, she had departed very
far from the Quaker rule. " I have not told you of
my resignation : he would not receive me if he knew ;
and Nancy, dear," she took my hand and held it, " my
heart bled for thee, so young, so beautiful, condemned
to languish in obscurity, or to endure the wooing of
some sanctified Yea Verily. Heavens, my dear! if
thy mother saw thee, this morning—eyes bright, face
clear, she would forgive this deception by which I
have rescued thee, and by which I hope to keep thee
for awhile. What is it, after all? I was born in the
Church of England. I was grown-up when I turned
Quaker. (Your mother would be amazed to mark the
difference.) I only joined the Society to please my
Reuben. For his sake I would have become a Mo-
hammedan, had he wished it. (Your eyes, Nancy,
are like lamps, and your lips like rosebuds !) As long
as he lived I said 'thee' instead of 'thou' and 'you.'
Oh! the pride and the pretence of it! While he
lived, too, I dressed always in his fashion, which I was
happy to discover is not unbecoming to a fine woman
like myself." My cousin was a tall and handsome
woman with large eyes, an ample cheek, and fullness
of figure. " Not at all unbecoming if the dress is
made of fine materials." Certainly I had never before heard talk so easy and so voluble, accompanied
by so many smiles and nods and little gestures of

head and lips and hands. "My dear, I was never more than half a Quaker. They questioned me on my admission. Reuben, though a Broadbrim, was as anxious to marry me as if he had been a simple Churchman. That was why I loved him—because he loved me as a young man should. So he told me what to say, and they received me. But only half a Quaker, ever. I kept my harpsichord in a garret, out of the way : I used to go secretly to St. Paul's to hear the anthem. Oh! I like the Friends well enough. They are charitable to the poor, but they are stiff-necked : even Reuben believed there was no salvation except in his sect : and thy brother Joseph believes that even membership does not insure salvation. However, there is some safety in taking a Quaker for a husband : he will not go to bed drunk, nor will he indulge in those—rovings—or sallies—which most torment a woman's heart."

I understood very little of this long discourse, because the newness of everything bewildered me. However, one thing at least was plain : that my cousin had me, for a time, in her keeping, and that many other new things were going to happen.

So she went on talking, and I listening and looking about me.

"Why, my Nancy, the gloom has gone already. It was but sulks, I doubt, thou saucy girl! Yet it must not return. The cloud hath rolled away—already I see the sunshine on thy brow." She patted my check softly. She was, in a word, one of those women who would gladly see all their friends happy. "Why,

Nancy, I have seen for a long time that neither nunnery nor Meeting-house was designed for thee."
What did she mean? "Brother Broadbrim hath no
concern with this soft face, with those rosy lips, with
those big eyes, with this velvet cheek which hath already the returning rose—'tis now the time of roses :
thou art created for the happiness of a Man, not of a
Yea Verily." I ought to have remonstrated against
this talk, but, indeed, I had no power. "Well: we
shall show thee the Wicked World. My Lord and
Lady Vanity shall see the sweetest piece of Innocence
ever taken into the Park. I say the Park, my dear,
where the ladies of fashion walk, but I am not one of
them—although I go as fine as most—for Reuben left
money. I am not one of them. A mere tradesman's
widow who married a Broadbrim—yet his hat was the
only fault he had—one who for love put on the frock
of grey—I say that a tradesman's widow is not received by these ladies, though her beauty may make
them tear their hair for mortification, and though her
dress be finer than theirs, and her accomplishments
better. Well—I mind it not—so much have I gotten
from the Friends that I regard no more the preten-
sions of rank, and am afraid to stand before no man—
and no woman either, which is saying more. We shall
look at them in the Park, Nancy, and it shall not be
my fault, my dear, if they do not look at thee. Already thou art transformed : the thought of the silent
house like a great grave——"

Here she stopped suddenly and sprang to her feet,
for the mere mention of the silent house recalled to

my mind, in a moment, all that had happened: the
gloomy forebodings of everlasting perdition, Joseph's
triumphant proofs that no one should presume to
hope, the lonely brooding over those sad thoughts in
the garden, the dreadful day when I stood over the
black water of the pond, my thoughts blacker still;
and all the trouble returned to my eyes.   I seemed to
hear the rustling of wings—the return of Melancholia
—I turned ashy pale—I fell back in my chair.   When
I recovered, Molly was patting my hands with a cold
wet sponge, and my cousin was administering smell-
ing salts.

   " Poor lamb! " she was saying.   " She is weaker
than I thought.   Molly, never mention the house—
never speak to her about it.   We must keep her
thoughts from the past."

   " It was not the loneliness," said Molly.   " A body
may bear to be lonely : 'twas Master Joseph with his
everlasting asking who could be saved.   Oh ! they're
hard upon her with their Elected and their damned—
damned for nothing—as a body may say."

   " Hush, Molly !   She opens her eyes."

   So I sat up, and my cousin went on talking, looking
anxiously at me from time to time.   I think she
talked faster than ever, keeping my mind fixed upon
the new things to which she was introducing me.

   " When we are in the world, my dear, we must do
as the world does.   Lord ! a body must not be singular.   Therefore you will dress as they dress.   And you
must speak as they speak.   And you must learn the
pretty little nothings, the graces, the pretences, the

affectations: they mean nothing, but they please ; and the art of smiling and laughing—it will amuse you infinitely for a while to be a lady of fashion. And I have thought of a great moral lesson in it—oh! a most useful lesson. In the Society there are no temptations for a lovely maid: no one turns her head with love and compliments, flames and darts and burning hearts, bosky groves and laughing Loves: she knows nothing of these poetical snares which catch a girl and make her vain and conceited. But, my Nancy, which is better—to meet temptation and resist it, or never to be tempted at all? Think how meritorious it is to resist temptation."

If I am reproached with the readiness of this desertion of my own people, remember that I was not in a condition to resist, to question, or to object. The chief emotions in my mind at the time were bewilderment amidst these new surroundings, a newly awakened curiosity, and an ever-present terror lest the clutch of the demon—can I ever cease to believe that I was truly Possessed?—should again seize upon me. But of resistance I was quite incapable. I knew not, nor did my cousin know, that in putting off the Quaker garb I could never again put it on. I knew not, nor did she know, that in giving up their manner of speech I could never resume it. For dress and speech alike are connected with that time of Melancholia. Even now, after more than twenty years, when I think of the silent house where one heard nothing but the ticking of the clock, which was haunted by a fearful whisper threatening in my ears everlasting torment, a shudder seizes me. I shake and tremble: for a little while my mind is clouded: for a brief space the skies are darkened, and I feel again, as I felt then, that there is no hope, and can be none, for me, because I am not one of the few Elect, and that my unhappy soul is included among the innumerable multitude of those for whom Christ did not die.

CHAPTER III.

The Wicked World.

THEN did my cousin address herself very seriously to the task of making me observe, and imitate, the fashions of the world. And I have to relate how what was begun only as an experiment or a medicine proved in the end to be a necessary condition of life: in other words, how it became impossible for me to go back to my old way of life.

First, because this meant one's outward appearance, we engaged upon the subject of dress. To me there had-been hitherto but two colours (except those with which Nature had endowed the flowers)—namely, grey and drab: the men dressed in the latter, the women in the former. Yet colour, and the discrimination of colour, came to me as by instinct. And as for fashions—for the shape of a mantle or a sash or a hat; for stuffs of silk or satin; brocade or velvet; for ribbons, laces, gloves, embroidery, and such gear, it was wonderful in the eyes of my instructress to mark the rapid progress which I made. Yet I ventured sometimes—not every day—more feebly to protest against giving to these things the whole attention of a woman.

"Why, Nancy," said my cousin laughing, "what is the use of fine clothes? They set off and adorn a fine woman. And why should a fine woman set off and adorn her person? To attract the men, my dear. And why should she wish to attract the men? In order to gain power and have her own way. The men believe they rule the world. Not so. The women rule the men, who rule the world."

One need not believe all the idle nonsense talked by Isabel in her light and careless way, which, to one like myself, was wonderful. Yet there is (for a woman) a happiness (I know not why) in the mere putting on things that are beautiful and becoming; and not only in wearing, but in choosing them out of other things beautiful and becoming such as flowered silks, point lace, and the like. If clothes were invented only for warmth, a blanket and a leathern girdle would be enough. If they were invented to show the figure— but why should we wish to show the figure?—then hoops, head-dresses, sleeves, and many other things would have to be discarded. The figure has nothing to do with the fashions: if one were shaped like a pig the fashions might continue. If the figure alone were concerned the fashions would never change. But all human creatures love change; therefore the fashions change: and all women, if they can afford to buy them, delight in stuffs beautiful to look at and soft to handle.

In a word, I proved in this respect an apt pupil, and speedily learned almost as much as my cousin could teach me. And after a week or two you might have seen me, who had been clad in plain Quakers' grey all my life, now sitting in the shops of Ludgate Hill or Cheap, while the complaisant draper and his patient apprentices brought out their choicest fabrics, such as they do not use to set in the windows, and learnedly discoursed for our instruction upon the newest fashions and their changes.

Another point was the manner of speech. It would seem easy to change from "thee" to "thou" or "you" when one is not familiar, or to say "yes" and "no" instead of "yea" and "nay"; yet I confess that it cost me a great deal of practice before I spoke easily in the way of the world. Happily, a woman is not called upon to use the oaths and appeals to the Deity which are commonly the custom with men : thus I had nothing to learn except (which I did never learn) such familiarity with these words as might make them fall unnoticed on my ears.

My cousin was anxious on the score of an easy or a graceful carriage. It must be owned that the Quakers in this respect are greatly to seek : yet among them the stiffness of their carriage lends to those who are advanced in years a certain dignity. It is of the younger men and women that one would complain. I think, for instance, with a kind of shame of my brother Joseph, who moved and stood as if he was of a verity made of wood and jointed like a puppet. " My dear," said Isabel, " at Dartford one could hear the joints creak."

For the sake of grace I must needs learn dancing. "There is nothing," said my cousin, " that so takes the stiffness out of the limbs. The Society of Friends would make a woman believe that she hath no limbs and is nothing but a head on a grey frock. I should

like, my dear, to give you a wooden hoop and make
you run in the Park every day—but it is a censorious
world. We will learn to dance."

By this time I was quite ready to accept without
question whatever regimen might be prescribed for
me. Nor did I stop to inquire or to consider what
would be my brother's wrath should he discover that
I had learned to dance. To dance! Was there anything which filled the heart of the Quaker with greater
horror than the spectacle of young men and maidens
dancing—hand in hand—round the ring—setting to
each other, beating time with their feet: with curtsies
and inclinations: singing as they danced? All they
knew was the rude, coarse wake and village dance, not
the courtly, graceful, stately dance that my cousin
taught me.

One who has been cut off from the innocent pleasures of the world may well become, in a manner, in-
toxicated with them when they are at length placed
within her reach. I became greedy of everything,
and of dancing among the rest. The movement of
the body in harmony with the music: the expression
by the limbs of what music meant: the interpretation
of courtesy, respect, reverence, affection, gracefulness
by corresponding gestures and steps was a thing to me
so wholly unexpected and so new that I could not but
ask for more.

I learned, as well, to laugh. Yes: strange to say,
the power of laughing came to me unsolicited and
untaught. I cannot tell you when first I laughed, or
why. I learned to laugh, as a duckling learns to swim,

by observing others laugh. When one begins to
laugh, one finds a thousand things to laugh at : unexpected turns : the astonishment of some one : something said mal-à-propos; something said unwarily :
the accidental discovery of a little secret. The difficulty is to find out, not why one should laugh, but
why one did not always laugh. If we laughed when
Molly tripped on the carpet and fell down with the
dish of sausages, why did not my brother Joseph laugh
when a similar accident happened at his table? I
only note this trifling point because I desire you to
understand the great and wonderful transformation
which my cousin brought about.

I have said that my cousin's rooms were covered
with pictures, upon which I gazed with a pleasure always new. Most of these pictures are now hanging
on the walls of my own house : yet, after so many
years, the sight of them still affords delight to me, and
in each one I discover always some fresh beauty. In
some of them there are spiritual heights which are discovered by long contemplation, when the soul is
lifted to the level of the picture. It seems to me,
thinking over all that I have read and seen and experienced, that there are times when the painter or
the poet describes or paints things far beyond his own
reach of mind : there is, for instance, a divinity, sometimes, in the face of Virgin or Saint as represented in
certain pictures which the painter himself could never
perceive or portray. Therefore I say that the soul
must be lifted to the level of such a picture before it
can convey its message. Why, then, have my former

friends forbidden paintings? Because, I suppose, the founder of the sect was too ignorant to know what a picture is, or what high thoughts may be suggested by a picture.

Not only did my cousin possess these pictures in frames fitted to the panels of her wainscotting, but she had also portfolios full of prints and engravings, some of them most exquisite; some, it is true, of the earth, earthy (which one could pass over). In addition she could herself draw very dexterously in pencil outline, which she would afterwards fill in with colour. Her genius lay in drawing figures: thus she drew the soldiers marching out of St. James's Palace: the fine ladies in the Park: the beaux attending them: the divine and the lawyer: and the people in the street— the men and women who walk all day long about every street carrying everything that a house can want and bawling their wares at the top of the voice. Here are her drawings before me. I remember every one: the bandbox man with his bandboxes of every shape and every colour, the man covered up and almost hidden by his pile of baskets; the man who offered to mend your bellows, the man who sold brickdust, the woman with the cats'-meat, the girl who would mend your rush-buttoned chair, the man with the brooms, the knife-terror, the lavender girl, the boy with the matches, the old clothes man, the Turk who sold the slippers, the sandman, the strawberry-girl, and the sweep. They are all before me, drawn to the life. Why should these things be forbidden? What sinful emotion is excited in the mind by the picture of the knife-grinder? What by the picture of the straw-berry-girl?

Among the pictures were figured certain marble statues. Before one of them my cousin held me. " Nancy," she said, "this figure is the sweetest dream of beauty ever put into marble. Learn—for I am sure you do not know already—that the type of perfection, whether of Art, or of Learning, or of Holiness, is the human figure, and the female figure. The curving lines which artists love are taken by them to repre-sent the highest and most perfect attainment in every-thing. This form is the soul, blessed and purified ; or it is Song at its noblest : it is the Muse of this or of that. Regard it as a symbol, and ask only how far the figure corresponds with the ideal." But this les-son I learned gradually, and not in a single day. To understand these things is to understand that ancient art of which the connoisseurs speak and write with such enthusiasm.

Then Isabel showed me her books—she had a case full of them.

"I have always thought," she went on, "that the finest invention of man has been the book which por-trays the sufferings of imaginary people. In reading of them we forget ourselves: and though we boil with indignation we are restrained by the knowledge that nothing is real. So, my dear, we will to-day, if you please, begin the study of that most unfortunate of puppets, the real—unreal, imaginary—veritable, hero-ine, Clarissa."

In this immortal book the wickedness of man is so

unmistakably held up to execration, and the unhappy victim of a relentless passion is so movingly depicted that one rises from its perusal with a heart strengthened for virtue and religion. I confess that to me Clarissa is a real woman of flesh and blood. And to think that this book, with all other works of imagination which deal with the passions and sins of men and women, should be prohibited by the Society of Friends!

After reading " Clarissa " we exchanged novels for poetry. First my cousin introduced me to portions of Shakspere, Milton, Dryden, Pope, and others. She read these portions aloud. Many women, I think, would do well to study the art of reading aloud. My cousin read very well, and after study in the true modulation of the voice and with gestures appropriate to every emotion, she possessed a sweet voice and read with much feeling. It is in the reading of fine poetry that a generous heart most readily betrays itself. As she read she would stop to say, " Listen, Nancy—here is a noble thought—this is sweet and tender—this is a passage that women would do well to carry about in their minds . . . Here is a vivid description. One can hear the clanking of the armour . . . Here is a fine contempt for things base and low. Can one hear such sentiments at Meeting? This poet is all for giving up everything : our old friends are all for getting what they can—every man for himself, whether it is a seat in heaven or a hundred thousand pounds. They forbid the poets. Why? Because, they say, some poetry is not fit for a virtuous woman

"WHILE MY COUSIN PLAYED I SAT BESIDE HER." —*Page 55.*

to read. Then they may as well forbid a walk in the streets, where, to be sure, the things said are far worse than any poet has ever written. No, my dear, the same spirit which forbade poetry also forbade music and painting. It is a narrow and an ignorant spirit, my dear, which we have done well to put away."

One must not forget the power of music. Was not my soul uplifted a thousand times?—yea, clean carried out of itself into heights filled with blissful dreams and soft airs, by my cousin's playing? She knew all kinds of music—soft and gentle: loud and martial: tender, so that the heart yearned after something unknown: meditative, sorrowful. Much of what she played was music taken from Masses composed for the Roman service: that service which I had been taught to believe was all superstition and treachery and deceit. Yet the music was unspeakably moving. While my cousin played I sat beside her, my head on my hand, seeing nothing, all my senses rapt by those sweet strains.

Why—why—why — have the Friends closed this avenue, this gate of Heaven? Eye hath not seen the glories of the world to come, but surely by means of music the soul may be wafted upwards and so be vouchsafed a glimpse through the Pearly Gates. Never shall I forget the first morning when we heard the music in Westminster Abbey. The church itself amazed me : the tombs of the Kings and of the great men of the country filled me with emotion : these were the people—I had never thought them real before I saw their tombs—who were set upon thrones and

bidden to resist temptation not offered to lesser men ;
to be great and good and wise—for the sake of their
people. Well : all the people—kings and paupers,
wise or foolish, good or bad, great or little—the
Church receives them all. The Church receives them
all. And our little sect—our following small and narrow—refuses them all. The Church receives them all :
this building so wonderful in its height and length and
in the beauty of its pillars and its carvings stands for
the whole Church of Christ and is a symbol of the
Church of Christ : and it receives all—all—all within
its walls. Then, while I thought these things, the
sweet pure voices of the boys—they stood for the
angels—rose up and floated over our heads and rolled
about the roof and the arches and the aisles; and
after the anthem the voice of him who prayed was like
a whisper to us who stood outside under the tran-
sept. So great was the contrast between the univer-
sal Motherhood of the Church of England and the
straitness of my sect that my former opinions—all
that were left—fell from me as a mantle falls from the
shoulders. Come what might come, I would henceforth, I resolved, follow a creed which allowed me to
believe in the goodness and the love of the Lord.

"Child!" my cousin cried when I told her these
things. "What is this? They will surely say that it
was my doing."

"Dear Isabel! thou art all goodness to me. But,
indeed, I can no longer remain in the Society of
Friends."

Here I must stop. My education (or my transfor-

mation) was now complete. Look at me at the begin-
ing of this chapter. In dress, in speech, in carriage,
a Quaker among Quakers: my mind, except for the
narrow creed of that sect, empty, and ready for the
possession of any wandering devils who might be permitted to enter. Ignorant of the world: ignorant of
music, painting, singing, dancing: ignorant of manners.
In all these things my cousin was able to effect a complete change principally because she found me at a
time when I was weak and humbled, and above all
things anxious never to look back.

As I said above, my cousin did not understand that
in doing all this for me she was making it impossible
for me to return to the old life. Not even the memory
of my mother could send me back to a sect where I
found no hope—or if any, no more than a struggling
ray of light in the darkness scarcely visible. Let me
live under the wings of the Church which admits all,
as the Abbey buries all, within its walls. Here lie
saint and sinner: sinful King and innocent Queen,
martyr and murderess—the Church admits them all.
"Come," she cries. "All ye who have lived. Here
there is hope for all. Lie down and rest and trust."
And so, as John Bunyan journeyed through the Dark
Valley to the Hills beyond, I went through all those
agonies of terror and found myself at last standing on
the slopes of the Hills Beautiful.

CHAPTER IV.

The First Meeting.

You have heard from Lord de Lys how tradition
still attaches to a house in St. James's Place concerning a certain Person and a certain lady. It cannot be
more than a garbled and mangled version of the truth.
Not one of the persons chiefly concerned would ever,
I believe, speak publicly of this episode. Not Captain Sellinger; not the Corporal, who was afterwards
killed in action ; not my cousin, who died of smallpox
a year after this event ; not Dr. Mynsterchamber, who
went away under circumstances you shall learn, and
no doubt is long since dead ; not Molly, who remains
with me still; not Mr. Robert Storey, who shortly
afterwards fell into misfortune and the Fleet Prison.
In whatever version was spread abroad, I make no
doubt that I was depicted as a woman of the basest
sort, practising the allurements of Delilah, decked
with fine raiment and jewels, costly head-tire and
wanton looks : in short, such a woman as is described
by the Wise King in his Book of Proverbs. You,
however, who have read so far will understand that a
young gentlewoman with such a history as mine—for
which reason I have written what precedes—formerly
a Quakeress, and of the strictest kind, daughter of a

wealthy manufacturer, instructed in none of the arts
of allurement and only the simplest graces and accomplishments, would be unable—if she were basely to
wish—to attempt those arts.

This is a love story : for my own part I do not believe that any others are worth reading : I am indeed
sincerely sorry for all poor women who have no love
story of their own. One must not magnify the passion of love, but certainly there is no other passion
that plays so important a part in this transitory life,
especially for my sex. I say that this is a love story :
and I declare, further, that if any young man (whatever his rank) bestowed upon me his affections in the
springtime of my days, when I possessed some charms
of face and form, it was not on account of any allurements or snares, but solely on account of those per-
fections which a generous and noble soul (out of his
own nobility) imagined in a woman all imperfections.
The more noble the lover the deeper and the stronger
is his love, the more heavenly becomes the woman of
his imagination. Such a young man sees in the woman he loves a Living Well of Virtue, a Sealed Fountain, a soul all beautiful within and without. Happy
is the woman who is loved by so great a heart ; for
even before her death she may be led upward so as to
become an angel of heaven.

My cousin spent an incredible amount of pains upon
me for three months—namely, May, June, and July of
the year 1760. During that time she transformed me
into a woman of the fashion—that is to say, not a
great Court lady, but a woman who dressed like the

rest, spoke like the rest, and took the same pleasure in the things that delight all other women. Of friends we had not many, which afterwards proved an advantage to us. The other occupants of the house— namely, Corporal Bates, of the Horse Guards, and his family in the garrets, Captain Sellinger on the second floor, and Dr. Mynsterchamber on the ground floor, we knew, but had little intercourse with them. So much was I changed that I could not bear to think of the Society of Friends. Only to remember the house at Dartford made me tremble and shiver. I had ceased going to First Day Meeting, and had even begun to attend the services at St. James's, Piccadilly, with my cousin, who had a pew in that noble church. As for singing, painting, reading poetry, making music, embroidery, fine dress, and adornment of all kinds I was now as fond of these things as my cousin could desire.

It was on Wednesday, August 17, that the event happened which was destined to change the whole of my life. At half-past seven in the evening I was returning home from evening prayers at St. James's. It was a sermon day, which made the service longer. I was accompanied by Molly, who walked behind me, carrying my prayer-book. Many other ladies were also going home after prayers, either in their coaches or accompanied by footmen carrying sticks, or, like me, protected only by a woman-servant.

At such a time and in such a place one considers that there is no danger save from some gentleman whose attentions are uninvited or from some audacious pickpocket: who could look for danger at the

Court end of the town, in the most polite streets, with numbers of passengers, and in broad daylight? A gentlewoman may, surely, go to evening prayers and return home without fear of molestation within a few yards of the King's Palace. There is, however, another kind of danger to which one is exposed in every part of the town. One thinks little of it : one cannot guard against it : yet it always threatens : it is always possible : it can never be removed, so long as the world continues to drink rum, punch, port-wine, or beer.

However, being tranquil as to this or any other danger, and seeing many ladies and persons of respectable appearance in the streets, I walked along reflecting on the discourse which the congregation had just heard. It was one of the kind which the Church of England loves : the preacher had an argument which he expounded, followed up, and proved with a great display of scholarship and with that appearance of authority which the pulpit, the ecclesiastical wig, the black gown, and a full voice also contributed to his discourse. I know not, now, what he advanced or proved. There was nothing of himself in it : no " experiences," no claim to the special working of the Lord in his soul : nothing individual : he spoke as one in a collective Church, as if the individual shared with all the rest the gifts and graces of the Church, which receives all alike, treats all alike : gives the same promise to all alike. Nor did this preacher, as my brother Joseph was wont to do, take a text here and a text there and lay them side by side. Not so : he showed us what each text means in the original Greek, and what it means with reference to the passages that go before and the passages which follow after. Such a discourse to a person of my experience was like an invitation to rest and be happy in an Ark of Refuge.

We accomplished our short walk through Jermyn Street and down St. James's Street in perfect safety until we reached the corner of St. James's Place. When we turned into that very quiet place we were met full face to face by two gentlemen walking arm-in-arm, or rather, shoulder to shoulder.

They both wore the King's scarlet. One of them I knew very well. He was the Honourable Robert Sellinger, younger brother of the Viscount de Lys, Captain in his Majesty's Horse-Guards. He was at this time not more than five-and-twenty: a tall and proper person, upon whom the King's uniform sat becomingly: all women I am sure, like to see a young man in a handsome uniform. As yet the gout which afterwards cruelly afflicted him, swelling his joints, covering his face with unsightly blotches, crippling his feet, had not appeared. He was, however, so to speak, inviting and preparing the way for it: this he did by drinking too much port-wine or rum punch, so that already his neck was too thick and his cheek too flushed, for so young a man. In the morning, however, there was no better company: he was as well-bred a man as is expected in one of his rank: he had some knowledge of books: he was of the kindliest disposition: and he discoursed pleasantly. In appearance I say that he was tall: his nose was long and narrow: his eyes had a constant light as of sunshine in them: his lips were ever ready for a smile. To me and to my cousin he was attentive: he visited us frequently: he walked with us in the Park: he told us about the old King in St. James's Palace and the Princes in Leicester Square, and he paid me every day some new and pleasing compliment. But he did not make love to me, for which I am now thankful: indeed, the poor man, who had but this one fault, entertained love towards the bottle as his only mistress. Strange, that a man of parts and judgment should every night voluntarily fuddle himself! Why did he do it? Why do men, our superiors in strength of mind as well as of body, choose to deaden their finer senses for the sake of—I know not what—say, a few drops of sweetness, more or less?

Had Captain Sellinger been sober this evening I am certain that nothing would have happened. Sober, he respected me and all other women; drunk, he regarded all women alike, just as he regarded (I suppose) the impudent hussies in the Park, whom I have seen the gentlemen, with a disgusting familiarity, take by the chin. This evening, however, he was overcome, and he walked with difficulty, holding up his companion and being held up by him.

At the corner of St. James's Place, I say, we came face to face with this pair, insomuch that there was no way of avoiding them; nor would they suffer me to take the wall and pass, but, in a manner, spread themselves and barred the way.

" Captain Sellinger," I said, " will you let me pass? "

" Jack," he replied, speaking thickly, " 'tis Nancy—

divine Nancy. She hath been at her devotions—on her lovely knees. Jack, let us take her to Maryle-bone Gardens to finish the evening."

"T'other bottle," the other man replied still more thickly. He understood nothing.

"Let me pass, Captain Sellinger." But he still barred the way.

"Thou shalt take the maid, Jack," he continued. "Molly will do for thee. Hold up, man—and I will take the mistress. Call a coach—call a coach, Molly, for thy mistress and Jack and me."

So he went on in his tipsy way, about the lovely Nancy, the divine Nancy, and such nonsense as makes me ashamed to set it down except to show that he knew not what he said.

"Captain Sellinger," I said, "you have been drink-ing, otherwise you would not behave in this strange way. Please suffer me to pass. For shame, Sir; for shame!"

"T'other bottle," murmured his companion, drop-ping his head upon his chest.

"You shall pass," he said, " in my arms, in a chariot —in a chair—" he hardly knew what he said—"to Marylebone Gardens. There we will dance—you have never yet danced with me, fair Nancy. We will afterwards take supper—supper, and have—eh, Jack? —t'other bottle."

" T'other bottle," the other gentleman replied; but his glassy eye showed that he at least would not arrive at that stage, having certainly worked his way already through as many bottles as he could hold.

"Let me go, Captain Sellinger!" I cried, as he caught hold of my hand.

"We will go together," he repeated, firm in his drunken mood, "to Marylebone Gardens. The women shall expire—by Gad!—with envy and spite—bless their hearts! And the men shall burst—hang 'em!— with envy. We will show them Venus herself—Venus herself—fair Queen of Love. Willy-nilly, fair Nancy, needs must thou show thy face at Marybone."

"Nay, Captain Sellinger, this passes endurance. You are so tipsy that you are not yourself. You know not what you say. Will you let me go, or must I force my way through?"

Now, what he did I know not. He seized my hand, he tried to kiss my cheek. I know not, indeed, what he did; because to be accosted in this manner in such a place as St. James's Street by two drunken gentlemen terrifies a girl out of her senses. And to be told that, willy-nilly, she must go with these two gentlemen—almost unable to stand—to a place of public resort disturbed me so much that I can hardly tell what happened. However, I cried out for help, that is quite certain, and Molly screamed and pulled me back, and stood in front of me : and the poor Captain was so fuddled that he hardly knew the maid from the mistress, which, I suppose, was the reason why Molly boxed his ears. And then—then—this was the first meeting—there came running across the street two gentlemen, both young, the elder not more than one or two and twenty, and the other two years or so younger. They drew their swords. "Madam," said the elder, with great resolution in his eyes and in his voice, "have no fear, we will make a way for you."

So saying he stepped before me, drawing his sword and holding it before him, pointed at the poor tipsy Captain.

The other—the younger man—stepped to the right hand of his friend, and also drew his sword quickly, standing beside the first, yet a little in advance, and it seemed to me as if he was defending his friend, so watchfully did he hold his weapon. I noticed, besides, that the two young men were richly dressed : the elder, who was the taller and stouter, in scarlet, like Captain Sellinger, with broad gold lace on his hat and beautiful lace at his wrists and neck. His sash was also trimmed with gold lace. His friend, on the other hand, wore a blue coat with white facings, also decorated with gold lace. I was so ignorant at the time that I did not recognise the uniform of the Royal Navy.

Now at sight of the drawn swords the Captain showed an immediate and remarkable change of demeanour. All the soldier awakened in his breast ; he stepped back, leaving hold of his friend, who fell to the ground ; he stood upright and alert : he drew his sword swiftly : the wine went out of his head. "As you will, gentlemen," he said, "if you must interfere where you have no business." So he turned half round, saluted his enemy and crossed swords.

"Oh! Good gentlemen!" cried Molly, wringing her hands.

"Gentlemen!" I said. "They are drunk——"

As I spoke an extraordinary transformation fell upon Captain Sellinger. His face expressed suddenly a swift succession of emotions—doubt, astonishment, bewilderment, and recognition. "Good Lord!" he cried. Then he lowered his sword to the ground, the point touching the stones : he took off his hat, bowed low, sheathed his sword, and still with bowed head retreated backward, and so passed into the Park beyond.

For my own part, I was not so much astonished by this behaviour, because my people practise these courtesies of bows and bendings and reverences so little, that, indeed, I knew not what kind of reverence is due to this person or to that.

"So," said the younger of the two, "the adventure ends well. What about this other brave companion of the bottle?"

For Captain Sellinger's friend, on losing the support of his brother toper, fell forward on the kerbstone, and, not being able to get up, was fumbling about stupidly in search of his sword, which he was too drunk to find.

"Gentlemen," I said, "I thank you for your kindly help. As for this poor man lying here, I say again that he is drunk. Otherwise, pray, gentlemen, be so good as to put up your swords."

So they obeyed. And the elder, with a bow, asked me if I had far to go. I told him that at the end of St. James's Place lived my cousin, whom I was then visiting, and that I could now go home in perfect safety.

"Nay, Madam," he replied. "To the door at least you will suffer us to attend you."

So they walked, one on either side of me, for the short distance that remained. When we reached the door I thanked them again and wished them good-night.

"Madam," said the elder of the two, gazing into my face but not boldly or impudently—the word impudence can never, surely, be connected with him—"may we, at least, learn the name of the lady—or the goddess—whom we have this evening happily assisted?"

"Sir," I replied, ashamed to be called a goddess, "I am the daughter of the late Samuel Waldon, paper manufacturer of Dartford in Kent. I am here on a visit to my cousin Mrs. Isabel Storey, widow of my father's cousin, the late Mr. Reuben Storey, American merchant, of Great Tower Hill."

He received the information with a show of the deepest interest, and lingered as if uncertain.

"Come, George," said the other, "we keep this lady waiting on her doorstep."

So the elder of the two bowed. "Madam," he said, "I humbly hope for our better acquaintance."

"I too, Madam," said the other, "venture to hope for better acquaintance. If," he indicated his companion, "this gentleman be permitted the honour of calling——"

"Sir," I replied, "I have no right to accept or to refuse such an honour, being but a guest of my cousin."

"Sure, Miss Nancy," said the impudent Molly,

"there are not too many young gentlemen coming to
the house. Do you call, gentlemen, and you will find
a welcome, trust me. Good-night, therefore, gentlemen, and thank you for my mistress."

So they laughed and walked away. I turned my
head to look after them, and was punished for my curiosity like Lot's wife—for the elder of the two, he who
was called George, had also turned his head, and he
smiled and waved his hand. It made me blush to be
caught looking after him.

At his own door, half opened, stood Dr. Mynsterchamber, the lodger of the ground floor, in his ragged
old gown and his head wrapped in a nightcap. The
man was so long and lean and so much like a vulture
that I shuddered whenever I met him, and this was
almost every time that we went out of the house or
returned to it. He would then open his door an
inch or two, poke out his hooked nose and nod his
head, saying, "Good-morning, fair Nancy": or "Divine Nancy"; or "Lovely nymph, good-day," with
the privilege which we accord to age.

This evening his door was opened wider than usual.
and his whole head came out. "Lovely Nancy," he
said, "the beaux are beginning. Thy train will soon
drive other nymphs to madness."

"I have no beaux, Dr. Mynsterchamber."

"It is a magnificent beginning. One of them, at
least, will come again, doubtless. Have they told
thee, child, who and what they are? Ha! not yet.
In good time. Well, history is made by women. Love
rules the Court; love is victorious over the conqueror.

The Kings are led by Rosamond and Alice and Jane and Nelly and Gabrielle, each in his turn; each by one at a time. For a time they have their day—their little day "—his voice was like a raven's, hoarse and boding ill. "Well—the candle is lit: the pretty moth flies round and round : pure and clear burns the flame : see! the moth flies into it, and lies dying, all its colours burned up. The story of Semele is a parable."

"I know not what you mean, Sir."

"No, no. Best not ask their names. That they should come to this house—to this house—strange!" He shut his door and retired. As I ran up the stairs, I heard him muttering. His words made me uneasy. What did he mean by his long list of women? Who was the moth and what was the candle?

    *   *   *   *   *   *

"I wonder who they were," said my cousin. "So Molly promised them a welcome in my name. Molly is an impudent baggage. Yet, my dear, one would not stand in your way. They will come to see you. Oh, Nancy! that such a lovely face was condemned to go in grey, and to marry a man in drab! Monstrous! Well, they shall have a welcome. Heaven grant they may not prove to be profligates."

"They looked most virtuous, I think."

"Looked indeed! Who can trust a man's looks? Last year one of them—a mere adventurer—carried off an heiress, and was at Gretna Green before her parents knew that she was lost. To be sure, they say that she was nothing loth."

"I am no heiress, cousin. Therefore no one will carry me off."

"I don't know, child. There are other reasons for carrying off a woman. Besides, thy father was possessed of goodly bags of gold. There are hunters of nymphs as well as hunters of fortune. There are in the world always young men named Lovelace. Remember Clarissa, my dear."

I laid my hand on hers. "If Clarissa had lived with thee, dear cousin, Lovelace would not have ventured or succeeded."

CHAPTER V.

The Next Day.

IN the morning Captain Sellinger presented himself, making the excuses due from a gentleman. There was not much repentance in his looks, but some: he was not wholly without grace. His excuses were not too full of self-reproach: he had not lost any self-respect, because he was certainly not more drunk than becomes a gentleman, as was shown by the fact that he could still distinguish a lovely woman. "This," I said, "was the reason why you kissed Molly, the maid." The accident, he confessed, betrayed a momentary wandering of wits.

He owned, however, that he ought to have taken my refusal seriously and allowed me to pass. And he expressed himself as unfeignedly sorry for having caused me the least pain. In a word, he spoke as a gentleman should.

"Still, Captain Sellinger, I am pleased to think that Molly boxed your ears."

"I shall call Molly out. She must give me satisfaction. Can a man of honour sit down with ears tingling? You say that I mistook the maid for the mistress. That should be impossible in your case, Miss Nancy. I *have* seen maids—but enough. You say that Molly virtuously boxed my ears? Well, I cannot remember. And then, suddenly, so far as my memory serves me, who should jump out of the ground like a Jack-in-the-box, or a ghost at Drury, but the Prince of Wales himself, with his feathers on his head and a naked sword in his hand?"

" You are dreaming, Captain Sellinger."

" I suppose I am. But, Nancy, how came the Prince of Wales in St. James's Place?"

" How came he in your muddled brain? How can any one account for tricks of imagination? Besides, there were two gentlemen, not one."

" Na—na—na—do not make me out sober. I saw two gentlemen, which is a proof that there was but one. Had there been two I should have seen four. Everybody knows so much. There was one gentleman, I tell you, not two."

After the Captain came the Corporal.

Corporal Bates, also of the Guards, but not in Captain Sellinger's company, occupied the garrets of the house with his wife and family of six little children. All day long, unless it rained, the children played in the Green Park, while their mother made and sewed for them the clothes that they wore out as fast as they could. The Corporal maintained them (but with difficulty) by teaching the art of fence, the mathematics, drawing landscapes and houses, painting in water-colours, and fine penmanship, for he was a man of many accomplishments. When he was at leisure he drew up plans of campaign, plans of sieges, observations on campaigns, and military pamphlets of all kinds, but especially such as professed to extend the power of the country. None of these learned tracts would booksellers—who were in a league, he said, to crush merit—publish for him. All his talk was on military matters; and he lived in the constant hope (and as constant disappointment) of receiving a commission. In a word, he was a brave, loyal, honest man, who believed himself to be another Churchill, or a Turenne at least, in the art of war.

Coming off duty that morning he knocked at our door and appeared in his uniform, with a high hat, white cross belt, and long worsted epaulettes, which he played with proudly because they proclaimed his rank. To be corporal is to stand on the lowest rung of the ladder, but yet it is on the ladder.

"Ladies," he said, saluting us, "your most obedient servant. I come to offer my respects and my condolences. Truly I tear my hair to think that Fortune—cruel Fortune—forbade me the happiness which two unknown gentlemen enjoyed last night. Perhaps they were not even soldiers. I venture to hope that no evil consequences of the shock have ensued. Ha! had I been there—though he is Captain in my regiment—yet he should have seen what sword-play means. Captain or no Captain—even if I was broke for it." He looked as valiant as Mars himself, the God of War.

"Thank you, Corporal Bates," I replied. "But it was much better to have no fighting."

"As for consequences," said my cousin. "Miss Nancy did not even swoon, which proves her courage;

and Molly assures me that her own appetite is unimpaired, which proves her insensibility. Yet she was kissed."

" It is my sorrow, ladies," he repeated, bringing his feet into position, " that I was not so favoured as to be on the spot. In such a case, my commission they could not choose but grant me as a reward."

"Courage, Corporal. Another occasion will perhaps present itself."

" Madam, you will perhaps go again to evening prayers. The Church bell is the ladies' call of duty: it is their réveille. I most humbly offer my services as escort. I presume not to walk beside my convoy— I will walk behind with a drawn sword and a proud heart."

Here, at least, was devotion and gratitude. One would willingly be frightened a little if only to draw forth such proof of kind hearts.

" But, Corporal, valour, even when it has no chance of proving itself, deserves reward." My cousin took from the cupboard a bottle of port and a glass. " Sir, you must be thirsty."

" In the presence of Beauty, Madam, every soldier is thirsty." I do not know what he meant by this aphorism. " I drink your health, Madam—Miss Nancy, when Virginal distress next calls for the hero's arm, may I be there to help! "

Our next visitor that day was Mr. Robert Storey, the bookseller of St. James's Street. He was cousin to Isabel's late husband ; yet his branch of the family belonged not to the Society. He was at this time still a young man, not more than eight-and-twenty, having succeeded to his father's business two or three years before. In his dress he aimed at the outward semblance of the substantial citizen: he would be taken for one known on 'Change; therefore his coat was of black velvet, his stockings of white silk, and his buckles of silver; at his throat and wrists he wore fine white lace; his buttons were of silver, and silver lace adorned his hat; his powdered hair was tied behind with a large black silk bow; a bunch of seals hung from his fob; a gold ring was on one finger; and he carried a gold-headed cane. He stood at the door for a moment in a studied attitude: in his right hand he held his hat over his heart: in his left he held the gold-headed cane: he brought his feet into the dancing-master's first position, that which shows the white silk stockings and the shape of a good leg to advantage. He was, in fact, a personable young man of fair stature and reasonable face, though his eyes were too close together. He bowed low, first to his cousin, and then to myself.

"Cousin Storey," he said, "your most obedient. Miss Nancy, your most humble."

Then he came in and sat down. In all his actions and all his words, Robert Storey still preserved the air of one who performs a duty properly. He now held himself upright in his chair: his legs crossed: his left hand plunged into his waistcoat, his right hand free for gesture.

His shop in Pall Mall, which we often visited, was large and filled with books: folios on the lower shelves : quartos on the middle : and octavos on the higher. It was all day filled with book collectors, poets, scholars, divines, and certain persons for whom he entertained a profound contempt, yet employed them constantly, called booksellers' hacks. They are persons, it appears, who have some tincture of learning but none of genius : they are cursed with an ardent desire to write, a desire which unfits them for any honourable employment ; yet they cannot with all their efforts depict the passions, move the heart, or fire the imagination. They compile books which those who cannot distinguish treat seriously : such as essays for the magazine, at a guinea the sheet, poetry by subscription, translations of ancient poets already translated a hundred times, histories copied from better historians, travels in foreign countries (never having left their own), sermons for clergymen who cannot compose—in a word, they are hacks ready to do all kinds of work at any pay that they can get. It is needless to add that they will advocate any cause, write on any side, and—still at a guinea a sheet— would defend even the fallen angels.

Robert came often to visit us in the evening after his shop was shut. Sometimes he read to us ; sometimes he spoke of the poets, who made of his shop a kind of Apollo's Walk. It must be confessed that, although he despised the tribe of hacks, he spoke always with reverence of those scholars and poets and wits whose productions lend a lustre to this age—such men, I mean, as Samuel Johnson, Dr. Warburton, Lord Lyttelton, Henry Fielding, Tobias Smollett, the

Reverend Laurence Sterne, and David Garrick, if one
may include a mere actor with these illustrious names.
More often, however, Robert brought us news of
the great world, with anecdotes and scandals, which
he produced one by one, as a child picks out plums.
His shop, in fact, was a greater home for gossip and
scandal than even a barber's: scholars and men of
letters, I verily believe, love talking as much as women. He would deliver himself of these items slowly
and with intervals: and he was fond of concluding
any one, when he could, with a moral or a religious
observation.

This evening, however, he had no opportunity, for my
cousin instantly poured into his ears the story of my
adventure. He received it with a good man's horror.

"This," he exclaimed at length, as carried away by
righteous indignation, "appears to me one of the
most flagitious acts ever attempted by a profligate
aristocracy."

"Mr. Robert," I told him, somewhat surprised at
his heat, "the Captain was overcome with drink and
knew not what he did."

"Your ignorance, Miss Nancy," he replied with a
smile, "enables you to undertake the defence of that
bad man. The business seems to me (I am necessarily
acquainted with much of the wickedness of the world)
arranged beforehand: two men pretend to be drunk:
they waylay a young gentlewoman: two others pretend to rescue her. The conspiracy is quite easy to
carry out, if one has the wickedness to devise it and
the daring to carry it through."

"That, Mr. Storey," I replied, "seems, if I may say
so, nonsense, because how could they know when we
should pass? Besides, the Captain was really drunk."
He shrugged his shoulders and bowed his head.

"Miss Nancy," he said, "has, I know, been already
remarked. I have heard observations upon her singular beauty in my shop—from Doctors of Divinity. If
these reverend persons observe the beauty of a lady,
be sure that the profligate beaux and sparks of this
end of town have also done the same thing. However, let us hope that the business is finished."

"On the contrary, Robert," said my cousin, "these
gentlemen have expressed a desire, which does us
great honour, to improve their acquaintance."

"Ay? Ay? Dear! Dear! The wickedness of
this part of town is terrible : yet I have five satirists
in verse and eleven in prose on my books and in my
pay at this moment lashing the vices of the Great.
There is also a sermon every Sunday at St. James's.
Well, ladies, this is a very serious affair. You will
have to place it in my hands. Believe me, I shall do
justice to the occasion."

"It seems to me," I said, "that these are two well-
bred gentlemen who desire to pay their respects to
ladies who are indebted to them. I cannot understand, Mr. Storey, either your heat or your charges
of deceit and wickedness. Is it not better to believe
that a man is honourable until he shows that he is
not?"

"My dear young lady, you know nothing, believe
me. And my cousin here knows little more. How

can you know the kind of company into which you
may be led?"

"We have at least read 'Clarissa,'" said Isabel.

"Well, Mr. Richardson knows how to teach and
warn the female heart. Without raising a blush to
your cheek, Miss Nancy, I cannot describe the company into which you may fall. Know, however, that
these young Sprigs of Quality (if such indeed is their
station) live in a world which is different indeed from
our own. So much so that we cannot get into it, if
we would. I thank the Lord, however, that I desire
not to exchange my station for theirs. We are honest workers, they are unprofitable drones: we make
wealth, they consume it: we live with measure and
decorum, they without rule or order: we save, they
spend: we take thought for the morrow, their morrow
is assured: we live for the world to come, they for
the world that is: we fear God and keep His commandments, they continue as if there were no commandments at all: we are constant in our affections,
they continually mislead and deceive trusting women.
Miss Nancy, seek not further acquaintance with these
young men. They are so far above you, indeed, that
they are infinitely below you."

The last sentence so pleased him, inasmuch as it
sounded like a paradox from one of his essayists, that
he repeated it. The words impressed me at the moment as anything said sonorously which one does not
understand sometimes does impress a hearer—you
may hear such things in church. If you think of it,
however, it is a foolish thing to say, for it means that

the higher is a man's rank the more corrupt does he become : in which case his Most Sacred Majesty himself—but I hesitate to write the words.

" Ladies," he went on, " it is your singular privilege, also, to belong to this same class, which is as much above the common herd as it is below the nobility. What, to you, are the attractions of fashion and of rank ? These two gentlemen hope to get a footing in this house by an open and palpable trick, which they have learned from a novel of intrigue (unhappily there are such novels, but not published by me). What sort of reception should they meet ? From me, if I were here, they would hear the truth." He rose and stood in an attitude of one who rebukes. " ' Retire,' I should say, ' Retire in confusion ' "—he stood up and pointed to the door—" ' from this house of Virtue and Religion. Leave unmolested the Daughters of Innocence who adorn this house. Retire ! Repent of designs conceived in wickedness, or carry those designs to places which are more fit for their attempt.' These are the words, ladies—or words to this effect— which I should feel it absolutely necessary to use, on your behalf, were these gentlemen in my presence to attempt an entrance."

More he would have added, in the same elevated strain, for as a moraliser Robert Storey had no equal. But at that moment Molly came running upstairs and threw open the door, crying, without any ceremony, " Madam ! Miss Nancy ! The two young gentlemen are here ! "

And so, her honest face grinning from ear to ear,

she withdrew, and our two gallant rescuers appeared.

We all rose.

"Madam," the elder spoke, bowing first to my
cousin and then to me, "we have ventured to call, in
order to ask if Miss Nancy hath recovered from the
shock and affright of yesterday."

"Nay, Sir," I said. "If you call that a fright
which was but an affair of a moment, thanks to your
courage——"

"Nancy," my cousin interposed, "was naturally
indisposed at first, but with the aid of a little cherry
brandy, she speedily recovered."

I hastened to present her by name. "Gentlemen,
this is my cousin, Mrs. Storey, widow of the late Reuben Storey, American merchant, of Great Tower
Hill."

They bowed low again. "And this is Mr. Robert
Storey." They inclined their heads slightly with a
look of condescension—as if I had introduced Molly
my maid. They were dressed as the day before, but
their swords they had left outside on the landing.

We then sat down, and I waited with some trepidation for Robert's promised harangue. Alas! there
would be no harangue. The poor man stood confused
and terrified. His face expressed this confusion : his
hands hung stupidly : his stiffness and resolution had
gone out of him. Where was the proper pride of the
bookseller, which should have sustained him even
in the presence of a Baron ? Gone : it had left him.
When the rest of us sat down he remained standing :

he appeared unable to decide what to do : he opened his mouth and gasped : as for the words of fire where were they? Then he stammered a confused good-night to his cousin, bowed low to the gentlemen, and retired, falling ignominiously over the mat as he went out. So there was an end to the grand appeal in the name of virtue.

CHAPTER VI.

"My Brother, Sir George."

WHEN Mr. Robert Storey left us, in this sudden and surprising manner, before we resumed our chairs, the younger of the two visitors introduced his brother and himself.

"Madam," addressing my cousin, "our anxiety for the safety of Miss Nancy may, we hope, excuse our presumption in calling. Let me present to you my brother, Sir George Le Breton: I am myself—Mr. Edward Le Breton, of His Majesty's Navy. And, believe me, we are both very much at your service."

Sir George bowed low and looked about the room curiously, as if he were in some strange place.

"Gentlemen," my cousin replied, smiling sweetly— most grateful in her mind that she was arrayed becom. ingly! "I am indeed gratified by this honour, the more so as it enables me to express my sense of your gallantry last night."

They both disclaimed any cause for gratitude, and, compliments finished, we sat down and began to talk.

"My brother," said the sailor, "is a country gentle-man, so that he can stay at home while I go plough-ing the salt wave."

While he spoke, his brother was looking about the

room with curiosity. He appeared not to hear this remark.

"To be a country gentleman," said my cousin, "is a great thing. May I ask, Sir"—she addressed Sir George—"in what county lies your estate?"

Sir George started, and changed colour.

"I have property," he replied in some confusion— I know not why—"chiefly in Berks and Wilts: but also elsewhere——"

The elder brother was at that time in the first flush of early manhood: he was tall and strongly made: he · was much stronger, one would judge from his breadth and height, than the ordinary run of young men: his lips and mouth spoke of firmness: his features were regular and large: he moved and spoke with an unmistakable air of authority, yet his eyes, swift to change, betrayed the gentleness and softness of his heart: although at a time of life when youth is at its best and the spirits are at their highest, he wore an habitual expression of seriousness, as of one who contemplates grave responsibilities. His cheek betrayed by its rosy hue his splendid health.

It must not be supposed that this summary of his appearance could have been written after the first day of conversation. Not at all. I write down the description of the man as I learned to know him in three months of his society and conversation.

I must call the second, as he presently begged me to do, being always of a frank and even fraternal kindliness, by his Christian name. Not, therefore, Captain Le Breton, but Edward. As for him, vivacity was stamped upon his face; he was animated in speech, in look, in movement; he was always happy; he seemed to laugh whenever he spoke; not so much at the wit or humour of what was said, as that, being perfectly happy, he must needs laugh. Yet he could at any moment assume an air of authority almost as profound as that of his brother. In appearance he was smaller and slighter; his dress, which was that of a naval officer, of blue cloth with white facings, gold buttons, and a scarlet sash, was much less splendid than the silk coat worn by his brother. Yet it seemed to befit his character, which was entirely simple and trustful. And as his own soul was incapable of aught that was mean, disloyal, or treacherous, so he believed that most of the world was created after the same mould. I think, for my own part, that he who is thus constituted, and can so regard his fellows, is far more likely to obtain such happiness as the world affords than one who regards every other man as a rogue and a traitor : who finds mean motives in the noblest actions: and guards himself at every point against the possible treachery of a friend.

The discourse on this, their first visit, was much more formal than it afterwards became. Our friends manifested some curiosity as to the Society of Friends (Isabel made haste to explain our connection with that body), of which they had never before seen any members.

" I thought," said Sir George, " that there had been some distinction in dress. I heard something of a leather doublet which was never changed."

" There were formerly extravagances," my cousin
replied. " These have now settled down into a dress
of drab for the men and of drab or grey for the women. They wear no ornaments, as they practise no
arts."

" Miss Nancy is, therefore, not a Quakeress."

" She has not yet left the Society. While she stays
with me she dresses as fashion orders. When my
husband died I went back to the Church of England,
in which I was born."

" Madam," said Sir George very earnestly, " permit
me to say that you are quite right. There can be no
form of faith in which we can find so much happiness
or such solid assurance for the future. And there is
no other form of faith in which there have been and
are still so many scholars, divines, and philosophers."

" Add to which," his brother said, " that we must
not let Miss Nancy resume the grey and drab, or she
will make that fashion immortal. As it is, I look to
see no change in the present fashion while Miss
Nancy adorns it."

I take pleasure in remembering the little extravagances which please at the time, because they are extravagant, yet mean nothing.

" Perhaps," said my cousin, " Nancy may be persuaded not to return to the garb of the Quakeress."

" Grey and drab—'tis the habit of a nun. Miss
Nancy, we cannot believe that you were intended for
a nunnery."

So we talked on all kinds of things. Sir George admired my cousin's pictures, and examined them more

closely, my cousin explaining them. Mr. Edward and
I talked meanwhile. He asked me what people I
knew or visited about St. James's ; he expressed his
surprise that he had never met or seen us anywhere.

" Sir," I said, " I am not only a Quakeress, but also
the daughter of a manufacturer. On either ground I
can have no place in the fashionable world. We live
here, in the midst of noble people, but have no friends
among them."

" Yet I swear," he replied, laughing, " there is not
anywhere one better fitted to grace a Court."

Sir George had finished *his* round of the walls, and
now stood beside me and heard these words.

" Why," said Sir George, " you miss all the scandal.
This kind of life is full of scandals. You are happy
not to know how much Lady Betty lost last night at
ombre, and how Lady Charlotte has run away with
her groom. Pray, Madam, do not change in this par-
ticular. Do not let Miss Nancy join the goodly company of Scandal."

Presently turning over a portfolio of engravings, we
came upon one of a sea-fight. " Why," cried Edward,
" I myself am a mere tarpaulin. I ought to have
come in my petticoats." So he took up the picture
and began to talk about sea-fights, of which he had
seen more than one ; of engagements on land, and of
tempests and shipwrecks. Alas ! what a gallant lad
he was, and how the colour rose to his cheeks and the
light of his eye fired as he sprang to his feet and
cheered the striking of the enemy's flag ! His brother
listened, as much moved as ourselves. " Happy the

land," he said, "happy the King for whom these brave fellows fight!"

"Yet I was taught to believe that all fighting is un-christian," I said. "Our people hold the doctrine of non-resistance. They obey the Gospel precept. They turn the other cheek."

Sir George replied slowly: "Why, then, if fighting is unchristian, where is patriotism or loyalty? Where is the honour that despises death? Where is the sac-rifice of personal advantage? It may be that the time may come when the lion will lie down with the lamb: believe me, ladies, that time is not yet. For private slights and insults it may even be possible, with some, to turn the other cheek. As yet, how-ever, the words are to be taken as a prophecy rather than a command."

At nine o'clock Molly brought up supper. At the appearance of the tray, my cousin appeared anxious, but her countenance cleared when she saw what was on it. For our supper was commonly a slice or two of bread with a little soft cheese and a glass of wine. This incomparable Molly, finding that the gentlemen did not withdraw, stepped round to Rider Street, behind St. James's Street, and returned with a cold roast chicken, some slices of ham, a greengage pie, and two or three tarts—it was not for nothing that the maid had lived with a wealthy Quaker, at whose house, though the outlook of the soul was doubtful that of the body was always secured. Well might my cousin change countenance at the sight of so dainty a supper, which, when laid out on the clean white cloth, with the blue china and glass, the silver spoons, and the ivory-handled steel forks of which my cousin was justly proud—and embellished with a bottle of Madeira, her late husband's best—was a supper to tempt a nobleman.

" Pray, gentlemen," she cried with smiling mock humility, "do not leave us"—for they both rose at sight of the supper—"to our simple meal. I have but what you see, but indeed you will make us happy if you partake of it with us."

So they sat down, and my cousin carved, while Edward poured out the wine, not touching his glass until his brother had first tasted. " This," he said, " is a feast for the gods. Ah, ladies, could you but behold us a thousand miles at sea with our salt junk and our weevilly biscuit ! I thank you, Madam : the leg was ever my favourite part of the bird : let me give you a slice of ham. Brother, you let your glass stand too long—he is but a one-legged creature : he bears too heavy a load : lighten him a little. Miss Nancy —nay—one more glass." I think I see him now— making so much of this grand feast—laughing and talking. " On Saturday night," he said, " we give our- selves a little happiness in drinking to our mistresses: but it is a shadowy joy: a winter's sunshine, which only pretends to warm. This ham, Madam, must have graced a porker of Westphalia. The Madeira has been more than once to India—that I dare affirm without taking an oath in the presence of Miss Nancy."

" It has been three times to India," said my cousin proudly. " My husband was choice in his wine."

Supper over, they invited us to play on the harpsichord. My cousin obeyed, and I saw that Sir George
possessed a soul sensible to the power of music. My
cousin played with great taste and skill : she played,
first of all, some of the music of that famous composer,
Handel ; then she changed the theme, and played in
a lighter strain. Both our visitors listened intently :
but the elder was more moved. Then she struck into
the air of a song.

"Shall Nancy sing to you?" she asked. " I promise you she hath a charming voice, though as yet it
is not completely trained."

They begged and entreated, though I would willingly have been excused. So, while she played an
accompaniment, I sang a song which she had taught
me. The words were her own, set to the air called
" Drink to me only with thine eyes." Isabel wrote the
words herself one day after discoursing with me on the
wickedness of forbidding music to the people called
Quakers. She called the song " Life and Song "—

> The thrushes sing from yonder wood,
>   The lark from yonder sky ;
> And all day long the sweet wind's song
>   Among the leaves doth lie.
> Oh! gently touch the magic string,
>   Let soft strains rise and fall,
> So that our thoughts in concert sing
>   With birds and leaves and all.
>
> The birds love sun and light and air .
>   The glories of the day :
> The living things, both foul and fair,
>   Rejoice to live alway.

Oh ! gently touch the magic string ;
Let soft strains rise and fall :
So that our songs of praise we sing
In concert with them all.

The birds they sing : the birds they love :
List ! mate his mate invites.
All living things around, above,
They know the same delights.
Oh ! gently touch the magic string,
Let soft strains rise and fall :
So that our hearts of love may sing
In concert with them all.

"Let me thank you, Miss Nancy. Such a voice,
with such a face, is rarely seen." It was Sir George
who spoke. "Perhaps we may have the happiness of
hearing another song."

"No, gentlemen," Isabel said, shutting the harpsichord. "We would not tire your ears. If it pleases
you to come again, Nancy shall sing again and I will
play to you. And now let me offer you a simple glass
of punch. It is a custom of the City, to which both
my father and my husband belonged."

"Willingly, Madam." Edward spoke in the name
of his brother, for both. "Most willingly, especially
if you will permit me to make it, as we make it at sea
—I think you will own that even servants taught by
you cannot make punch so well as a sailor. Afar from
love—torn from his sweetheart—what comfort for the
sailor but his punch?"

So Molly brought the hot water, the lemons, sugar,
spice, and the rum in a decanter, with the punch bowl

—be sure that it was Isabel's best punch bowl—that reserved by her husband for the refreshment of the pious company which frequented his house—and a beautiful bowl it was, thin as an egg, painted with flowers, gilt-edged, and, if you struck it lightly, giving out a note as clear as a bell and almost as loud.

You could imagine that the making of punch was a mighty mystery, so great was the attention bestowed upon it by the maker of it. He pushed back his ruffles; he spread out his materials around him: then, with an air of boundless importance, he began.

There is this difference between men and women, that whatever men like to do it is with a will: they put into it, for the time, all their heart; women, on the other hand, save for what touches their affections and their dress, do everything as if it mattered not whether it was ill done or well done. No woman could possibly think that in the brewing of punch so much care was necessary. To be sure I have seen equal care bestowed (by a man) upon the boiling of an egg or the composition of a sallet.

First he cut his lemons; then he rubbed the bowl with the rind; after this he opened the decanter and sniffed at the contents. " Ha! " he said, " I have not been in the Navy for nothing. This is right Barbadoes; your true West Indian spirit—twenty years old, if it is a day. Your lamented husband, dear Madam, knew punch as well as Madeira! "

" He also knew Port and Rhenish and Canary—and, indeed every wine there is. He had no equal as a connoisseur."

"It is to be hoped "—Edward began to squeeze his lemons—"that where he now goes to Meeting, these gifts will not be wasted." Then he put in the rum: added a glass or two of Madeira: measured out the sugar and the spice with anxious eyes: and lastly, poured over all the hot water. Then he placed the spoon in my hand, and begged me to stir it. "For," he said, "the one thing that is lacking at sea is the light touch of a woman's hand. Believe me, Miss Nancy, there is a persuasiveness in the stirring of the bowl by a lovely woman which induces the materials to combine and mix with a will and a completeness, which not even the youngest volunteer at sea can induce."

So I stirred, laughing, and presently Edward declared the punch ready, and, indeed, thanks to my stirring, perfection.

He poured out five full glasses and bestowed one upon each, including Molly, who stood by wondering and pleased. Then he stood up and addressed his brother. "George," he said, "a toast."

"I drink," said George, "to the fair Quakeress, Miss Nancy." So, with a little maidenly blush which became him, he drank half a glass and set it down. But his brother drank two glasses one after the other, saying that the toast deserved nine times nine.

Then, for it was now already ten o'clock, they departed, promising that they would speedily call again.

"The elder," said my cousin, when they were gone, "is a young man whose face announces, unless I am mistaken, both honour and resolution—I think that he

"SO I STIRRED, LAUGHING." — *Page 94.*

is rich because his brother deferred so deeply to his opinion. Younger brothers do not so regard their elders where there is no estate to inherit. I observed, Nancy, that while the younger brother talked and laughed, the elder sat gazing tenderly."

"Nay, cousin, at his first visit? Curiously, perhaps. He looked about the room with a strange curiosity. He seemed unaccustomed to such rooms as these."

"Well, child, unless I am mistaken, it was—tenderly."

"Isabel! What can he know of my mind?"

"Truly, very little, my dear, unless the face proclaims the mind, in which case he need be under no apprehensions. Nancy, child, it is not a woman's mind that a young man inquires after : her face, to him, proclaims her mind : her lovely face, my dear, and her bewitching form proclaim possible virtues and all possible wisdom."

CHAPTER VII.

The Opinions of a Gentleman.

EVERY woman is at heart a match-maker. This proposition is generally advanced as an accusation or charge against the sex. On the contrary, it should be considered as a part of the eulogy which must be pronounced on women by every candid man. For, that every woman should be a match-maker proves the natural kindness of her heart, and that in spite of the (so-called) feminine jealousies commonly attributed to her. Nothing is more desired, or more desirable, by a woman than love : all her instincts lead her to desire love : it is love that raises weak woman to be mistress instead of servant : nay, it is love that makes her a willing and happy servant, though the mistress : it is love that distinguishes and glorifies her : it is love that makes her live by the work of other hands not her own : it is love that gives her more than the full share of her lover's good fortune, and enables her to mitigate and console him in adversity : it is love that removes from her the loneliness of the soul apart : finally, it is love, and love alone— even past love—which lifts her out of the apparent insignificance of her lot.

Every woman knows this: if every woman, knowing this, desires that another woman should be loved as well as herself, then must every woman's heart be truly soft and kind, and anxious for the general happiness.

My cousin was no exception to the rule. She assumed from the outset that love brought these two gentlemen to visit us. Why else should they come? "My dear," said Isabel; "one of them is in love with a certain person. Of that we may be assured. The other comes, I suppose—unless he, too, is in love —to lend support and countenance."

"I do not know," I replied, being as yet unmoved. "They make no signs of love. What is a woman to do whose lover, if there is one, makes no sign?"

"I cannot tell which it is"—we were still at the outset. "Nothing astonishes me more than this difficulty. Sometimes I think it is one: sometimes I think it is the other. I have seen the elder brother gazing upon you the whole evening through: the next day, perhaps, it is the younger. However, let us have patience. The flame will break out before long. Meantime let us attend, my dear, with even greater solicitude, to our ribbons and our rags."

It is not difficult to study the mode when one lives in St. James's: one has but to walk down the street, which is filled all day with fine people: or in St. James's Park: or in the Green Park; to see how the ladies of fashion dress and rouge and patch.

"We are by right but City Madams," said Isabel. "We ought to be living within the sound of Bow Bells; yet we can show as well as any how a fine woman may set off her charms. And as for charms, my Nancy, what can they display at Court—in face or figure—finer than can a certain person, who shall be nameless?"

At first this kind of talk shamed me. Was, I asked, a woman to be praised according to her points, like a horse or a dog? Did love mean nothing more than admiration of these points?

"Nay," said my wise cousin. "We have Nature behind us, and before us, and within us always. We build upon Nature. Dress, for instance, keeps us warm, but we do not wrap ourselves in a blanket: we build the structure called Fashion upon that blanket. Love begins with the attraction of beauty, but with civilised beings it doth not end there. My husband once owned that first he loved me for my face, which he was pleased to admire; but afterwards he found other things—those which belong to the understanding—which he also admired. Yet a lovely face must ever give a woman the highest advantage. Do not despise Nature, my dear."

I understand, now, that she was right. After all, it is easy for a girl to be reconciled to the rulings of nature when she has been endowed with what men call charms.

"A man, in a word," Isabel continued, "is first caught by a face and afterwards fixed—if ever he can be fixed—by the heart, or the mind, or the capability, or some other charm, real or imaginary, of which the world knows nothing. Thus fixed, it is for life. My dear, the only man a woman of sensibility as well as

beauty has to fear is the dull man—the stupid man
—who cannot understand more than what he sees,
and, when he tires of one face, flies off to another.
Now let us go back to where we began, that is, our
ribbons and our rags."

Every one will believe me, I am sure, when I confess that, although a Quakeress by breeding, I quickly
discovered how great a pleasure may be found in considering dress and fashion : stuffs and shape : trimmings and ribbons : to sit in a shop and have spread
out before you dazzling things in flowered silks, satin,
brocade, or velvet : to imagine a frock glorified with
ribbons, lace, and trimmings : to choose : to order :
to try on before a long glass : I confess that to my
newly awakened sense it was enchanting. Every
woman will understand me. But let no man, except
those of the Society, blame me : let him try to understand that a woman's dress is far more to her than his
own can be to him : to the latter it is always, more or
less, his working dress, like the leathern apron of the
blacksmith ; the sign of his occupation, like the red
cap of the brewer, or the brown paper cap of the car-
penter : or his fighting dress, like the cuirass and the
helmet. In a woman dress is never intended for work
but for adornment : in youth it proclaims, and en-
shrines, and sets off the newly blossomed flower of her
beauty : and in age it conceals, as well as it can, the
decay and final disappearance of beauty. It also proclaims her wealth and her rank. To be sure I had no
rank, yet my cousin dressed me as fine as any coun-
tess, and when we walked in the park the other women

stared at us with the rudeness of envy, or the equal rudeness of curiosity. Even the highest rank, I have learned by this experience, does not always confer good breeding. It is not well bred, even for a duchess, to stare after a new-comer with the air of asking what right she has to appear among a well-dressed company, herself well dressed.

I am not therefore ashamed to confess that during this period I spent much time standing before the mirror, or sitting at the counter of the mercer's shop.

"Cousin," I said, "what if my brother should see me now?" 'Twas when my first really fine frock came home, and I stood in grandeur, hoop and all, ready to sally forth into the park.

"Quakeress," she laughed, speaking in the old style. "Will thee still be thinking about thy brother? Thee are but a goose. I do not think that some one will ever suffer thee to go back to him."

Did I, then, lay myself out, consciously, to attract and captivate a man, like the woman in the Book of Proverbs? Nay: that can I never confess. Sure I am that if any woman should read this page, she will forgive me for wishing to appear becomingly dressed.

These friends of ours called upon us a second time: and a third time: and again and again: they made excuses for calling: they brought presents—an engraving for my cousin: some fine silver-work from India for me: a book, because we loved books—always something new. Of course when they had offered their gifts, they sat down and talked. After a week

or two, they came every day, either in the morning or
in the evening.

In August the fashionable part of town is empty.
The great people come up from the country in Janu-
ary and leave in June. The park is therefore nearly
empty during that month. Sometimes we walked
with our friends in the deserted paths of St. James's
Park : sometimes we saw the soldiers exercising in the
Green Park : sometimes we watched the Trooping of
the Colour at St. James's Palace. Many times as we
walked with them, Sir George beside me, and Edward
with Isabel, hats were taken off and people gazed upon
us curiously, especially upon me. " They are, I suppose," he would say carelessly, " acquaintances of
mine. A great many people know me. Not everybody. Yet they gaze upon you, Miss Nancy, for very
good reasons which I need not explain."

Meantime, I could no longer disguise from myself
the knowledge that Sir George came to see me, and
that the brother came simply to accompany him.
And it was manifest that the younger brother's deference to the elder was always most marked and un-
usual. On the other hand, Sir George accepted this
deference as if it were his due—yet not arrogantly.

I have told you that Sir George was a young man
of singularly fine appearance. Let me talk about him
again. His large and open face showed the nobility
of his soul : honour, truth, loyalty, bravery, were
stamped upon it ; his eyes were always full of light,
and—oh ! to think of it !—I have seen them full of
love and tenderness. He wore his hair powdered and

tied behind in a bow of black ribbon ; his gold lace, his gold buckles, were of the finest ; his dress was that of a rich young man. In his speech he was rapid, but authoritative ; his voice was musical and sweet.

In his manner he was extremely affable : he wore habitually the gracious smile that belongs to a good heart. I have since learned that he could be peremptory, and even harsh on occasions : as when his orders were not obeyed. For myself, I cannot understand how he could ever be harsh. The mere look of reproach in those eyes, always so kindly, would have made me sink into the earth.

It is a pleasure for me to recall some of the opinions and judgments which he delivered in my presence ; and, indeed, addressed chiefly to myself. And since it is interesting to the world to know what were the private sentiments and the opinions of a great man in his younger days, while still a (comparatively) private person, I propose to pause in my story in order to set down some of those which I remember. There are times when I seem to remember every word that he ever said : there are other times (those of depression) when many of his words seem to escape me. His opinions may have been founded on imperfect knowledge : but they were always such as a noble mind would form and hold.

Sometimes we read poetry, but neither of the brothers cared greatly for verse : they were not open to the influence of the Muse : they were not moved by poetry, though my cousin read, or declaimed, as well as any actress. When I ventured to remonstrate

with Sir George on this apparent insensibility, "If I
were a woman," he said, "I should read poetry. Men
act, women look on : they like to hear, if they cannot
see, how a thing is done. The poet fights the battle
over again for their instruction."

"But, Sir," I ventured to say, "the actors are few,
the spectators are many, and they are not all women."

"Let us say, then, that poets write not for men of
action. That is to say, not for kings and princes ;
generals and admirals, statesmen, lawmakers, judges,
bishops, divines. See how large a number are excluded,
for these are the men of action, who care little how
a thing is described so that it is done well. For myself, it is possible that I, too, shall be numbered here-
after among those who act. Do you think that I
shall concern myself about the gentry who are trying
to make *crown* rhyme to *frown?* It is a necessary
condition imposed upon the man who acts that he
should be the prey of the man who writes. Poets
eulogise the men who are successful. They are the
slanderers of the men who are defeated. Miss Nancy,
the poets do not write for the leaders, but for those
who are led : they write, I say, for the spectators : for
the herd : for the people who obey, and for the women
who look on. For my part, I cannot for the life of
me understand the admiration with which the world
regards the poets, or the vanity with which they regard
themselves."

"Does not their vanity spring from the world's
admiration?" I ventured to ask. "If we did not
admire and love their works they would not be vain?"

" Yet—what is it we admire? A feat of arms finely
described : yet, Miss Nancy, the feat of arms is neither
better nor worse for the description. The poet does
not make it. He only talks about it."

" He makes kings immortal, Sir. Who would know,
after all these years, anything of the Siege of Troy but
for Homer's Epic and Pope's Translation?"

" A general or a prince should so live that he should
carve his name himself in immortal granite never to
be forgotten. I hear that they accuse the King of
neglecting poets. What should he do for them? If
they are good poets they become so without the
King's help. Why should the King encourage them?
Elizabeth did not encourage Shakspere, who got on
very well, I believe, without her support. Kings must
encourage the soldiers who defend the nation and
extend her glory : and statesmen who administrate the
country : and merchants who increase her wealth : and
scholars who preserve her religion : but poets! Let
those for whom the poets write maintain the poets.
Therefore, Miss Nancy, I prefer those who make the
history of the world : that is, the Kings who rule : to
the men who write verses upon them."

" But, Sir," I said, " there are other poets besides
those who write epics. There are pastoral poets, religious poets : those who write love poems : those who
write drinking songs : satirists——"

" There, indeed," he said, " I congratulate you, Miss
Nancy. The pastoral poets talk about the warblers
in the bosky grove and the enamelled lawns. When
I walk in my gardens at Kew I see the flowers and

I hear the birds. It would make me no happier if I could repeat dozens of rhymes upon them. As for drinking-songs, you would not like my brother to troll out in this room some low sailor's drinking-song : and as for satire, it is, truly, a fine thing to invent lies and to take away another man's character. Of love-songs, however, I must speak with respect, because my father, who loved the arts of every kind, wrote at least two. One, which I remember, was addressed to his mistress—that is, his wife."

We begged him to recite it.

"I would rather sing it for you," he replied.

This was a new discovery. He could touch the harpsichord and sing. His voice, I have already said, was musical : it was also true to time and tune. The words which I took down were as follows. I give the best—which were the first two verses and the last—

'Tis not the liquid brightness of thine eyes,
That swim with pleasure and delight,
Nor those two heavenly arches which arise
O'er each of them to shade their light.

'Tis not that hair which plays with every wind,
And loves to wanton round thy face :
Now straying round the forehead. now behind,
Retiring with insidious grace.

No : 'tis that gentleness of mind, that love
So kindly answering my desire :
That grace with which you look and speak and move
That thus has set my soul on fire.

After this he often sang to us. "At home," he said, "when I sing, they all fall into ecstasies. Sure never was heard so fine a singer! Never was heard so fine a voice! From your lips, dear ladies, alone can I learn the truth and have my faults corrected, and so improve. If singing is a trifle worth doing, it is worth taking trouble about." My cousin had told him that he hissed his consonants too much, and ran words together which should be separate. "Nay—but, indeed, I thank you for your criticisms. Perhaps another evening I may prove that I have laid your instructions to heart."

Of books and authors he entertained as poor an opinion as of poets. "If a gentleman chooses," he said, "to entertain the world with his thoughts, I suppose he may do so, though it would be more dignified to communicate them to his private friends only, as many learned scholars and wits prefer to do. But as for these ragged fellows who hang about booksellers' shops; write vile pamphlets on either side for money; sell their pens to all comers; praise or slander according to pay, and supply whatever is wanted at a guinea a sheet—this, I hear, is the rule—why, I think such a trade most contemptible and most hateful."

"But," I said, "authors move the world through the imagination, either by a play, or a poem, or a romance."

"Why, if so, how is your author better than a buffoon who makes the people laugh? He is but a Jack Pudding and a Merry Andrew at best. If we condescend to laugh at such a fellow we despise him still. Pitiful trade, to make idle people laugh or cry ! But perhaps there are people who do not think so. Otherwise no one would be proud to take up the trade."

I submitted with humility that many of these authors wrote with a serious intention, for the promotion of Virtue. And I instanced that remarkable work, "Clarissa," by the ingenious Mr. Samuel Richardson.

"I have heard of the book," he said : "I doubt, however, whether virtue can be advanced by the delineation of vice or the contemplation of virtue brought to ruin. Besides, this advocacy of virtue belongs to Divines and to religion. Tell me, Miss Nancy, if the Gospel, which contains the Word of God, fails to inculcate virtue, can we expect success from a printer of Fleet Street ? "

He would, in fact, admit only as worthy of encouragement, books of instruction, such as works on agriculture, inventions, medicine, surgery, arts and crafts, and the like. Much reading, he thought, made a man rely on books more than upon himself. "Consider a gardener," he said. " I dare swear that none of my gardeners know how to read. Yet, what a vast field of knowledge belongs to them : they know the trees and the flowers and the roots and the vegetables, with everything belonging to them : each kind of tree, and how it lives and flourishes: its soil: its health and diseases. They know all the birds and their customs : there is no end to the knowledge of a gardener. What book can teach this knowledge ? "

One must confess that this kind of knowledge cannot be imparted by books.

"As for me," he went on, "I find that I learn best if I learn by the word of mouth. Whether it is in the art of war or the art of government, I do not care to read so much as to listen : then I turn over in my mind what I have heard, and there it sticks. How much better is this than the printed book, where one always sees the peacock author strutting about and crying, ' Hear me! Behold me! See these fine feathers! How clever I am!'"

Such were his opinions on poets and authors. He did not advance them with the diffidence that one finds in most young men : such diffidence, for instance, as is due to the presence of older or more experienced persons: such diffidence as one acquires by frequenting places where men congregate: as the halls and common rooms of colleges; coffee-houses and taverns. This young man spoke as if he had been encouraged to think his own opinions of the greatest importance : this, indeed, as you will presently understand, was the case.

His opinions, again, were such as one would expect of a young man living out of the world : that is to say, apart from the folk who do the work and are anxious about their daily bread. His views of human nature were not based on a sufficiently wide observation. Yet they were remarkable, you will own, for their sound justice.

We spoke of plays. I mentioned that I knew them only by reading, for I had never been to the theatre.

" A play," he said, " is the representation of history
or fable by action accompanied by dialogue proper to
the situation. If you only read a play you have to
imagine a succession of situations, which continually
change as they follow the course of the story. I confess that my own imagination is too dull and the
effort is too great for this. If you will permit me to
accompany you to the play you will see a thousand
beauties in the story which you never guessed by
reading."

I said that in my youth I was taught that the theatre is the house of the Devil.

" Why," he replied, " so is this house, and every
house, unless we keep him out. Miss Nancy's face
would frighten him even out of the playhouse."

" But," said my cousin, " I have always understood
that vice is open and unrestrained at the playhouse.
How can a gentlewoman venture into such a place ? "

" At first," he replied, " you will wonder what a
gentlewoman has to do in such a place : you will see
the people fighting in the gallery, brawling in the pit,
the fellows staring at the pretty women in the boxes,
the painted Jezebels laughing loud and staring at the
men, the footmen in their gallery whistling and calling
and bawling, the music making noise enough to crack
your ears, and the orange-girls shrieking above all.
But as soon as the piece begins you forget all that
offended you before : your eyes will be fixed upon the
stage : you will be carried quite out of yourself : you
will think of nothing but the story which they act.
They are not afraid—these actors—to place even Kings

and Queens upon the stage: the Majesty of Kings, which is conveyed to them by the holy Chrism, they cannot, of course, imitate : but the dignity of a Queen have I seen represented with wonderful power. That, Miss Nancy, is, I suppose, because all women are born to command."

" Well, but," I said, still thinking of the authors and the poets, " every play must be written by some one, who invents also the fable or plot."

" Nobody asks who wrote it. The playwright finds his plot somewhere ; he does not invent it. He arranges it first, and then writes the words afterwards. But the words are nothing: it is the scene and the situation that carry us out of ourselves. The play is not made by the author, but by the actor, to whom alone should be given the credit."

Now to this opinion, that the words are nothing, and that the play is made by the actor, not the author, my cousin, who loved the reading of plays, demurred, and a long argument followed, which I omit because nothing was settled, and to this day I know not whether a play owes more to the poet or to the actor.

In a word, he loved the play, which moved him deeply, but he cared nothing for the fine poetry or the noble sentiments : what moved him were the situations, the things that happened : Richard the Second in prison filled him with pity : the fine verses put into the King's mouth by the poet moved him not at all.

" If I were a schoolmaster," he said, " I would teach history by means of plays, to be acted by the boys.

The schoolmaster would arrange the play and the boys would make their own words."

Sometimes we sat down to play cards. His favourite game was that called Comet. I believe that the Founder of our Society called them the Devil's pictures, or something equally severe. Surely, had he seen our innocent games, at which no one wept at losing or rejoiced at winning, he would have changed his opinion. Cards, I apprehend, like wine, dress, and many other things, are what we make of them. On this subject he was quite clear and decided. He played with interest, but it was the interest of watching the chances and varying fortunes of the cards, which sometimes wantonly strip a player of all he has, and at other times, with no more reason, load him with wealth.

" A gentleman," he said, " must not play above his means : let him lose no more than he will never miss, and win no more than will not make him rich. Let us not see your lovely face, Miss Nancy, distorted by the anxieties of the gamester. Sometimes, at my mother's card parties, I watch the ladies over their play. Heavens ! If they only mark the havoc which play can make upon a woman's face ! What lover' would not fly in horror from his mistress when he saw her snatch up her cards ; bite her lips ; turn white and red through her rouge : when her eyes are filled with tears : when her voice chokes : and her brow wrinkles with rage and despair? Yet the next night they are ready to begin again ! Miss Nancy, you have again all the luck of the cards."

He spoke often and willingly on religion, in which
he was firmly attached to the Established Church:
holding in pity all those persons who dissent from the
Thirty-Nine Articles; not, as some clergymen of the
Establishment do, treating them with hatred as if
they were criminals: or derision, as if their judgment
were contemptible: but with a sincere and deep-
rooted pity that, owing to some early prejudice or
confusion of brain, they should not be able to discern
the truth. He knew all the arguments against the
Catholics, and wondered openly why the Pope of
Rome did not acknowledge the English Church as the
only true form: the Jesuits, and the Pretender's
brother, he supposed, kept him from reading the simple arguments against Popery. As for the Protestant
sects, he knew some of them—their name is legion—
and what was to be said against them. As for the
Society of Friends, he had been, till he knew us, in
complete ignorance. How could a young gentleman
grow up in ignorance of the Society? In every town
the Friends are to be found: always in trade; always
wealthy; spoken of continually on account of their
refusal to pay tithes; having colonies in America; belonging more largely than most sects to the history of
their country: and here was a young man of two-and-
twenty who knew nothing of them. " Who are they?"
he asked. " Why were they called Friends? Why
did they offer no resistance? Why did they refuse to
pay tithes and Easter dues? By what arguments did
they defend their position? If we were all equal it
would be right for all to wear the same dress: then we

ought all to have the same fortune." He took the greatest pleasure in knocking down the doctrines of my people. This, I daresay, was not difficult with two women, only half-hearted, against him.

" I take my doctrines," he said, " from the Arch-bishops, the Bishops, and the Divines of my own Church. These doctrines, I understand, were origi-nally laid down for us in Hebrew, Chaldean, and in Greek—perhaps in other languages, none of which do I understand, even if I had them laid before me. How, then, can I pretend to judge of these doctrines, what they were and what the translation should be? Do the Quakers understand these ancient languages? I think not. Yet they venture to construct their own interpretation. This is presumption! Do they also profess to expound the law which has been made for them by successive Kings? Dear Miss Nancy, there is no safety among such people, believe me. In things religious, above all, the wise must lead the igno-rant."

These words I have remembered ever since. Of their wisdom I have now no doubt. Scholarship and learning are of small importance except for the acqui-sition of wisdom and the imparting of knowledge. It is to the Divines that the world at large must look for their opinions.

Sometimes he asked questions about the people—how they live, how they work, what they think, of their loyalty, their religion, their manners; betraying a strange ignorance of the lower classes whom we of the middle sort continually meet and know.

"I suppose," he said, "that I ought to know something of these people. My excuse is that while my brother Edward has been to sea, and so knows the world, I have had to live at home—for reasons which I will spare you. Few indeed are the houses into which I have gone: few are the people outside my own—relations—whom I know. Therefore, all that you tell me interests me."

My cousin, for instance, told him how the City people of the better class live: she described her own life before she married a Quaker: the cheerful life of a London merchant's daughter, with the assembly once a week in winter: the country drives in summer —to Hampstead and Highgate in the north, to Dulwich and the hanging woods of Penge in the south: the card-parties in the winter evenings: the river parties: the City feasts: the church and the sermons: the visits accompanied by a 'prentice with a club and a lantern: the sets and coteries and the different ranks and stations: all of which she depicted with much vividness. The differences in position he could not possibly understand. "Rank," he said, "very rightfully belongs to the Sovereign. A peer would not condescend to know a craftsman : but why is a lawyer above a schoolmaster?—a merchant above a shopkeeper? They are all commoners."

"The quarterdeck cannot associate with the fo'c'sle," said the sailor.

"There, brother, we have the officer. That is rank. That we understand."

This strange ignorance of the lower walks of Society seemed connected with the fact that his mother, as he told us, was a foreigner.

"For myself," he said, "it is my chief pride that I am born an Englishman."

Then he raised his hand, and recited these verses— "I spoke them," he explained, "as a prologue to a play when I was thirteen or fourteen—

> *" Should this superior to my years be thought,*
> *Know—'tis the first great lesson I was taught.*
> *What ?   Tho' a boy !   It may with pride be said ;*
> *A boy : in England born : in England bred :*
> *Where freedom well becomes the earliest state,*
> *For there the laws of Liberty innate."*

These lines he pronounced (as he did everything) with the utmost sincerity.   He could never understand the differences in position (rather than in rank) which make the pride (or the misery) of so many of our City dames.   I suppose that to one who stands on a pinnacle, or looks down upon the world from the summit of some high mountain, the smaller differences vanish : all becomes a plain surface.

"As for our own class," said my cousin, "it is that of the sober and successful merchant, who is raised above the shopkeeper by his superior education and knowledge : by his superior wealth : and by the magnitude of his enterprises."

He made haste to compliment her as to her own class.

"Madam," he said, "your class is the chief glory of the country : you make its wealth : you employ the people.   Believe me, we are truly sensible of the service which London has always rendered to this country.   As for myself and my brother, we hold it a singular happiness that we are permitted to join the society of so much virtue and so much refinement as that of yourself and Miss Nancy."

We both acknowledged this compliment.

" Here," he continued, " I find amusement without rudeness: wit without coarseness, and "—he rose, for it was nearly ten—"friendship without self-seeking."

He bent his head and kissed both our hands, with a humid eye which betrayed his sensibility.

CHAPTER VIII.

The Christening of a Convert.

EVERY history is like a journey: there are long stretches of road dusty or muddy with joltings and jostlings in the deep ruts: then come periods of rest, of smooth road, of pleasant company. One such moment of rest and refreshment I would note here, if only to show the natural piety of heart which distinguished my lover, whom I must still call, as his brother called him, Sir George le Breton.

I write these words in my summer-house: there are two windows in it: one of them looks upon the valley of the Lea. I can see the barges towed up and down the river: it is a broad flat valley, a marsh in winter, a meadow in summer: day after day, year after year, I sit and gaze across this expanse broken only by the meandering stream. Beyond it are the low hills of Essex. As this landscape so is my life: it is the stream which always goes on towards the end: and there is no change in it: nothing happens.

The other window looks upon my garden—a brave garden full of fruit and flowers. The garden speaks to me daily. It says—I gave it to you—I who loved you well—yet not as he—the other—loved you. Do not forget either of us—this garden is so full of fruits and flowers because it is a garden of Love. When you walk in it: when you look upon it: remember.

As if I could ever forget! The days pass: the nights pass: the suns rise and set: I desire nothing: I expect nothing: I hope nothing: I have no friends: I live only in the past: I do not wish to die because the memory of the past is precious and I would not lose it: I console myself concerning inevitable death with thinking that we shall preserve the memories of the past. There was once a poet who wrote that there is no greater misery than the memory of past joys. No, no, no: that is not so. I would not for all the world part with the memory of my past joys. They make my life happy; they give me pride: even though, I know, the people at church whisper that this is the lady who was once—— What does it matter what they whisper? Alas! A woman's heart rules her in everything, even in religion. Sometimes when I read Paul's promises concerning the future life—where he tells us—this great consoler—that eye hath not seen: nor can man's mind understand: the glories, the joys, that await us in the other world, I, being only a humble and unlettered woman, feel that unless one person is there with me, I shall be insensible to those joys. Again, since all human delights, all the joys and pleasures and ecstasies of which we can form any conception (being limited by what we can see and understand here) have their roots in corruption, but soar high as the highest human nature can allow: we may understand how out of the basest desires may spring the highest spiritual gifts: and since of all sources of human happiness love is the first, the most copious, the most satisfying, it is therefore the counterpart of the supreme joys, whatever they may be, of Heaven. In which case, my lover will come back to me. There, at least, will be no talk of rank and birth and barriers of love. For I was his first: I was his first: before the Other came across the seas.

By this time, there was no doubt possible. He came every evening, sometimes in the morning: he gazed in my face with such love as one could hardly believe. What was it that he saw in my face? Indeed, I know not why a man should be so overcome by a woman's face. I knew very well by this time that he was of high rank: I understood what he meant when once he spoke of the story about Lord Burleigh and the village maid, saying that he was wrong to take her to his great castle, but should have left her in her native village or placed her somewhere in a cottage surrounded by flowers and orchards where she would be happy in her own way, and where he could find rest from the cares of rank and station. And to this story he often returned. As for things that have been suspected, no one, I am sure, who reads this history will continue to believe them. Never —never—never could this noble soul stoop to anything disgraceful. How could I respect him otherwise? How could I, otherwise, think him worthy the love and respect which still I bear towards him?

It was at this time, and in consequence of his desire, that I was baptized and received into the Church of England.

It was a desire very greatly at his heart. He urged the cause of the Church with singular spirit and full conviction. It was the ancient Church of Christ purged from corruption : it taught nothing but what the Bible sanctions and commands : it has its organised authority, as the early Church had, with bishops, and priests, and deacons : the ancient sacraments : the ancient forms of prayer. He showed me that the Church was the mother of a great number of divines, scholars, and philosophers. Further, that my own poor sect was founded by simple men who were governed by the letter—and that an uncertain letter, because they knew not the ancient languages.

"One thing only," he said to my cousin, "is lacking in this sweet girl—she is still a schismatic."

"I think that she will never return to the Society again."

"Yet she is not baptized. Nancy, the Church waits thee—she waits with open arms."

In a word, I repaired to the rector of St. James's, Piccadilly, and laid my case before him. This excellent man was so good as so devote some time to my instruction in the doctrines of the Church, showing me at the same time how they rest upon the solid Rock of the Word.

When I fully understood the meaning of the things which are prohibited by the Society of Friends—as the efficacy of the sacraments : the baptism of infants : the kneeling posture : the chanting and singing : the litanies and forms of prayer : the declaration of absolution : and so forth—when I had learned the

Catechism and read the Articles (which my tutor kindly allowed me to accept unquestioned), I was baptized.

The ceremony took place after the Second Lesson of Evening Prayer. My cousin appeared as my god-mother, to present me at the font: very few people were present: Sir George stood retired under the gallery, where he could see, but was not observed.

Thus, consenting at first to receive instruction out of a desire to please my lover, I found myself a daughter—I hope a true and loyal daughter—to a Church which numbers in its illustrious company of children an infinite number of scholars and divines: poets and philosophers: statesmen and soldiers: mar-tyrs and confessors.

When the awful service was over and my vows were pronounced, my soul was filled with solemn thoughts. I felt myself regenerate, in a sense which would never be admitted by my brother: I was lifted out of a barn, so to speak, into a palace: out of a fold sur-rounded by wolves into meadows safely guarded.

At the doors of the church, after the baptism, Sir George met us.

"We are now," he whispered, "of the same faith and of the same mind. What I believe, you believe: what I think, you think. I am now completely happy." Not one word of love had yet been pronounced. Yet I, like him, was now completely happy.

This day is one of those which mark the course of the journey. It can never be forgotten. My heart is full when I think of it. For the first time in my life,

I understood what it was to be a member of the Christian Church : not one of a little flock apart, torn by fears and saddened by doubts, but one of the whole great company of human creatures for whom our Lord came to earth : He loved that whole great company : not one or two among them. And now those evil shadows fled from my soul : these demons of terror and doubt left me for good. I have no fear now. I am one of that great Company. My lover led me into it. I owe to him, in a sense, even my certainty of Redemption.

Two days later, in the same church, I was confirmed by the Lord Bishop of London, alone. It was at the special request of my lover that this learned prelate consented to receive me. "A gentlewoman of great piety and many virtues," the Bishop was told. No one was present except my cousin and the verger. The doors were shut, and I received, in a kind of solitude, the blessing and a brief exhortation of the Bishop. The solitude, had I understood it, should have foreshadowed the solitude of my after life, with the blessing to console and comfort the lonely woman.

On the following Sunday I completed my entrance into the Church of England by communion at the Sacred Table.

CHAPTER IX.

King's Favourites.

I SUPPOSE it was natural that we should feel some curiosity as to the family to which our friends belonged. They had a mother living: she was of German birth; they spoke as if she lived in London, and with her sons; their father was dead. Sir George had a country house at Kew; Edward had a younger son's portion; there was a grandfather of whom both spoke with a reverence not usual, I believe, in young men; in fact we knew, as we thought, everything about them, except the extent and the position of their estates and the history of their family. " Everybody," said my cousin, " knows about the Storeys. There is always a Storey of good repute on 'Change. In City names I am learned, and can tell you of any one, whether he belongs to a good City family or not. But of these people of rank I know nothing." Therefore we were in ignorance as to the history and position of the Le Bretons.

And yet—it was truly wonderful—everybody about us knew perfectly well the history, the position, and everything concerning that family and the two young men who belonged to it. Thus, Captain Sellinger knew: Corporal Bates knew: the Doctor knew: Robert Storey knew: what is still more wonderful, no one told us who they were: everybody, on the other hand, supposed that we knew.

As for the Doctor, his behaviour surprised me extremely, because I could not for the life of me understand what he meant. I think I have already mentioned him. He was the old man whose means of living were not apparent. He occupied the front room on the ground floor. He called himself Mynsterchamber, which, as we now know, was an assumed name. We called him Doctor, I know not why, for he did not practise. For the most part he seemed to be sitting like a spider with his door ajar, watching the people pass in and out. He had many visitors of his own: some of them he let out privately by the garden door, which opened upon the Park. Whenever my cousin and I went out or returned, he would throw open the door and stand there, a long, lean figure with a hatchet face, a cunning foxy face all wrinkles, with a pair of keen bright eyes. Then he would laugh gently and rub his hands while he passed some extravagant compliment. I expected these compliments: they amused me: one knew how foolish they were: yet they amused me. It was, " Miss Nancy will kill all the swains this morning": or " Miss Nancy, I protest, hath called up all her angelic soul into her eyes." And so on. Why, we might defend a compliment as a homage to virtue: it cannot harm a woman to be reminded that an angelic soul is much to be desired: she may then be induced to raise her own imperfect soul. Cold would be the world: it would be a world after the fashion of our Society : in which the exact truth, and nothing more, was told. In that kind of world the Doctor would have saluted me some morning with, " Miss Nancy, I vow, doth express in her sour and peevish countenance the whole of her detestable temper." That, I am quite sure, would have made me very angry.

One morning he not only threw the door wide open and passed the usual compliment, but he invited us to enter his room. Out of curiosity to see the lodging of this mysterious person, my cousin accepted and we went in. The room was furnished most meagrely. There was a low and narrow wooden bed covered with a blanket : there was a table littered with papers : two or three common chairs : and a cupboard with shelves containing his wardrobe. There was also a large wooden box strengthened with iron. His hat, sword, and coat hung from the wall : his wig hung from another nail : he wore a white cotton nightcap tied round his head like a turban, and a long, ragged nightgown of faded silk.

" The place," he said, " is simple, as you see ; yet it does very well for an old soldier."

He handed us to chairs. " I believe," he said, " that this is the first time during my residence here, of ten years, that I have been visited by a lady. What can I offer?" He went to his cupboard and brought out a bottle of curious shape and two little wine-glasses, into which he poured some liquid. " This," he said, " is a cordial made by certain monks in a place called the Grande Chartreuse. Taste it, ladies. Be not afraid :

it is strong, but I have given you only a few drops."
It was, indeed, the most delicious nectar that I had
ever tasted, but too strong for a woman's drink.
While we tasted this cordial he went on talking.
"This is my humble lodging: hither come a few old
friends from time to time to visit me: we exchange
recollections and experiences: like all old men, we
praise the days that are past. Alas! They come no
more. Age has few pleasures except wine and recollections and the snuff-box." He produced his own
and illustrated the remark.

He spoke with something of a foreign accent.

"You have travelled abroad, Sir?" my cousin
asked.

"I have travelled over most of Europe. I have
seen the Courts of Kings and the cottages of the people. I speak most of the European languages. That
man cannot be said to travel who cannot speak the
language of the country."

"You must have observed many interesting
things?"

"The differences between peoples appear interesting at first. When one grows old, they become insig-
nificant. All men and women in every country are
the same. And their highest virtues are simply those
which we teach to children."

"What teaching do you mean, Sir?"

"I mean, Madam, the elementary virtues which are,
I believe, taught in your Church Catechism: Honesty,
obedience, chastity, industry, loyalty—nothing more
is wanted. Were these virtues actually practised in

the world, there would be no poverty, no discontent,
no lawyers, no prisons, no gibbets, no sermons. Nothing is wanted in spite of your Thirty-nine Articles
and your libraries of theology but the simple virtues.
Honesty to beget confidence and trust : obedience to
preserve order and authority : chastity to preserve the
dignity of women : industry to supply the world :
and, above all, and before all, loyalty to keep the
social machine from falling to pieces."

"Is loyalty to be put first, Doctor? To be sure, in
this favoured land, we are all loyal."

He made a wry face. "All loyal, Madam?" he
repeated. "All loyal? I would to Heaven we were!
Loyalty, Madam, to the lawful sovereign—not to any
usurper—is the first of all duties. He who is loyal is
everything : he is ready at all times to spend and be
spent in the service of his King. There may be a bad
King, yet some time or other he dies : whatever may
be said of him he fulfils—he cannot choose but fulfil
—the function of a King. When he dies there comes
a better. The King is the keystone to the arch : the
only stone that belongs to that place. If all the world
were loyal there would be no rebellions, no heresies,
no false prophets, no mischievous liberties : we should
all think alike, hold the same faith, and, if need be,
should die alike."

He spoke earnestly, and his face lost for a moment
its habitual look of cunning.

"When a man is loyal," he went on, "he will do
cheerfully whatever he is bidden to do by his superiors, even if it cost him his fortune and estate : even

if it ruins his children : yea, even if it orders him to
carry out the basest of tasks; even if his loyalty cover
him with infamy, he will dare it cheerfully. A man
who is loyal will place more than his life—he will
place his honour—at the disposal of his King."

"Could a King take a man's honour from him?"

"In politics and statecraft, Miss Nancy, everything
may be possible—even necessary."

"Of course," said my cousin, "everybody must be
loyal."

"Madam, believe me : it is the superlatively good
thing. Remember all the miseries—the civil wars—
brought upon this country by disloyalty. Henry the
Fourth takes his cousin's place. Presently the country is red with rivers of blood. Charles the First is
murdered, with more rivers of blood. James the
Second is deposed, and what end do we see to the
troubles that followed that act of wickedness?"

"Nay, Sir!" My cousin opened her eyes. This
was a strange theory to hear in the reign of George II.

"Loyalty remains in the country still. There are
the martyrs of 1715 and those of 1745. Derwentwater's spirit yet survives——"

My cousin jumped up.

"Nancy!" she cried. "This gentleman is a Jacobite."

"Nay, nay." He spoke as one who coaxes.
"What matter the opinions of an old man who can no
longer fight and is not a pamphleteer? You shall
have your own way and be as loyal as you like. Sit
down again, and I will show you something." We

sat down, and he opened his box. "You must know, ladies, that I have a poor house—in the country—a country house. Here I have certain collections—an old man likes to collect things. I have some paintings : some china ; some curiosities of all kinds. Since I have been in London I have made a little collection of miniatures which will interest you, I am sure. They are portraits—real or imaginary—of lovely and celebrated ladies—not one so lovely as Miss Nancy, who will, I am sure, be the most celebrated of them all." He took out a box about a foot long and placed it on the table. It contained a large number of miniatures set in gold frames. I took them up one after the other. They were, as he said, portraits of really beautiful women.

"That portrait," he said—I was looking at one representing a girl wearing a Scotch plaid over her shoulder—"will never be given you, Miss Nancy, by the gentleman who visits you every day."

" Why not, Sir ? "

" Truly, I cannot say. If you do not know, I do not. It is the portrait of Flora Macdonald, a very distinguished loyalist, who saved the life of Prince Charles Edward."

" The Young Pretender," my cousin corrected him.

" If you please—Prince or Pretender—she saved his life. The Prince has been—though there is still time for fortune to change—singularly unfortunate hitherto : misfortune dogs his steps : he is continually pursued by misfortune : yet he has had his consolation in the women whose portraits are in this box.

Clementina Walkinshaw : Jenny Cameron : Lady Mac
kintosh : and not the least the subject of this piece,
Flora Macdonald.   Now Miss Nancy, I repeat, would
your friends give you this picture ? "

"Why should they not, Sir ? "

"Indeed, I repeat, I cannot say. If you do not
know I do not.   Will you choose to look at the rest ?
They are all the favourites of Kings and Princes. See
—here is Agnes Sorel, beloved of Charles the Seventh
of France : here La Belle Gabrielle, mistress of Henry
the Fourth of France : here is La Vallière : here
Madame de Montespan : all French ladies.   Here,
again, are some English portraits.   Fair Rosamond—
but I doubt the genuineness of this portrait : Alice
Ferrars : Jane Shore :—they are all sad in the eyes.
I know not why, but the King's sweetheart is never
happy for long.   Here is Nell Gwynne——"   .

"Put them up—put them up, Doctor Mynsterchamber.   Are these things to be shown to a young
lady ? " My cousin was greatly moved.   The Doctor
grinned, with such a meaning look that though I
knew not what it meant I shivered and shook as in
the presence of some evil thing.

"Come, Nancy, come," she caught me by the hand.
"This is the last time, Doctor Mynsterchamber, that I
shall enter your lodging.   Do not dare, Sir, so much
as to speak to us !   Rosamond and Nell Gwynne, indeed ! "

She pushed me out, very indignant.   "What does
the old villain mean ? " she asked.   "As for the
French pictures I know nothing about the persons,

and, I am sure, I do not desire to know anything : but the English creatures one has heard about in history. What does he mean by the loyalty of Derwentwater? My dear, the creature is a Jacobite. That is certain. And what does he mean by saying that our friends would not give us the portrait of the Scotch woman?"

CHAPTER X.

Robert Storey.

IT was somewhere about this time that Mr. Robert Storey paid me a remarkable visit. He came in the morning, when (I suppose) he knew that Isabel would probably be out with Molly and a basket, somewhere about Shepherd's Market. I was, in fact, alone, for that reason. Since the evening when he fairly ran away, frightened by the mere aspect of our visitors, he had not once called upon us. For my own part, as I did not think of him, or miss him, I asked not why he came no longer, who had before that event come so often.

This morning he was dressed in the plain brown cloth in which he served his customers and showed his books. One expected the studied respect of the counter: the self-satisfaction with which he stood before me was out of place in the workaday dress. A certain anxiety, however, was in his eyes and his salutation showed some doubt or difficulty in his mind by the omission of some of his ceremonies.

Yet he remembered, on sitting down, to thrust his right hand under his waistcoat, which is an attitude denoting authority. A suppliant, if you think of it, doth never sit upright, with his hand in his waistcoat over his heart.

" This is unexpected, Mr. Robert," I said. " The cares of business, I believe, generally occupy your mornings."

" I have left a shopful of poets and authors soliciting, as usual, my patronage. They must wait. I come at the call of duty. Consider me, Miss Nancy, as a man who never flinches at the call of duty."

" Indeed, Sir! I am honoured, whatever the cause."

" Where ruin threatens one in whom a man takes a friendly interest, or even a warmer interest, he would be below a man were he not to obey the voice of duty. In such a case to flinch would be degrading. Vanish, safety! Welcome, danger!—so that duty points the way."

" Really, Mr. Robert! You are doubtless right. But—does the occasion justify these noble sentiments?"

" In some cases," he went on, " as in old friendship, or in blood relationship, a man has a right to intervene: in other cases, the right has been conferred upon him by circumstances: as when two persons have been lovers. The recollection of the past preserves a tender interest, and confers that right. He who hath once loved, always loves. He who hath once loved retains the right of intervention. So sacred, Miss Nancy, is the passion of love."

He must have got this exordium off by heart: with so much dignity and roundness of phrase was it advanced: indeed, in what followed as well, he seemed like one who is saying a lesson ; or like a schoolboy reciting, with studied gestures, the words of another.

As for me, I understood not one word. What had
Robert Storey to do with love? Why should he
speak to me about the sacred passion of love? Never
had I suspected, never did my cousin suspect, that
the man entertained towards me any sentiment of the
kind. As for myself, as you know very well, I had
no thought of love from any quarter until a certain
person began to occupy my heart.

"Love," he went on, grandly, "even when rejected
and scorned, confers rights. To love a worthy woman
—that is, a woman worthy the affection of a merchant—not only raises the woman but also the man,
in whom love confirms and strengthens his former con-
spicuous virtues. It is a patent of nobility. Venus
borrows the sword of Mars and lays it over the
shoulders of the lover." He repeated the last clause,
being carried away by admiration of it.

I know not how long he might have gone on with
these extravagances, had I not stopped him, being out
of patience.

"Pray, Sir, for Heaven's sake cease talking language
fit for one of your starving authors and come to the
point. What do you mean, once for all, by your
rights and your duty and your sacred passion of
love?"

He turned very red, took his hand out of his bosom,
and leaning both hands on his knees, he bent down
and whispered hoarsely, though there was nobody else
in the room, "Miss Nancy, I can never forget that I
was first in the field."

"What do mean, Sir?"

" First in the field. That you cannot deny."

" I do not wish to deny anything that is true. But, if you please, what field?"

" First in the field, I say : you know very well what I mean. For two months my attentions—those of a plain substantial merchant—a sober, godly citizen—pleased—until the Other came."

" Attentions! To me, Mr. Robert?" This did astonish me, because, I repeat, I had no kind of suspicion at all that he had ever paid me attentions Speeches of a highly moral character he had made, often : but these I could not take for attentions.

" Understand me, if you please, Sir. I have never received any attentions from you, to my knowledge. You have behaved to me in no way differently than to my cousin. I am certain that Isabel has never suspected such a thing. Put it out of your thoughts, therefore, instantly and for ever. I cannot admit that you have any rights, or that I have ever heard you speak to me except as Isabel's cousin should be al-lowed to speak."

Perhaps I spoke more strongly than was necessary : but I confess that the claim made me angry. Rob-ert Storey ever my lover! This smug, self-satisfied man of second-hand maxims and third-rate phrases! Robert Storey ever to occupy the heart afterwards filled with——oh!

In reply he sighed heavily, joined his hands, and sat back in his chair with his eyes raised as if appealing to Heaven. " So quickly may the world corrupt! So quickly may the most transparent soul be clouded!

So quickly may coquetry—heartless coquetry—grow
up even in the Quaker heart!"

"Now, Mr. Robert Storey, you become rude. I
assure you, once more, that I was quite unconscious
of any attentions on your part."

"Alas!" he replied. "That Miss Nancy should so
stoop! How can I believe such a thing? Did I not
lend books? Did I not come here instead of going to
my club where I am an honoured member?"

"I am sorry, Sir. I was brought up in such seclusion
that I understood not what these attentions might
mean."

"Nay—think—you allowed me to believe: you suffered me to flatter myself: that I was not displeasing
to you."

"Displeasing? Why should you be displeasing?
Besides, if you were I could not tell you so in my
cousin's house."

"Then, suddenly, there appeared upon the scene—
Another—one who dazzled—and I am forgotten and
cast aside. This gives me, I say, the right to warn."

I was silent because what he said was quite true. I
had forgotten him. Persons for whom we do not
greatly care, pass out of our minds very easily. I had
forgotten him. Yet as to these intentions, indeed I
did not even suspect them.

"These young—gentlemen—are admitted every
night : the honest merchant is turned out of doors."

"Not turned out of doors. Remember, Mr. Robert,
you ran away. We do not keep you out of doors.
Come back if you please."

"You know that I cannot pretend to associate with these two—persons."

"You were once, if I remember, convinced that they were highwaymen or impostors of some kind. Do you now own that you were wrong?"

"If," he replied slowly, "it will help you to return to your senses, I do own that I was wrong. They are young men, as you know, of high place. Their world is not mine. I cannot presume to sit in the same room with them."

"You also thought that they are profligates. However, that matters little. What is your present grievance?"

"They are admitted here every evening, Miss Nancy. Have you considered—has my cousin considered—the construction which the world may put upon such an intimacy?"

"We live so much out of the world that we do not hear what the world says."

"No woman can afford to disregard the character which she bears in the world. As for me, my cousin's name is also concerned. This adds to the apprehensions with which I contemplate the situation."

"It is very good of you, Mr. Robert, to caution me against the world. Meantime, I doubt if the most censorious can find anything to say against visits paid openly to two women—one of them a widow—by two brothers, who always come together."

He rose : he made as if he would speak : he checked himself : he walked to the window and looked out : he came back and stood by the table.

"You shall hear what is said. Only the day before yesterday you passed my shop in Pall Mall, I was standing on the door step conversing with a customer, concerning a certain person. As you passed he said to me 'Those are the ladies whom he visits.' As he spoke he turned away his head."

"Is that all? Why, it is quite true."

He groaned so unaffectedly that I did not laugh at him as I was at first inclined.

"The world will always think the worst. Oh, Miss Nancy! you know not the wickedness of the world."

"But—what have we to do with the wickedness of the world? These gentlemen come not alone, if it is a sin for a man to call alone upon two ladies: I do not receive them alone, but in the company of my cousin. Believe me, Sir, they never transgress—they could not—the rules of good breeding. They are well-bred young men, with whom it is a great pleasure to converse. I am sure that they have no place in the corrupt society of which you speak——"

"That is as it may be—but why do they come? I will tell you, then, in so many words, why they come."

He sat down again and delivered himself of the suspicions which filled his soul.

"I will tell you," he repeated, "why they come. They are not highwaymen or adventurers, or impostors of any kind: you pretend not to know their rank: well, I will not know either."

"I wish to learn the truth when it pleases my friends to tell me. Besides, Mr. Robert, I could hardly believe you on this subject, after your mistake as to the highwaymen. Go on, however."

" I will begin, then. In this country "—Robert Storey always affected, as you have perceived, the preacher, or lecturer, or moral philosopher. " In this country where there exists a hierarchy, which is a word derived from the Latin meaning a ladder, there are levels in which each of us is born. To take your place on the wrong level brings misery and repentance. Those on the higher levels must not marry with those of the lower. Yet, sometimes, to the irreparable injury of the women concerned, the men of the upper levels make love to the women of the lower. They either dazzle the poor creatures with their ribbons and their gold lace ; or they make promises which they never mean to perform : or one makes his society so pleasing to a woman that—poor wretch ! —she cannot live without her lover, and so—and so— the rest is easy."

" The rest, Mr. Storey ? " I sprang to my feet fired with indignation. " What rest, pray ? What rest, I say ? "

" The rest ? It is what happens whenever a woman like yourself listens to a man like either of these two. There can be but one rest, Miss Nancy ; there can be, I say "—he rose quietly, forgot his affectations, and spoke quite plainly straight to my face—" but one termination to such an affair as that. If no one else will warn thee, I will. What ? Can you suppose that a person of that position can marry one of the trading class—can marry a Quakeress—one of that despised

sect? A Quakeress? If he were to do such a thing
in the heat and madness of his passion, he would have
to conceal and to deny the fact. How would you endure the slights, the rudenesses, the cruelties, the suspicions which such a position would bring upon you?
What friends would you have? Your own? Not so:
they would not meet your husband. His friends?
They would not meet you. The men would not concern themselves about you: the women would hate
you. They would leave no stone unturned to make
mischief between your husband and you. Nancy,
you know nothing of the fine ladies of London.
They come to my shop, and I listen to their talk:
they regard me not. I am only a shopkeeper: a
servant. They say what they please before me: what
do they care about a servant's opinion about them?
Their lovers call them angels, but they are fallen
angels. They are as false as Belial: as cruel as Death:
as vain as peacocks: their cheeks are painted: their
hair once belonged to some poor, honest girl: beneath
their fine clothes they are made of wood and of whale-
bone: they are selfish, greedy, grasping, insatiable as
the daughters of the horseleech, and as pitiless as a
slave-driver of Virginia."

He spoke with so much fervour that he moved me.
Yet what grounds were there for his outbreak? Nothing could be charged against our friends: neither of
them had begun to make love, although I felt and
understood the truth very well. As for the fine
ladies, he had probably received some affront in their
behaviour to him which caused this outburst of wrath.
What could he know about them?"

He sat down and wiped his forehead with his handkerchief. Then he composed himself once more,
ashamed of his heat, and represented the man who
has delivered a message or a prophecy and now smiles
gently over the recollection of an effective speech.

"Mr. Storey," I replied, "I think that what you
have said passes all bounds; yet I am willing to believe that you are in earnest. Understand, however,
that there is no ground for this suspicion at all--none.
And now, if you please, we will end the conversation."

"One word more, if you will permit. The danger
exists: of that I am quite sure: my cousin Isabel
ought to perceive it, and to avoid it—even by flight.
My passion has perhaps betrayed me into speaking
with greater heat than I had intended—pray forgive
me. And now, Miss Nancy, hear me quietly on
another subject. All these suspicions and whispered
scandals can be avoided in one simple way—by marrying me."

He rose again, took one step forward, held out both
his arms, and threw his head back in an attitude
which he believed to be one of admiration or passion
controlled by virtue.

" By marrying me," he repeated. " Miss Nancy. it
is in your power to make a good man happy, not
a——"

I stepped back, and took up a position which en-
abled me to have the table between us.

" By marrying you, Mr. Robert ? "

" It is the only way. Then the voice of the world,
which does not concern itself about honourable wives

of sober citizens, will pour its calumny upon the name
of some other woman. Marry me, Nancy."

" It is impossible—quite impossible."

" Nancy, when I think of that other Person playing
with thy heart my own is like to burst with rage. Believe me, Nancy, I love thee. Thy image is always
before my eyes, day and night. Sometimes I come at
night and stand under the window here—and think
with madness that those two are upstairs with Isabel
and you. Nancy, I cannot bear it."

"Mr. Robert," I said, " it is impossible. Say no
more. Leave me now."

" I must say what I came to say. Consider again :
these friends of yours are only playing with you.
For you, if not for them, it is playing with fire. For
myself, I have no other desire than to make you my
partner for life. You know me—I am personable : I
have good manners : I come of a good family. In
the trade I hold a good position. I have money
saved and a reasonable income. I possess shares in
many important books. As for reading, few have read
more books. For religion, I am a sidesman of St.
James's——"

" It is no use—oh ! no use at all. Please go away
and leave me."

" I shall prove a fond and loving husband."

" Mr. Robert, I could not marry you, even if these
gentlemen had never come here."

He looked at me fixedly for some moments. Then
he picked up his hat, which had fallen on the ground.

" Your eyes are hard, Nancy. I perceive plainly

that another presence, not mine, is wanted to make them soft. I say no more for this time. Only, Nancy, when trouble comes, remember that there was a man in your own rank who once loved thee, but was driven away. When trouble comes—it must' come— there is no help for it—it must come : remember that it would not have come had you taken that good man, that religious and respectable man, and embarked your money in his business."

"Thank you, Mr. Robert." I offered him my hand, but he would not take it. "If trouble comes, I will remember that the same kind of trouble would not have come with you. Believe me, Sir, I would rather have that sort of trouble without you, than any other kind with you."

So he went away, without any attitudes, quite naturally, and with his face full of rage. He loved me, in his fashion, I dare say, but how could I endure him after that Other?

This conversation for a time disquieted me. Not all of it. I cared nothing about the difference of station : if two people love each other heartily what matters difference of station? Nor did I care what he said about the women of fashion, except for the curiosity of it, and to think of the smiling, bowing shopkeeper all the time listening with both ears to the talk of these persons! No : the part which con- cerned me most was the statement that the time may come to every woman so courted when she can no longer live happily except in the society of the man who courts her.

Was that time already come to me?

With flushed cheek and beating heart I put the question by.

CHAPTER XI.

The Masquerade.

THUS slipped away the months of August and September. Oh! the happy time! The sweet and happy time! In the evening we sang or played cards: sometimes we danced: sometimes we read: continually we talked and laughed: continually I saw in the eyes of one that look which no woman, not even the most innocent, can misunderstand; and in the eyes of the other a look of interest—I will call it brotherly interest—with something of anxiety, which now I understand. Always we laughed and were happy. Kind Heaven gives to youth that power of happiness; but only for a short time, lest men and women should cease to bethink them of the world to come. Should not that glad time of spring warn us that there are joys of which we know not, even sweeter than the joys of love and youth?

Sometimes, but not often, we walked together in the morning. Then, as I have said before, people sometimes stared at us: hats were doffed—it becomes more and more wonderful, the more I think of it, that we did not discover the names and the rank of our friends.

London is full of places where the men amuse

themselves. There are theatres, masquerades, dancing places, gardens such as those at Bagnigge, Vauxhall, Marylebone, Sadler's Wells, St. George's Fields, and others : there are races, fairs, taverns, clubs, coffee-houses, cock-fighting, boxing, bull-baiting, quarterstaff, wrestling, and other things. Some of these amusements—not many—are open to gentlewomen. The rest we gladly leave to men, with the drinking, rioting, fighting, and robbing that go on afterwards. We talked of these amusements, none of which had either of us seen. They proposed to show us some of them. What would we choose ?

"Madam," said Sir George, "it has been our happy fortune, so far, to accept your favours. Suffer us to become still more indebted to you by accepting from us in your turn some amusement, however trifling."

"What say you, Nancy ? Sir George is very kind. What would you like ?"

"Should we walk in St. Paul's, or go to see the Royal Exchange ?" I asked, not knowing what else to say.

The brothers looked at each other doubtfully. Sir George replied, with a little hesitation, that there was little pleasure in walking about crowded streets, and being possibly followed and mobbed and stared at.

"Why should the crowd stare ?" I asked.

"Because, Miss Nancy," Edward replied quickly, "they always stare at every handsome woman, and they always mob and follow her if she happens to be very handsome."

It was prettily said, and there was no answer possible. At least none occurred to me. Yet I knew very well that this was not meant.

"Should we," I said, "go to see the Court? We are told that any one decently dressed is admitted in the afternoon? I should like to see his Majesty, if only once."

"I fear not," said Sir George quickly. "The King is old : the Court is now very quiet : it is, I am told, greatly desired to keep it quiet. Your loyalty, Miss Nancy, were better displayed by keeping away. Yet a chance may occur when I might show you St. James's."

"Then, Sir George," said my cousin, "should we not leave the choice to yourself?"

"It is a grave responsibility, Madam," he replied. "Nothing less than to make or to mar the happiness of two most amiable ladies for a whole evening. I say the evening, because at that hour there is less danger of being followed and mobbed."

This was one of a hundred indications which he gave of an unwillingness to be recognised. For my own part, I could see no reason why any young man should fear recognition, or dread being followed.

"No one will recognise you, George," said his brother, "outside St. James's Street. But, if you please, let us choose the evening. We will go where we can find company, music, dancing, and supper. Will that please you, Miss Nancy?"

"What is there, Edward?" asked Sir George.

"To-night there is a ball at Carlisle House, Soho —one of Madame Cornely's subscription balls."

Sir George shook his head. "You can afford to go there, Edward, perhaps. I cannot."

"What do you say to Vauxhall?"

"The last time I went there it was full of tallow chandlers."

"So long as they leave their tallow at home, what matter? What do you say to Ranelagh?"

"To walk round and round with a crowd of chattering women all talking about each other. Our friends, brother, would quickly tire of Ranelagh."

"Well, then, there is a grand masquerade to-morrow evening at the Marylebone Gardens."

"We could all wear dominoes, I suppose. The place could not possibly be worse than Vauxhall. It might amuse our friends to witness the amusements of the people."

We looked at each other. A masquerade! Surely this was not a form of amusement which decorum allowed to a lady.

"You have never seen a masquerade, Madam?" I suppose we both looked astonished.

"I have always been given to understand," my cousin replied, "that none but females who have lost respect for their reputation are ever seen there."

"I observe, Madam, with admiration, the jealousy with which City ladies regard their pleasures. It is true that after midnight these masquerades often become scenes of riot. Before that hour, they are generally amusing, and sometimes full of surprises and of vivacity. Believe me, dear Madam, we would not invite you to an orgy, any more than we would escort you to a cock-fight or a prize-fight."

"To be sure, Sir, we can trust ourselves with you. If you think that we could go——"

"I not only think you can, but I think you should, as to a sight worth seeing. Briefly, dear ladies, if you care to be present at a scene of harmless merriment and good-natured frolic, we will attend you there. I think I can promise that you will experience no other inconveniences or rudenesses than one may expect among persons all disguised." He spoke with animation, as if he was anxious that we should go.

My cousin still hesitated, thus showing that some traces yet remained of her Quaker experiences. For myself, I was now quite abandoned, and ready for any innocent pleasure that the world affords, especially in such company.

Well, after a little demur, she acquiesced. For my own part, I confess I was most curious to see a public assembly, particularly one in which everybody was in disguise.

"I am the widow of a sober merchant," said Isabel. "What would that sober merchant—himself a member of the Society of Friends—say and think if he saw his relict at a masquerade disguised and wearing a domino?"

"He would call it the enlargement of your mind, Madam. He was, no doubt, a reasonable person, although a Quaker, and has now discovered that the amusements of the world are not only innocent, but laudable. Else why were they created? Doubtless, he now regrets that on earth he had no share in them. We might even picture," he added gravely, "the soul in Heaven regretting that it never learned to dance on earth."

It was agreed, then, that we should go to the masquerade, provided that we were not to remain after supper, when revelry would come in, and manners would go out. As for the characters we were to assume, it appeared that if we put on something, or carried something appropriate to the character assumed, or to its history, that would be enough to indicate our intention. Otherwise it might be difficult to obtain a dress such as that worn by the character assumed, or, as in the case of that chosen for myself, even impossible.

We then, sitting round the table, with great solemnity proceeded to pass in review famous women, beginning with the history of our own country and going on to other countries and even back to remote history. You would not believe, if you have not already enjoyed this experience, how difficult it is to choose a character for a masquerade, especially if your friends are jealous of your reputation. First, I remember, we thought of Queen Boadicea, but she would be useless without her chariot and her two daughters, therefore she was dismissed. How could we introduce her chariot into Marylebone Gardens? Next Fair Rosamond was proposed, but Sir George objected on account of her character: he could not bear, he said, that Miss Nancy's name should be coupled with one whose conduct might be forgiven, but could not be forgotten. The same objection was raised to the character of Jane Shore, even if I presented myself barefooted, bareheaded, in a white skirt and carrying a wax taper, doing penance. "I suppose," said Edward, "that we must not so much as mention Nell Gwynne or Lady Castlemaine?"

"Certainly not," said Sir George, colouring. "How can we even name such persons in this presence?"

"There is Anne Boleyn."

"The mother of Queen Elizabeth. But, if we choose Anne Boleyn, it would be taken as a protest against her execution. One would not choose to condemn the judgment of the King."

"There is Mary Queen of Scots."

"For private reasons," said Sir George, "I should take it as a personal honour if Miss Nancy played that part"—I knew not what he meant—"for I believe that if ever any woman was maligned Mary Queen of Scots is one. But I cannot deny that there are grave historians who believe her life to have been what her enemies pretended. Therefore we will pass over the name of Mary. Miss Nancy," he spoke earnestly, "you could not take her part without interesting yourself in her history, which is, I assure you, a tangled mass of invention and lies."

Some one suggested Queen Elizabeth. "Her features," said Sir George, "were strongly marked: her eyes were piercing: her hair was red: her port was imperious. Miss Nancy, whose eyes are all gentleness and softness, and her face all maidenly sweetness, could not possibly represent that part."

What were we to do then? Where to find an illustrious woman? Observe that none of us were students of history. However, we proceeded to think of names in ancient history, of which the gentlemen seemed to know something. Most of the names proposed were strange to me. For instance, there was the name of Helen of Troy. I had read somewhere that she was the loveliest woman of her time (for which reason it would have been a pleasant piece of presumption to represent her). It now appeared that she had actually run away from her own husband. This deplorable act not only caused a ten years' war and the destruction of a noble city, but also prevented me from attending the masquerade in her character. Queen Dido, for much the same reason, as I concluded, for I knew not the history of that sovereign, was next rejected. So also were other Queens and great ladies. Zenobia, Cleopatra, Aspasia, Theodora, and others whose names and actions I have forgotten if I ever knew them, all of them, it appeared, though great in other respects, were (unless they were maligned) cracked in reputation.

"Should I go as a Vestal Virgin?"

"What!" cried Sir George. "You to go as a woman who has forsworn love? Why . . . Miss Nancy, you were born for love."

"We might," observed his brother, "cause her to accept a lover publicly, and so to break her vows. This would make an interesting play for the masquerade. At the same time, for a Vestal to break her vows was anciently thought to be the worst possible omen, and to be productive of the greatest national calamities." He looked strangely at his brother as he spoke.

"No Vestal Virgin, then," said Sir George. "We will avoid national calamities."

What was to be tried next? After ancient history, sacred history. It was then suggested that Deborah, Miriam, Judith, or Esther might be attempted. But I could not consent to take into a masquerade—a place containing many scoffers—women belonging to the Bible.

"Let us try the women of the poets," said my cousin. "There are the creations of Shakspere: Portia the lawyer: the loving Cordelia: the unfortunate Ophelia: Juliet, the child of fourteen: Rosalind in the dress of a boy——"

"Nay," said Sir George impatiently—I have said that he loved not poetry—"Miss Nancy must not wear the dress of a boy. Let us leave the foolish poets and find something for her that the world will understand."

"We waste our time," said his brother. "What character can we find more fitting for Miss Nancy than Venus herself, the Goddess of Love?"

"Venus?" cried my cousin, looking up at a certain picture on her walls, "why—how in the world would you present her?"

"Nothing more easy. She will go in her ordinary white dress, in which Venus herself could not look more divine: she will have a golden belt about her waist: everybody will understand that—all the women who have been compared to Venus by their lovers; and every man who has been flogged through his Latin Grammar and his Ovid. The golden belt will proclaim her: perhaps you might add a flowing robe of muslin—say blue—to look like the old God's Heaven: and she might carry a sceptre in one hand, and a golden apple in the other. You remember, brother, that the shepherd bestowed the golden apple upon Venus as the most beautiful."

"Did he?" Sir George was not greatly concerned with mythology. "Perhaps he was right, so long as Miss Nancy was not there."

I laughed. "You are both bent on making me blush with your compliments. Let me have the golden apple, if you like; but my sceptre shall be my fan."

So that was arranged. Then came my cousin. How was she to go? "As Diana," said Edward. "Madam, as the huntress with a quiver at your back filled with arrows; a bow in your hand, and a crescent moon above your forehead, the whole world will swear that you are Diana to the life."

"Shall I be asked to shoot any one?" asked my cousin.

"If any one should be rude, you will turn him into a stag and hunt him. You must take care of the whole party, most dread Diana. There is one thing, however, I learned once, that gods and goddesses are jealous. Will the real Venus forgive one before whom her beauty pales? Will the real Diana burst with envy at the sight of her supplanter?"

So, after a great deal of talk, this important matter was decided.

The next morning we spent in the manner customary (say necessary) for women who are going to an entertainment where all the world will have on their best frocks. We sat together, that is, with our whole wardrobe spread out before us, and considered what we should wear in the evening. Oh! Friends, once truly Friends! Oh! Society of Friends! Oh! solemn Meeting House and silent congregation! Oh! Brother with the broad brim! Oh! Sisters with the flat straw hat and the grey stuff! Alas! How changed was this damsel, once so meek and silent, once wrapped in continual meditation upon things which she could never understand, and tortured by terrors which she could never drive away. Behold her now, full of anxiety—not about her soul—but about her frock; about her head; about the decorations of that worthless person which she had been taught to consider was already, even in comely youth, little better than dust and ashes!

"Yes, dear child," said Isabel: "the world has pleasures which draw us on. For my own part, I am certain that we were designed by Heaven always to seek after happiness. When we have settled these things of real importance, I will prove to you by argument that we do right to be happy when we can."

While we were thus debating, Molly running up and down between kitchen and parlour, grappling with the double cares of dress and dinner, there came a messenger—Molly said he was a footman with a most splendid livery—who brought a large parcel. Imagine our delight when we opened it! First of all there was Venus's belt of gold—I did not think them in earnest about it, but they were. It was a belt of pure gold—what is called filigree gold, of the kind they make in Venice, I am told: it was open-work about three inches broad, with a buckle set with pearls: never was a more delightful belt or girdle. It fitted my waist so perfectly that it would have been miraculous had not Molly confessed to giving the measurement. With the belt was an apple, a large pippin gilt and pierced so as to admit a ribbon with which to tie it to my wrist: and, for sceptre, there was a fan—a large and beautiful fan—painted on one side with Cupids flying, Cupids shooting, Cupids lying hidden behind flowers: and in the midst Venus herself rising out of the waters. All this was meant for me. For Diana there was the bow—about three feet long and adorned with ribbons—a quiver of open silver wire twisted together, and half-a-dozen sticks, feathered and gilt, to represent the arrows of the huntress. In addition, there was a thin silver plate shaped like the crescent moon; and a fan like mine, but representing the miserable fate of Actæon when he surprised Diana bathing in the river.

"My dear," said Isabel, "these things are vanities, indeed. What would your brother say? But Nancy, they mean—what do they mean? They are rich young men. I sometimes think that they may be of higher rank than they confess. Well: for to-night let us enjoy ourselves—low rank or high rank: they are but men: and when a young man is in love speak he must ere long—or die. I say no more, my dear."

My frock was the best I had, you may be sure; of

white satin over a great hoop: given to me by Isabel.
I was all in white: my cousin's lace adorned my
throat and my wrists: I wore a white silver chain
about my neck, white gloves and white ribbons in the
lofty structure of my head. Our hairdressers came at
four, and finished us before six ! Oh ! what a day was
that, spent altogether in making oneself fine ! As for
my cousin, she swore that she had never enjoyed such
a day since she was herself a girl, and went to her first
assembly at Grocers' Hall. "To dress thee, Nancy,
recalls the day of my first ball before I met my
Reuben and turned Quaker. That was a day ! Alack !
That youth should so quickly fly ! Well—to-night the
folk shall see Venus herself. And I know who longs
to say so—but I say no more, my dear."

Our escort arrived at about seven with a coach and
four horses. They brought the dominoes—oh ! the
pretty little black things. How saucy could one be in
a domino, with no one to know her name !

" Put it on before you get into the coach," said Sir
George. " Then no one will recognise you."

For themselves, they waited till we drew near the
place where the crowd began to be thick, before they
put on their own. They were dressed with great rich-
ness and magnificence, in crimson coats lined with
white silk, flowered silk waistcoats, and gold buckles
on their shoes.

Marylebone Gardens lie in the fields (which are now,
I hear, mostly built over) north of Tyburn Road.
The gates are opposite Marylebone Church, a neat
and handsome structure. They are approached by a

lane called the Marylebone Lane. Outside the gates
and half-way down Marylebone Lane there was col-
lected a crowd of people come to see the dresses and
the disguises : link-boys ran along with the carriages,
and the people looked in and shouted their approval
or the reverse. For ourselves, we received, one is
pleased to remember, a continuous roar of approbation. "They are so polite," said Sir George, "that
one would almost like you to take off your domino."

For myself, as this was my first experience of the
nocturnal pleasures of London, I felt a strange timid-
ity of expectation as we entered the gates. There
were already a considerable company assembling :
and more arrived continually : all were walking in one
direction, which we followed. The way led through
an avenue of trees, lit with lamps hanging from
the branches, but at rare intervals, so that at best
there was but twilight in that avenue beyond the
gate. Suddenly, however, we burst upon the main
avenue. Then, indeed, I started with surprise and
admiration. The avenue was broad and long: it had
rows of beautiful trees on either side : coloured lamps
hung in festoons from tree to tree : there were thousands of coloured lamps : we walked beneath these
lights, the ladies' dresses showing a quick succession
of varying hues : at the end there were certain erec-
tions standing out in a blaze of light. As for the
company, I paid no attention to them, being wholly
absorbed in admiring the beautiful lights. When we
came to the end of the avenue we were in an open
space, which was boarded over and already crowded

with people. In a balcony covered over to keep off rain the band was playing an accompaniment softly, while a woman richly dressed was singing some song, the words of which I could not distinguish. Half the people, however, were not listening.

On the other side rose another building also filled with light. Behind and between the trees were alcoves illuminated with colored lamps. In these alcoves parties were already gathered over supper and bowls of punch.

" Behold our masquerade," said Sir George. " We will do what all the world does. First we will walk round the Hall, and then we will come out to see the mummers."

We followed the throng and entered, Sir George walking first, with me : and his brother following after with my cousin. I found myself in a large square room : the walls, painted a light blue, were decorated with pictures of nymphs and swans; Loves and god- desses : flowers and fruit : there were also large mir- rors at intervals, in which I observed that the whole company gazed as they passed. A gallery contained accommodation for a band : the floor was smooth for dancing : but to-night, the weather being fair and warm, the dancing was to be outside : round the wall were seats if any chose to rest.

" We walk round," said Sir George, " and look at each other."

All the women wore masques, and nearly all were in character of some kind. One in black silk and carry- ing a lute, was the Muse of Comedy. A Turkish

Sultana in short skirts and full trousers wore a crown
to mark her rank : two Greek slaves followed her,
clinking their gilded fetters : Queen Elizabeth ruined
her part by inattention to the points which we had
considered : Dido wept perpetually—when she remembered to weep. Queens, mistresses, characters from
plays and poetry followed in rapid succession. I
know not how many came as Fair Rosamond—you
knew her by her bowl of poison : I remember three
Jane Shores, all in white, with tapers : Nell Gwynne
was so great a favourite that one hopes her history
was unknown : Joan of Arc was there in multitudes :
as for mythology, one could not have believed that so
many women understood the Deities of Olympus.
Nymphs of every kind : of the wood : of the stream :
of the ocean : displayed their charms with liberality :
all the greater goddesses were there, including at least
twenty Dianas and a dozen who pretended to play the
part of Venus.

They were all, I have said, in domino. The gentlemen with them were divided about equally, some being
in disguise and some not ; some wearing a domino
and some not. I observed that the gentlemen, though
they affected the finest manners possible, paying
extravagant compliments to the ladies, and even walking backwards, did not possess the ease which alone
can give to fine manners their charm : their studied
gestures reminded me of Robert Storey : when I
turned to my partner I observed at once the great
difference. Yet they all took infinite pains to show
their breeding, handling the snuff-box, for instance,

with all the ceremony and pretence which that performance demands in the polite world. It has always seemed to me that one secret of good manners is to assume or to pretend that everything is of the greatest value and rarity—even a pinch of snuff : a glass of wine : a slice of chicken : a hat or a wig : a man's opinion : a lady's smile : a woman's face. But all this, which is charming when it is done with ease, just as a good actor will play his part so naturally as to appear not an actor at all, is ridiculous when it is clearly pretence and imitation.

My escort looked about him with an air of good-natured disdain.

" I wonder," he said, " who they are, and where they come from, and why they think it becoming to mock the manners of gentlefolk."

" How do you know that they are not gentlefolk ? They are well dressed." I knew for my own part that they were playing at good manners : but I wanted to hear what he would say.

" Dress maketh not the man," he replied. " What I see is that all this parade of compliment ; this making legs and brandishing hat and snuff-box, is acting—and mostly bad acting. I should like to see their real manners off the stage of the assembly floor—in their counting-house and their shops."

" Remember, Sir George, that I also am but the daughter. . . ."

He turned his eyes from the crowd to me. " I care not whose daughter you are, Miss Nancy. It is sufficient for me to know that you are the most beauti-

ful woman in the world, with the finest manners and
the best breeding. There is not, believe me, a single
Court lady to be compared with thee." He took my
hand and pressed it tenderly. The open Assembly
Room of Marylebone Gardens is not the place for
making love, however, so, for the moment, he said no
more. And then I observed with astonishment that
he wore on his breast a splendid great star, blazing
with diamonds. I was not so ignorant as not to know
that this badge denoted high rank.

" What," I asked, " is the meaning of this star, Sir
George? You have hidden something from me, have
you not?"

" Have I hidden anything from you, Nancy? Believe me, dear child, there was good reason. I will
tell you what it is, if you desire to know."

" Nay, I am content to wait for your good pleasure.
Tell me when you please, so long as you do not treat
me as you treat these people, with a domino. Let
me see your face and read your mind, Sir George."

I said no more, but I confess that my heart sank a
little. What did I want with rank? We continued
to walk round the room, the people falling back at the
side. So great is the respect of the English for rank
that they show respect even for the star that indicates
it, not knowing even the name of the person it adorns.
Yet so much of the Quaker remains in me that I respect the man first and his rank next.

" That Marquis of Exeter "—Sir George went back
to the story which had so taken his fancy—" the one
who wooed a village maiden and married her and took

her to Burleigh House. He did wrongly. He should have kept her in her village all her life. It would have been happier for him to exchange his rank and dignity for the life of a simple country gentleman; and for her to live in ignorance of irksome rank with all its cares and responsibilities. Ah, Miss Nancy!" he murmured; "if it could be my happy lot to live with such a companion—so pure and sweet and innocent— untouched by the world—free from ambition, greed, or self-interest—content to love her Lord——" He stopped and sighed.

We were once more come round to the doors of the assembly room, having walked round it twice or three times in such discourse as the above. At the doors, his brother, with my cousin, was waiting.

"George," his brother called him, "they are dancing on the boards outside. Come out and dance just once. Do you know," he whispered, "you have forgotten to take off your star? Never mind now. Perhaps they will take it for your disguise: there is another star among the crowd much finer than yours —the diamonds from Drury Lane, I imagine: they mark, no doubt, the rank of a merchant's rider or his accountant."

Then the Master of the Ceremonies, a very polite gentleman, came up, and with smiling obsequiousness, bowed low to the star.

"If your Lordship," he said, "will command a minuet *de la cour :* if the Queen of Love "—he recognised the emblem—" will consent to walk a minuet with your Lordship——"

"If fair Venus condescends." Sir George led me by the hand into the middle of the floor before all that multitude of eyes. I know that they were asking each other to whom the star belonged and who was the lady his partner. I knew that they were expecting to witness the manner and style of the dance as practised in the highest circles. Alas! my dancing mistress was but the daughter of one City merchant and the widow of another; my style was that of the City assembly.

The band struck up the first bars. The dance began. I have reason to remember that dance because it was the first and the last dance that I ever performed in a public place.

You have seen how I sometimes danced with Sir George at home. I therefore knew, at least, his style, and had borrowed something, perhaps, of his dignity. He moved, indeed, through the dance with a courtliness and an authority quite in keeping with the spirit of the dance, which is intended, as some say, to indicate the true position of our sex, and to show how we should be treated with the greatest possible honour and respect, if only to make us endeavour after the virtues which the men attribute to us. Others there are who see in the minuet the progress of a courtly amour. The whole company stood round and looked on while we two alone occupied the floor: and probably on account of the star, they all applauded loudly when we finished. Then we retired, and they made a lane to let us pass.

"Nancy," said my cousin, "we are proud of you. Everybody was charmed."

" No one so much charmed as her partner," said Sir George.

Then the masques ran over the floor and seized it, so to speak ; and some began to dance—the music playing a noisy tune—in country dances, while others ran about making jokes and rough play. For half a dozen would get together and get something that belonged to their characters: there were clowns and French Pierrots all in white : there were dancing harlequins : there were sailors in petticoats dancing hornpipes : there were shepherds and shepherdesses with crooks and ribbons : there were negroes: there were milkmaids : there were queens without dignity ; and judges without authority : there were devils who caused no fear ; in short, it was a scene of pure merriment and of simple frolic, so far, without apparent rudeness or license. As we stood aloof, yet were the object of much attention, some of the mummers came out and ventured to pray to me as to a goddess.

" Fair Venus," cried one, " soften the heart of my mistress or I die "; or, " Great Goddess ! incline my mistress's heart," and so forth. One brought a censer, such as they use in Roman Catholic churches, and swung it before me.

" Come," said Sir George, " we shall presently have too much of this, brother ; let us to supper."

In one of the alcoves we found waiting for us some partridges, with a salad and a bottle of Lisbon ; and, after the Lisbon, a bowl of punch.

From our supper-table we could look out upon the revellers capering and acting and laughing on the

dancing-stage. Now while we sat there, the gentlemen over their punch, I was surprised to see under
the trees before our alcove Dr. Mynsterchamber himself. What was he doing in this place, at his age?
He had three or four gentlemen with him. They
were all masked, but I knew the Doctor by his long
lean figure and by the old brown coat which he wore,
frayed and threadbare. What was the Doctor doing
in the Gardens? Why did he and his friends keep
looking into our alcove? Why did they stand outside waiting, while all the other people walked about?
The sight of that old hawk made me uneasy, I knew
not why.

Then I observed another strange thing. Under the
trees in a place not illuminated, I discerned, having
eyes both strong and quick, two figures familiar to
me. Presently I made out that they were Captain
Sellinger and Corporal Bates. Strange. The Captain
at the Gardens in company with a corporal! Was he
drunk? No; he stood upright, a cane in his hand,
without the support of any one. What were they
doing?

About half-past eleven, when the music was at its
loudest, the mummers at the merriest, and queens,
goddesses, nymphs, and heroines were all jumping
about like Blowsabella of the Village Green: when
from the alcoves near us men were bawling songs,
whose words, happily, were lost to us, we rose to go,
sorry to leave the scene of so much mirth, yet anxious
not to witness the scenes of disorder which take
place later. Many ladies were directing their steps

towards the gates at the same time and for the same reason.

When we stood outside the alcove, just before we started, the Doctor and his friends moved forward. With what object I know not. At that moment Captain Sellinger stepped out of the shade followed by the Corporal. They marched straight to the place where we were standing : and there they stood beside us, but facing the Doctor and his party.

No one seemed to notice this movement except myself. We then walked along the avenue of trees, Sir George leading me and Edward, my cousin. Behind us, but at some distance, walked the Captain and the Corporal ; behind them the Doctor and his party.

When we reached the gates and got into the coach, I looked again. Just within the gates stood the Captain barring the way. And the Doctor and his party stood irresolute. For some reason or other I felt sure that they were baffled, and for no reason at all I connected their proposed action with the gallant youth who held my hand in the coach.

CHAPTER XII.

Molly and the Corporal.

HITHERTO I have told you what I saw and did and heard myself. I must now ask you to read something which bears upon this history, yet was confessed or delivered to me by another or by others.

It is nothing less than the reason why Captain Sellinger was at Marylebone Gardens that evening.

Servants, especially women, are always listening and prying, the ear at the door ajar, the eye at the keyhole. It affords them, I suppose, some pleasure, unintelligible by ourselves, to find out what is going on, even when there is nothing to conceal.

My own maid Molly, a person of great curiosity, though in other respects an excellent woman, when she was not watching her mistress and trying to make out which was the lover, turned her attention to the other residents of the house. The Corporal and Mrs. Bates had become her intimate friends: Captain Sellinger provoked no curiosity—a man who is drunk every day cannot be interesting to a woman who naturally prefers Apollo to Bacchus: therefore there remained only the Doctor.

" There is something wrong," she said—one cannot

stop the tongue of a woman when she is dressing your hair. " The Doctor keeps the key of the garden door " —it opened out upon the park. " He has friends calling all day long: they come in at the front door, and he lets them out by the garden door. He thinks I can't see out of the kitchen window for the shrubs, but I can. They whisper in the passage : sometimes they go out quite late at night."

One did not encourage her in these confidences; but it was strange. What was the man doing that he should receive visitors by day and night in this secret manner ? He might be a wizard, perhaps : or a fortune-teller, or an astrologer : there are always plenty of these gentry about for those who wish to learn the future and make themselves miserable beforehand ; to be sure, the Doctor looked like a gentleman though he went about with torn ruffles and ragged skirts. However, the subject concerned us not, and, besides, there were more pleasant things to think about.

But Molly communicated her suspicions to the Corporal, who frequently took a pipe of tobacco in the kitchen of an evening with a tankard of our small ale, to which the honest fellow was truly welcome.

He listened carelessly, at first, as not concerned with a prying woman's chatter: a gentleman had a right to receive his friends at one door and to let them out at another if he pleases. There is no law against whispering in the passage : one is not compelled to go to bed at midnight.

" But," said Molly, mysteriously, " they talk a foreign jargon."

"What language?" he asked. "Molly, it may be pure Yorkshire or Welsh."

"It may be French," she replied. And at this the Corporal sat up, attentive.

At that time, as everybody knows, we were at war with France. If it was French, what did Frenchmen do in St. James's Place? The Corporal, therefore, became thoughtful: he put down his pipe and considered the subject. Presently, after binding Molly over on the New Testament to secrecy, he told her that he thought it might be worth his while to become, for the first time in his life, a spy; he would watch and listen: he would find out why this company talked a foreign language. A spy, he explained, was a person whose occupation justly stinks; yet in such a cause as this: for country and King: as a soldier: a man must not shrink. Besides, he confessed, much advantage, in case of the thing proving important, might accrue to his own interests.

He was moved, therefore, to turn spy, and to watch the Doctor closely and constantly.

"The thing," he said, "must be done by rule and plan, as one lays siege to a fortification. Let us consider. At two the Doctor goes to his dinner: he returns at six. He, therefore, after dinner, sits in the coffee-house. His habits and his hours are fixed. Molly, I shall procure a master-key. That in our hands, we will to-morrow shut the front door when the Doctor goes out, and I will then secretly make a first examination of the country."

This he did. He found the room as you have

heard. There were papers on the table which he did not disturb; but he examined the wall. The room was wainscotted like our own upstairs. He measured a certain distance from the fireplace at the height of his own eye : he then came out having touched nothing on the table, nor opened the cupboard or the box. " That will do for a beginning," he said. " You can open the front door again, Molly, and the Doctor may return when he pleases."

He then returned to the kitchen, the walls of which were plastered with a yellow stuff : he scraped away a square space at a place corresponding to his measurements in the other room, and with some difficulty removed two or three bricks from the party-wall. He could then put his eye close to the wainscotting in the other room. " A small skewer, Molly," he called. With this he made half-a-dozen little holes in the wainscotting which would be invisible the other side. " Excellent ! I can now command the table, and I think I shall hear what they say. Molly, there must be no talking in the kitchen while these bricks are out. Every evening I shall take them out : every evening I shall put them back : you must cover the place with a frying-pan or something in the daytime."

In the evening, about nine o'clock, the Doctor's friends arrived : there were four or five of them, and they entered by the front door singly and without knocking at the door, which stood open.

The Corporal took down the frying-pan, removed the bricks, and stood prying through one of the holes, and listened intently.

" Molly," he murmured, " they are talking French.
A fortunate chance indeed that I should understand
that language."

So he listened again, very earnestly. " Molly," he
murmured presently, " they are the greatest villains
unhung. They are traitors: they are rebels: they
are . . ." Again he applied himself.

In a word, save for occasional whispered ejacula-
tions, the Corporal stood there till eleven o'clock,
when the Doctor arose and let out his friends by the
back way, Molly blowing out the candle so that he
should not suspect.

The Corporal replaced the bricks, hung up the frying-pan, and went to bed, where he lay awake all
night long, thinking what he had better do.

In the morning he came down, greatly moved and
agitated. " Molly," he whispered, " not a word, even
to your ladies. You have sworn. There will be murder if you talk. Not a word, Molly, on your life.
And now go call my wife downstairs." She came
down, the poor patient thing, so hard-worked, so anxious about her brats. " My dear," he said, " cheer up.
Let us rejoice. Look out upon the world with smiling face. Behold the sun : the clouds fly, the rain
stops, I see fair weather coming. My dear, something
is going to happen—some great thing—I know not
yet what ; but some great thing. I must drink to my
good fortune. If you please, Molly, a tankard—we
will all drink. Give it to me. Ha !" He poured out
a glass and held it up to the light. " It foams and
sparkles, and the bubbles rise. They rise like me, my

dear. For thy husband this day is a made man. It shall mean—I swear—my commission—long deferred —nothing less." He still held the glass to the light.

"My dear," said his wife, "has trouble driven thee distraught?"

"Distraught? I? Nay, it is not trouble before us, but joy. My dear, I am like unto one who lights on buried treasure. I see before me a splendid future. Let us drink first to the Lieutenant—that is, to me myself: next to the Lieutenant's charming wife—to thee, my dear: then to the Captain's lovely consort— to thee, my dear; and lastly, to the Colonel's honoured lady—to thee, Madam, to thee."

"Oh! what does this mean?" she asked.

"I drink to you, my dear—always to you—in silk and satin, the Pride of the Regiment!"

He finished the tankard and set it down. "And now," he said, "I go to consult Captain Sellinger. I am the bearer of State news—State Despatches. I am a Royal Messenger!"

"Well, Sir," said Molly, "the Captain was put to bed last night, and he will be sleeping still."

That was, in fact, the case. The Corporal had, therefore, to wait until noon, when he waited upon him while he was dressing.

"Sir," said the Corporal, "my errand shall prove, I make bold to say, an excuse for this intrusion upon your privacy."

"Corporal, you have your Lieutenants: you have the Captain of your troop. If your business concerns your troop, go to them."

"It does not, Sir. It is a business of so great importance that I crave permission to pour it into your Honour's ears. After that, if you so direct, I will take it to my own Captain."

"Go on, then, Corporal. But first give me the tankard." The Captain took a long drink of that refreshing creature, small ale, with which he would always revive his spirits in the morning. "So," he said, "the night was cheerful : the punch was strong." He sat on the table in his shirt sleeves, his stockings down at heel, his hair not dressed. "Now I am ready ; go on, Corporal."

What he heard was what you have already surmised. The Doctor on the ground floor was both a Jacobite and a French spy. His friends, also Jacobites, appeared to be of English descent, but, as they spoke French fluently, were probably the sons or grandsons of those who formed the Court of James II. in exile, whom he created earls and barons. They were talking over the chances of a rising or demonstration in favour of the Pretender whenever the King, who was already seventy-seven years of age, should die. For greater security, as they fondly thought, they conversed in French. As for their hopes they were assured of support in many quarters—it was not, remember, more than fifteen years from the Rebellion of 1745, which so nearly succeeded.

That was the general purport of the nightly meetings.

"You say," said the Captain, thoughtfully, after another draught of ale, "that they have papers and lists with them."

"They were lying on the table."

"If the Doctor has them in his keeping we can secure them easily. However—Hark ye, Corporal, this business should be told to your Captain. If it becomes a case for trial, you must show that you went to the right quarter."

"By your leave, Sir, one minute more."

"If they want to proclaim James Francis Edward"—the Captain went on—"let them. I would counsel encouraging them till they grew confident. We shall then know who are his friends in the country and shall be able to hang 'em all and so an end."

"But this is not all, Sir."

"Not all! What the devil would the fellow have? Will they carry off the King?"

"You shall hear, Sir. They have hatched a most diabolical plot, which will be carried into execution this very evening: or to-morrow evening, as the circumstances will allow."

"Go on, man. Come to the point. What is their plot?"

"In one word, Sir. Two young gentlemen, as your Honour very well knows, come to this house often and always in the evening. Your Honour knows their faces very well. So do I, although but a corporal, and for the same reason. Well, Sir, they shall be nameless. At ten o'clock, or thereabouts, they come downstairs, thinking of nothing: the stairs are dark: suppose an ambuscade of half-a-dozen men in the dark passage : suppose the Doctor's door suddenly thrown open: there is a rush: the two gentlemen are

seized—gagged—handcuffed. In the place outside
waits a coach : at Westminster Bridge stairs waits a
boat : in the pool lies a ship ready to weigh anchor
and drop down the river, and so cross to the coast of
France."

The Captain sprang to his feet, dropping the tankard and spilling the beer. " Corporal Bates," he cried,
" I believe you are a liar of the first water."

" I wish I was, Sir. But for my truth and honesty
I might now be commanding my company."

" This is the most desperate villainy ! This is un-
heard of ! The King so old that he may die any day
. . . How many of them are there ? "

" Not more than six, I should say. But there may
be more behind."

" Yes—more behind, perhaps—but no more for an
attempt in a narrow passage. Corporal, if you are
lying . . ."

" Sir," said the Corporal, taking a Bible which lay,
more for show, I fear, than for use, in the window, " I
swear, upon this sacred volume "—he kissed it—" by
all my hopes of eternal happiness ; by the sacred
name of God Almighty, that every word is true. Captain, this evening will show that I am no liar. The
ship which waits for them is a brig called the *Tower of
Brill*, Amsterdam. The captain has been bought,
though I believe he does not know the names of the
gentlemen he is to take across. He will sail into
French waters and will become a French prize : the
coach has been hired : it will be driven by one of the
conspirators : they will assemble to-night, and in the

Doctor's room : they have not yet decided whether to make the attempt on the stairs or as the gentlemen are walking out of the door."

The Captain looked at him seriously. "I cannot choose but believe you, my man. Well—how best to tackle this villainy?"

He proceeded to dress leisurely, turning upon the Corporal at intervals with a question, while he turned the matter over in his mind.

"Corporal, you are ready to fight in this cause?"

"Sir, I ask nothing better. And I am a master in the art of fence, which I teach, with fortification and the forms of siege."

"Corporal, you can be silent?"

"Sir, I am a soldier—therefore silent. I teach the art of war, with the soldier's duties, to all who come."

"Corporal, you have a wife, I understand. Can she hold her tongue?"

"The poor creature knows nothing of this busi‧ ness."

"Corporal, you appear to be a man of courage."

"Will your Honour give me the command of a for‧ lorn hope?"

"Does any one in this house, or out of it, know these visitors?"

"I think not, Sir. Molly, the maid, knows that they come. You and I are the only two who know."

"Hark ye, Corporal. This is not an affair to take to Bow Street. It is one in which your loyalty will be best shown in keeping the thing dark. If it were to succeed the Lord only knows what would happen. If it were to fail with a fight and half a dozen killed and wounded and the noise of it spread over the whole world, there would be a proper kind of scandal indeed. No: the attempt itself must be prevented. Now, Corporal, you and I must prevent it for the sake of the ladies. Our services will not be put in the *Gazette*: there will be no promotion for us: yet I take it upon me to assure you that you shall be no loser."

The poor Corporal hung his head. Silence and secrecy! And he had dreamed of a fight: slaughter of the conspirators: and himself the hero of the fray! And, after all, silence and secrecy!

" I repeat, Corporal, you shall be no loser. Very well. You and I must mount guard together every night from the time these villains arrive till the time they go away. And we must escort these gentlemen unseen home. Meantime, you are sure that the ladies know nothing about it ? "

" I am certain they do not."

" Humph! Give Molly, the maid, this guinea to keep her mouth shut. Very good. Let me think." He sat on the table again and buried his nose in the tankard, now empty. Custom connected the attitude with the assistance of thought.

The Corporal, meanwhile, pulled out of his pocket a paper, which he unrolled and smoothed upon the table. " It is a plan, Sir, drawn to scale, of the ground floor. Here is the Doctor's room : here the stairs : here is the kitchen : here the back door, the garden, and the garden door. I drew it this morning for your Honour's use."

"You are a man of infinite accomplishments, Corporal. This is admirable. Well, I think a little sand in the lock of the garden door will stop their retreat, in case we come to cold steel, which I doubt. This, evening, Corporal, you will patrol the passage and the back garden. If you find a man or two in ambuscade, run him through. I will take the consequences —run him through."

"I will, Sir." The Corporal drew himself up and smiled satisfaction.

"Have a candle burning in the passage or at the bend of the stairs: have another in the kitchen. Don't hide yourself: make a little noise to show that you are there. I will take the court and the front door. Remember, man, we want to prevent them, not to draw them on: we want to save certain gentlemen from a scandal and certain ladies from things which would be believed and said about them."

That night the Doctor's friends were assembled: the coach was waiting: those who were to hide under the stairs found a candle burning in the passage and a soldier carelessly walking about: the man on the coach-box observed that another, an officer, was standing on the door-steps or walking backwards and forwards before the door: one or two came out of the Doctor's room and observed him. At about ten o'clock there were steps on the stairs: the Doctor's door was opened and his head was poked out. The two gentlemen came down: they stood on the door-step: behind them was the Corporal, beside them was the Captain. They walked away: after them, at a little distance, followed the Captain and the Corporal. Then the Doctor's friends got into their coach and silently drove away.

We knew nothing about this nightly watch, but the guard at Marylebone could not be passed over. I asked Captain Sellinger what it meant. " We are not Princesses," I said, " to want a guard of honour."

" Nobody more deserves a guard of honour, Miss Nancy." He looked at me strangely and anxiously.

" But you seemed to come after us."

" Highwaymen are about: foot-pads are hanged every day by the dozen : pickpockets, hustlers, ruffians, are as common as oysters. Ladies must be protected."

" Thank you, Captain Sellinger," I replied. " But ladies do not ask for better protection than that of their own escort. We have two very gallant gentlemen for our escort."

" Villains abound. London is full of dangers. There can be no other reason, Miss Nancy, since you know of none."

CHAPTER XIII.

A River Party.

AFTER the masquerade, the next event of interest was our party on the river. It took place one evening early in October, when the sun sets soon after five. The weather, however, in that year was, for the season, open and mild—even warm, so that the freshness of the air upon the river and its coolness were pleasant.

When our friends first proposed this excursion, I looked forward to nothing more than to be tugged up the river by two pairs of brawny arms, and to be regaled by the horrid language of the rowers: in short, such a pleasure-party as may be seen upon the river whenever the weather is fine. We should probably, also, be splashed with water during the voyage. Therefore, I looked forward to it with no great pleasure, except for the society which I had—alas!—already learned to desire so much.

It was arranged that we should be at the Whitehall Stairs, whither Corporal Bates escorted us, at the hour of half-past four. Whitehall Stairs, formerly the stairs of the Palace, of which little now remains, are not a very convenient place for two gentlewomen to be kept waiting, though they are less frequented than many others, and consequently less disgusting for ears of delicacy. I wonder if there will ever arrive a time when the watermen of London will learn to speak with decency and to affirm without blasphemy.

But we were not kept waiting, for, true to time, the boat which was to convey us came sweeping up the river, and was held by a hook to the long pole or mast at the end of the stairs. Boat, do I call it? Why, Queen Cleopatra herself, whose barge is represented in one of my cousin's pictures, never had so beautiful a vessel: nor had Queen Elizabeth anything, I am sure, half so fine when she took the air upon the river: nor has the Lord Mayor a finer vessel when he comes up the river on the ninth day of November: nor has any City Company a more beautiful vessel. It was a barge capable of holding I know not how many people: within and without it was all carved work, bright paint and gilded wood: most lovely was she—every boat is feminine—to look at as she lay upon the water: her bows rose up high, with a figurehead representing a maiden, all (apparently) of pure gold: in the middle she was low, and she rose again in the stern: she had six oars on each side: the men wore a scarlet livery: the man who took the helm was also in scarlet: two or three footmen, also in scarlet, stood about beside the steersman: a cabin or chamber was constructed in front of the helm: that is to say, neither in the middle nor in the stern, but between the two: the roof was supported by slim and elegant intertwined pillars of carved wood: the sides were open, but there were velvet curtains to be drawn if the air should prove cold: round the sides were cushioned seats: in

"SO HE HANDED US INTO THE CABIN."—*Page 183.*

th₁ middle stood a small table, at present with nothing upon it : in the bows was a band of music, hautboys, horns, harps, violins, and other instruments.

When we came down the stairs the harpist ran his fingers over the strings and struck up the old air, " How should I my true love know ? " This I received as a compliment to myself, because I once said that a harp moved me more than any other instrument and another time said that I liked the tune of " How should I my true love know."

" Heavens ! " murmured my cousin. " Where did they get this splendid barge? It is not one of the City barges, or I should know it."

" Welcome ! " said Sir George, stepping on to the stairs. " We have luckily secured this barge. I hope it will prove comfortable." So he handed us into the cabin and placed us at the end, taking his own seat on the right-hand side by me, and his brother sitting opposite on the left-hand of Isabel.

And then they pushed off the boat, and the voyage, which remains graven upon my heart to this day, began. Oh! that the happy day could come back again! Oh! that one could not only remember past joys and recall sweet words, but also see the lovely youth once more, rejoicing in his manhood, full of love and happiness! But for the hope that, somehow, we cannot imagine in what way, vanished joys will be restored to us, life would be too sad for endurance. We should accuse Providence, and die hopeless. They pushed off the boat, I say, and we dropped down into the open stream. Over our heads hung or streamed

out a long silken pennant : thus were flags flying in
the bows and at the stern : the boat was all glorious
within and without : my heart beat : my colour came
and went : my eyes, I know not why, filled with tears :
and Sir George gazed upon me fondly and fixedly as
if he could never have enough.

We passed without accident through the arches of
Westminster Bridge and pursued our stately way, the
oars lifting and falling without noise, up the river beyond the houses and buildings which cease at Lambeth
and are followed by low shores with trees, fields, and
market-gardens, and a house here and there.

The course of the river at Westminster is nearly
north and south : before reaching Chelsea the river
bends to the west : here we faced the sun, now wester-
ing rapidly : before us the river lay spread out like a
sheet of red gold reflecting the sky above, which was
truly like a vision of the New Jerusalem.

" This is a dream of fairyland," said my cousin.

" I have seen many sunsets on the Atlantic," said
Edward ; " both sunsets over a rough sea and sunsets
over a sea as smooth as this river to-night ; and I have
seen sunsets in the Mediterranean : but give me still
the river Thames."

" My brother is happier than I," Sir George added.
" He is a sailor and can travel. I must stay at home.
Therefore I rejoice to hear that our Thames is as
beautiful as any of the famous rivers of foreign lands."

The tide was flowing and nearly high : the river
seemed brimming over, it was so full : the water was
covered with swans floating about by twos and threes—

there were hundreds of the graceful creatures ; there were also many boats on the river. Mostly they contained girls and their sweethearts (one supposes they were sweethearts) enjoying like us the freshness of the air and their own society : and there were many of the huge unwieldy barges filled to the water's edge with hay or with casks or coals or iron, working their way up stream with the tide, the men on board tugging at their long sweeps.

The scene was so beautiful that we sat in silence, ravished by the sight. And all this time the harper played to us, changing his tune continually into something still more sweet and beautiful. Thus he played, " Early one morning, just as the sun was rising," " Drink to me only with thine eyes "—when Sir George began to sing my song softly—" Begone, dull care," " Sweet, if you love me," " The dusky night rides down the sky " ; and more. The smaller boats, as we swept along, tried to keep up with us for the delight of the music : but could not, so they huzzaed and let us go on our way. Presently the sun sank, and before long there fell upon the world a soft and sweet twilight, on which rose a moon glorious and beautiful.

" Will the ladies take their regale now, brother ? " asked Edward.

" Sir, can you speak of eating in such a scene as this ? " replied my cousin.

But she sat up as if in readiness—while two of the footmen quickly spread the cloth and laid upon it the supper. Truly, the supper would tempt an ankress, if any ankresses yet remain to mortify their appetites and serve the Lord by starving. For there were pheasants and grouse—the latter bird brought out of Yorkshire, we were told, by flying post, so that the brace on our table had actually been shot two hundred and fifty miles away, two days before. And there was fruit of all kinds, pears, peaches, plums, grapes, the most costly and the most delicious that the country can produce.

It was now nearly dark. Then a new surprise awaited us. For, as if by magic, there appeared hanging round'the high bows of the barge a kind of crown of gleaming lamps of all colours, and a footman lit candles in our cabin, and we found ourselves sitting in a blaze of light. Then the harpist stopped, and the horns and the hautboys began tossing the music out upon the waters, which tossed it on to the shore, and so it came echoing back. If this world, I thought, can be made so heavenly, what must Heaven itself be like?

"Come," said our host, when we had exclaimed and applauded, "let us see what they have given us for supper. It will be found, I fear, a poor offering in return for your great kindness in coming."

Their poor offering was, I have said, a most delicate little banquet. One wanted nothing: the fresh air, the gleaming lights, the music of the horns, the company and conversation of our entertainers, were as exhilarating as the wine and as staying as the chicken and partridge. It must be confessed that we did justice to these viands, cheered as they were by the lively sallies of Edward, and the graver discourse of his brother.

Supper finished, the footman who had been standing behind the cabin came in and rapidly carried off
the dishes, leaving in their place a bowl of punch. He
also extinguished the candles in the cabin and left us
in the light produced by the glass lamps in the bows.

Beside me sat Sir George. He had been pensive
and even melancholy during the supper, gazing from
time to time upon me with eyes that now I understand. Sad is the lot of the woman upon whom those
eyes have never rested : eyes full of tenderness, and
respect, and longing. The memory of those eyes
remains with me to comfort my lonely age : "Once,"
they say, " thou wert fair and a man loved thee for
thy beauty : once thou wert so fair that a man believed thee to have all the virtues that belong to an
angel : once wast thou thought so fair that a man worshipped thee as one worships a wood-nymph or a
goddess of the heathen."

"What think you of our music, fair Nancy?" he
said, bending over me.

It was now, I say, almost dark in our cabin save for
the lights in the bows : the rowers lifted and dipped
their oars noiselessly : the music was gentle : the air
was soft : my heart was well-nigh full of happiness.
And now I was to be lifted out of myself—yea—to
the seventh heaven—with such joy as I never thought
could fill a human heart.

"The music," I replied, "seems to celebrate the
happiness of this evening. Yet for a touch I could
weep. Why does music move one to tears?"

He laid his left hand timidly round my waist : with

the right he took my hand and kissed it. "Sweet Nancy," he whispered, "believe that I would die rather than bring a tear into those eyes. If the music makes thee sad, sweet girl, it shall cease."

"Nay, but there are tears of joy as well as of sadness." I tried to withdraw my hand, but he held it firmly. Besides, it was the kind of capture to which a woman is resigned ; and, again, his words, his grasp, the pressure of his arm upon my waist all together, suddenly and swiftly, awakened me and changed vague yearnings into strong love—strong as death—yea—stronger. From that moment I was wholly his—all my heart, all my soul, all my thoughts—were his, and his alone.

It costs me no pain now to remember these things ; a few tears of regret, perhaps : but such regrets console the season of age : the memory of those days ennobles me : it makes me proud and happy : sometimes when I have thought long over them I take down a book which, in spite of all the Divines pretend, I find full of earthly love. I mean the Song of Solomon : and I read the verses concerning my beloved with that sense of experience which makes me understand them all.

"My tender sweetheart!" he whispered low, while the music drowned his words, and the others could not see. I hear that soft, sweet whisper still; 'twill comfort my dying moments: it is my consolation from day to day, from hour to hour, to remember it. Oh! I was the first in his heart : the first. Yes, the first : before the Other came across the seas : I was

the first. " My tender sweetheart! My most beloved
mistress!" Then he drew me gently to his bosom,
and laid my head upon his shoulder and kissed me on
the forehead and on the cheek and on the lips, mur-
muring, " Oh, my tender sweetheart! Oh, my most
beloved mistress!" This was all he said. It was not
so dark in the cabin but that the others might see
something; but I know not how much they saw.

How long did this declaration last? Indeed, I have
no recollection, because I lost myself. Presently I
heard his brother's voice.

" George, we are near the Stairs. Are you asleep?"

" No, brother. I have never been so wakeful, believe me. Are we really near Whitehall Stairs again?
Oh! let us turn round and have it all over again!"

His brother laughed. " I wish we could. But
there are other things to do this evening."

" True—a most tedious card-party awaits us, Miss
Nancy. Alas! here we are, and the evening is done."

It surprised me when we landed at the stairs to find
a link-boy waiting for us, and Captain Sellinger, quite
sober, with Corporal Bates, in attendance.

" By your leave, Sir," said the Captain, taking off
his hat, " I will escort the ladies home."

" If you please, Sir." Sir George seemed to know
the Captain. He stooped and kissed my hand once
more. " I shall never forget this evening," he whispered. " Never, so long as I live." So we landed,
and the barge pushed off again and went down the
river.

I was also greatly surprised to see on the stairs Dr.

Mynsterchamber and two or three gentlemen with
him whom I knew not. They whispered to each
other : they looked at the barge and at Captain Sellinger. When the barge pushed off they walked
away.

The Captain walked home with us, the Corporal
marching behind.

" You know Sir George Le Breton, then ? " I asked.
" Have you known him long ? "

" Sir George Le Breton ? Oh ! yes—yes ! " he replied, with a little confusion. " Oh, yes—I know—
Sir George—Sir George Le Breton."

" Do you know him intimately ? "

" No, certainly not. I have not that honour. But
of course—I know him. Not so well as you know
him, Miss Nancy."

If I blushed the night concealed that sign of guilt.

" We find him and his brother most agreeable company, Captain Sellinger."

" It is quite certain that they find most agreeable
company in St. James's Place."

" They are young gentlemen of many virtues, Captain Sellinger."

" So I have understood—especially Sir George.
He has all the virtues there are. It is his inheritance.
His father had all the virtues before him ; so has his
grandfather. All the virtues reside permanently in
the family."

" I know not what you mean, Captain Sellinger.
But they do not get tipsy in the evening."

" Which is best, child : to repent in the morning

with a headache, or to be sorry in the morning for an evening thrown away?"

By this time we were arrived at our own door. "And now," said the Captain, "that I have left you in safety at the door, I will go to the Cocoa-Tree and drink. There is still time. Good-night, ladies. It is indeed a most wonderful thing."

What was most wonderful?

"We must talk a little, Nancy," said Isabel, sitting down.

"What shall we talk about?"

"Let me look in thy face, Nancy. Oh! she says 'What shall we talk about?' We will talk about St. Paul's Cathedral, my dear, if you wish; or about Dartford Paper Mills; or about your brother Joseph of pious memory; or, indeed, about everything except what you want to talk about."

"Cousin, what do you mean?"

"Oh! you know very well. The cabin was dark, but not so dark but I could see one head bending over another. The oars made a splashing and the water lapped against the side of the boat, yet I heard a whisper on the other side of the cabin. Nancy, why was that head bent down? What did that whisper mean?"

"Oh! Cousin "—I threw my arms round her—"I am the happiest, most joyful woman in the whole world! He loves me!" Then I broke from her and ran into my own room, because I must needs be alone to sit and think.

In the morning she asked me no more questions,

being always so kind and so thoughtful about me; and after breakfast I went out to walk by myself in the Green Park to think over the thing which had befallen me.

When I came back I was waylaid by the Doctor, who came out of his room to meet me.

" I hope, Miss Nancy," he said, bowing profoundly, " that you enjoyed your voyage on the river last night. I saw the boat landing you at Whitehall Stairs. With a cavalier the river may be delightful. Without, it may provoke a sore throat. Miss Nancy, I beg once more to offer for your acceptance one of the miniatures"--he drew it out of his pocket—"which I showed you once before. It is a truly beautiful piece of work—see! it is set with pearls. Believe me, it is worthy even of your acceptance."

I took it in my hands. Yes: it presented a most lovely face with a strange sadness in the eyes: a face having blue eyes and light hair—like my own.

" 'Tis none other than the portrait of Mademoiselle la Vallière, first mistress of Louis Quatorze : once as good and beautiful as yourself. She was dazzled by the passion of the young Prince. She was the first love of Louis. They say he never truly loved any other woman. Take it, Miss Nancy. Take it—keep it. See—there is a touch—turn it to the light—just a touch of yourself, Miss Nancy—it may be my imagination—in those eyes. Keep it. She was a Prince's first and only love."

I had no suspicion why he forced this gift upon me : not the least suspicion. But now I know. Well, I took it : I have it still : when I take it out in these latter days, when the past is so far off and I so changed and the whole history dim except to me, I see that the Doctor was right. There is in the eyes a touch— a touch of sadness—a touch of myself. And I am glad that I never showed this miniature to my lover. Henceforth I can call him my lover.

CHAPTER XIV.

The Guard of Honour.

I NOW return to the events which were not con-
ducted in my presence ; namely, those concerned with
the Corporal's discovery and the Doctor's conspiracy.

You may be sure that it was not long before one of
the two brothers—the younger—discovered the fact
that these two sentinels were posted at the door every
night, and that they formed a voluntary escort out of
St. James's Place. As for Sir George, this was a thing
which he would not notice. The presence of an escort
would seem to him natural and no more to be questioned than the following of a footman. As elder
brother, he was more accustomed to these attentions
than an officer in the Royal Navy. Besides, he left
us every evening, I am quite sure, with his Head as
full as his Heart. For the Head said, "She is only a
daughter of a bourgeois : of no family : of no connec-
tions except those of trade. She is far, far below
your rank. You must put her out of your thoughts."
And the Heart said, "Nay ; but you love her : you
have told her so : she loves you : to leave her would
be the basest cruelty : arrange some plan, with your
Head, so that you may love her still." And always
Conscience whispered, "Remember, George, those in

high place must not set base examples." With these conflicts going on, do you think it wonderful that he did not notice certain things?

One evening, therefore, the younger brother, after allowing George to enter his own house, stopped in the street outside, and called the Captain.

" Hark ye, Sir," he began with some roughness, " I observe that in the exercise of a zeal which, I suppose, does an officer of Horse Guards credit, you have constituted yourself into a special Guard of Honour to my brother and myself."

Captain Sellinger bowed low. " I would explain, Sir," he began.

" Sir, I know you very well by sight, and you, I suppose, know my brother and myself, also by sight."

" I have that honour, Sir."

" Well, Sir, your zeal, let me tell you, is uncalled for and meddlesome. I beg—I command—that it be discontinued."

" When I have explained, Sir——"

" What? When a gentleman wishes to preserve an incognito: when he pays visits which he does not wish to be proclaimed by beat of drum : when he carries his own sword, and is not afraid to use it : to have his privacy invaded by a volunteer escort? Allow me to say, Sir, again, that it is meddlesome."

" Sir," said the Captain quietly, "you are able to say what you please——"

" Well, Sir, I will say what I please, and I will give you satisfaction afterwards like any other man. Why not bring your troops and trot along beside us? They

would look well drawn up every evening in St. James's
Place, would they not? Certain ladies of your acquaintance would receive this delicate attention with
pleasure, no doubt."

"Sir, I desire nothing but permission to explain.
Indeed, Sir, I shall show you the gravest reasons. Believe me, neither presumption nor meddling. . . . But
if you will not hear me."

"Go on, then. Explain if you can." He stood upon
the doorstep leaning against the pillars of the porch.
"Explain, then."

"I will not take long, Sir. To begin with, there is
a person on the ground floor of that house who, I
have discovered, is a rank Jacobite, and possibly a
French spy: of the former there is no doubt."

"Jacobite—Jacobite." He threw up his arms impatiently. "What does it matter, man? Are you so
foolish as to believe in that cry? Why, Sir, the Young
Pretender is forty and childless, and his brother is in
the Romish Church! Jacobite! Let him go to the
Devil for a Jacobite! He is a French spy, too, is
he? Well—St. James's is not Portsmouth Dockyard.
What is he to learn? What mighty secrets will he
pick up? Have him to Bow Street and hang him. Is
it because there is a Jacobite scoundrel in the house
that you think fit to dog my brother's steps every
night?"

"Pardon me, Sir. I said there was the gravest reason. I will tell it in short. It is this. Every evening
there assembles in this man's lodging on the ground
floor of that house in St. James's Place a company of

half a dozen: they are, apparently, the grandsons of those English and Irish who followed James into exile: they come and go without suspicion because they talk English perfectly: they are over here in the desperate hope of reviving a lost cause. Meantime, they have another matter in hand—which is the grave reason of which I spoke."

" Well, Sir?"

"To-morrow night, Sir, you may remark, if you choose, a coach in waiting. That coach is driven by one of themselves: at Whitehall Stairs there is waiting a boat, manned by two of themselves: down the river off Redriff lies a vessel waiting for them. The ship is called the *Tower of Brill*, of Amsterdam: the captain has been won over in the usual way: when he has received certain passengers, who will be carried up the ship's side, he will drop down the river: he will then make for Calais, and be taken by the French, who will learn when they get into port the names of the passengers."

"The names of the passengers? Who are they, then?"

"Your brother, Sir, and yourself."

" The Devil! How are they to get hold of us?"

" I have told you, Sir. Every evening that company is assembled in that Jacobite's room looking for an opportunity to seize you both at the bottom of the stairs, and carry you away, prisoners, to France."

"To seize us—seize my brother? To carry us away? Man—this is some foolish joke."

" No joke at all, Sir. It is plain truth, as I can

show. Now, Sir, with this conspiracy before you—
say—was my interference justified? Was I to lay the
matter before the magistrates and cause those ladies
to give evidence, and——"

Edward put up his hand. "Captain Sellinger," he
said, "this is a serious business. I must think for a
moment."

He was silent for some minutes. "Are you quite
sure of your information?" he asked. "From whom
did it come to you?"

"From a Corporal in the Horse Guards—a man of
education, who speaks French and overheard their conversation. I can show you this evening, Sir, how he
operates. The coach you can see for yourself."

"Then, Captain Sellinger," Edward replied, "I
thank you." So he held out his hand, which the
other, bowing low, touched with his fingers. "Forgive me, Sir, for my haste. I am to blame. I should
have known that a gentleman must have had his reasons. What do you advise?"

"With submission, Sir, that we continue the nightly
watch. There will be no attempt, I am sure, where
there is the certainty of a fight. A sudden and unexpected rush of five or six upon two might succeed:
not a rush provided for against four armed men.
These kind of conspirators are mighty coy about the
clashing of steel and waking the neighbours. They
desire a noiseless abduction, with gags and handcuffs.
If they still persist, it would be well to warn them."

"The business wants careful handling. We must
keep the ladies out of the affair: we must keep my

brother out of it. No breath of it must get about to his detriment. This Corporal of yours—is he an honest fellow?"

" I believe him to be so. He is a fellow of many accomplishments and vain. But honest and zealous."

" For my own part I should like a brush with the villains—you beside me and the gallant Corporal distinguishing himself behind. I am not sure whether we can contrive to keep my brother in ignorance. However I shall try. Above all things, his name must not appear publicly, and his person must not be put into any danger, if that is possible. Tell your man, Captain, to continue his silence. We will talk of this business again when I have turned it over in my mind."

For some days nothing more was done; the coach was brought every evening to St. James's Place, where it waited : the Doctor's friends came every evening to his lodging, where they waited : and every evening they were baulked by the accidental presence of Corporal Bates in the kitchen and about the passage, whistling and singing so that there could be no doubt concerning his presence, while outside in St. James's Place for some purpose of his own, doubtless to meet a girl, Captain Sellinger strolled about the Place or waited in the doorway. From time to time the Doctor would get up and look out, as if to ascertain the weather: his door was kept ajar, so that any footsteps could be heard : regularly at ten o'clock, when the two gentlemen came downstairs, the Corporal was standing at the bottom of the stairs ready with a salute, and the Captain was standing on the

doorstep; and if the conspirators made a rush it would
be met by these two defenders first.

What did the Doctor suspect? I cannot tell. The
coach, I say, continued to come every evening. I
conjecture that they were resolved to wait until an
opportunity should occur, and that they thought this
opportunity would certainly occur before long. I
conjecture, further, that they had no thought of murder, which would be useless, but of seizing the person.
If they had desired murder they might bring six or
more against four and so set upon them; but it was
plainly their interest to avoid bloodshed: now when
swords are crossed even in self-defence, one cannot
say who will receive a thrust. Meanwhile it is also
certain, in my mind, that they had no suspicion that
their purpose was discovered. Else why this perse-
verance in making everything ready night after night?
Their very security showed that they had no suspicions: for this security would have been impossible
if the plot had been known, in which case there would
have been no delay, but they would all have been
seized, committed, tried, and executed in the usual
way. These considerations account for the fact that
they made no attempt to fly or to disperse themselves.

"You walk abroad late, Captain Sellinger," said the
Doctor, one morning. "Last night I went forth to
watch the stars, and saw you in the Court: the night
before, if I mistake not, I heard your footsteps."

" Doctor, if a little friend sometimes came to talk
to you in this quiet Court, where there is no one ex-

cept a cursed mysterious coach which waits every evening for some one, would you like to be watched?"

"Oh! If a woman is in the case, Captain—one has been young——"

"The nights grow cold. In a few days I fear she will come no longer."

That night the coach came not, nor did the company gather in the Doctor's room. Yet soon after the coach appeared again, and the men came again. They had not lost their hopes of an opportunity.

On another occasion—"Captain," said the Doctor, "advise me. The fellow who lives in the garret— Corporal Bates by name——"

"What of him, Doctor?"

"A noisy fellow. He disturbs me in the evening. When one would be writing or reading, or perhaps sleeping, he walks about the passage whistling. He goes in and out of the kitchen and drinks."

"He is not in my Company, Doctor. I cannot speak to him. But bid Molly the maid tie a dish-clout to his coat-tail. Or make his wife jealous."

That was all that the Doctor and his friends got by their interference. Yet it showed uneasiness. It is certain that they feared all was not right.

As for my cousin and myself, we knew nothing. For my own part I lived in a Fool's Paradise, i. e., in the Paradise which every woman desires for herself, the Paradise of Love. This gallant young gentleman loved me: so brave and so handsome; so rich and so highly placed, he loved me, when he might have chosen among the noblest ladies of the land: he had chosen me : he loved me : he loved me. While I sat with those words day and night ringing in my brain, downstairs went on the plots and conspiracies of those villains and the devotion of those two, the Captain and the Corporal, thwarting and preventing.

The patience, both of conspirators and of guard, is shown by the time during which the former waited for an opportunity, and the latter continued to interpose obstacles. Consider the time that the watch continued. Yet the thing was worth patience and watchfulness incredible. We went to Marylebone Gardens on the last day of September ; the plot was then discovered and in the possession of Captain Sellinger. He began his watch and escort and continued both, as you shall see, for more than three weeks. When the coach was waiting in the Place, the Captain and his companion patrolled the open square and guarded the steps and the stairs. What put an end to the business you shall learn in due course.

CHAPTER XV.

The Palace and the Court.

YOU have read how Sir George turned the conversation when my cousin or I expressed a desire to see the Court and Palace of St. James's. The King was old : one must not annoy the King: our loyalty would be best shown by not attempting to enjoy the privilege of seeing the Palace : and so forth. Therefore we were greatly surprised when he offered of his own accord to show us what was to be seen. "Come," he said, "to the Colour Court, which is that within the gate, at the Mounting of the Guard, to-morrow morning, and I will try to let you see everything."

You may be sure that we joyfully accepted the invitation. For my own part, I understood that something, I knew not what, was intended for me, especially, by this invitation, and I dressed with some trepidation yet with happy expectancy. What he chose to do would be well done.

The Mounting of the Guard at eleven every morning is a pretty sight : we had often witnessed it from the end of St. James's Street. First marches the band headed by the drum major, a very majestic person, over six feet high and carrying a gold-headed staff : after him the "trumpets and shawms," that is to say, men in cocked hats and scarlet uniforms blowing strange instruments : then two little boys, pretty little fellows, who look as if they ought to be still in a Dame's school, with drums : then a great fat negro with a turban carrying the big drum, and on either side another negro with cymbals and tambourine. Then a company of twenty-four drums and fifes : then the Captain or Colonel with his sword drawn marching before the ensign who carried the colours ; lastly, the guard of the day, fellows so well shaven and so finely dressed that you would not believe their daily work was that of the humble, though useful, coal-heaver.

At eleven the next morning, therefore, we repaired to Colour Court. When the Guard had left the Court Sir George came to us dressed in scarlet with his star and a glittering order on his breast. " I am here," he said, " as a kind of official : do not be surprised when they salute me. I have ordered that none are to be admitted except on the King's business while you are here. You will have the Palace to yourselves, ladies, except for the private apartments of the King."

So saying, he led the way. I observed that wherever we met one of the Palace servants, or any gentleman belonging to the Court, our guide was saluted in the most respectful manner possible, everybody falling back out of our way and bowing low or saluting.

I forget most of the things we saw, and, indeed, it does not greatly matter, because the importance of

the morning lay not in the State rooms of the Palace,
but in the words which were spoken in them.

First we went into the Chapel, where the King
every year makes his offering of gold, frankincense,
and myrrh. Here, also, we learned, the Sovereign
formerly touched for the King's Evil, working miracles daily.

"If," said our guide, "the King reigns by Divine
permission, there would seem nothing ridiculous in
the function which George I. discontinued."

"But," I said, "we all live by Divine permission:
and all we do or say is only what we are permitted:
yet we do not work miracles."

"I do not press the point," he replied. "What
divines ordain or decide that do I accept with humility. The King touches no longer, by the ruling of
the Church. It is enough. Let me show you, next,
the State rooms."

These rooms are called Queen Anne's Room, the
Throne Room, the Armoury, and others which I
forget. The rooms were large and lofty, opening
one out of the other: in one or two there were card-
tables and chairs: all had thick carpets and heavy
curtains: there were gilded chairs and sofas: there
were very large looking-glasses, hanging chandeliers,
carved cornices and chimney pieces with coats-of-
arms and crowns and initials: among them those
of Henry VIII. and Anne Boleyn. There were
also pictures, chiefly portraits. Here were the two
Princes of Wales who died young: Arthur, son of
Henry VII.; and Henry, son of James. Here is Jane

Seymour, the Duchess of York, Charles I. in Green-
wich Park: and I remember a famous picture of
Adam and Eve in the Garden of Paradise. As for
the rooms themselves, they were full of memories. I
looked about in curiosity. Here Queen Mary died—
in great misery and deserved: here King Charles
slept—if he could sleep—on the night before his execution: here Queen Anne lived and died: these rooms
are full of history: great Lords and Ladies fill them
in the imagination: here are held the grand Levées and
Drawing-Rooms: here the King and the Court hold
their great gambling nights at the New Year: here are
the Court Balls: here the foreign Ambassadors are received and the Deputations from the City of London
and elsewhere: here the Privy Council assemble.

"Yes," said Sir George, " the rooms have many
memories. For my own part, I think more of Westminster than of St. James's. A King in Westminster
Palace was a King indeed. One would rather be Edward the First than—even—George the Second.
However, I will now take you to a part of the Palace
which the public are not allowed to see."

He took us by some corridors, empty and deserted,
to a door which he opened. A porter, sitting on a
chair half asleep, jumped up and stood with his hands
down, ready for service. " Where is the King?"
asked our guide.

" His Majesty is in the Palace Garden, Sir," the
man replied.

" We can walk round, then. I am going to show the
King's own private rooms. And first, these "—he led

the way—" are the private rooms of the late Queen."
It was a suite, or collection, of rooms containing the
bed-chamber with a great bed richly hung with velvet
and gold fringes: the little bed-chamber for the
Queen's personal attendant: the room for the robes:
the dressing-room: and the withdrawing-room. "All
is kept exactly," whispered Sir George, "as the Queen
left it: the furniture undisturbed: the robes hanging
as they were. She was a great woman, greater than
the world will ever know. Come."

We left the room hushed by the presence of death
and the emotion expressed on our conductor's face.

"You have spoken with the late Queen, Sir George?"

"Thousands of times. She was good enough to—
to—love me."

I said no more and he led us away.

He showed us next the King's private rooms: his
bedroom: his writing and reception-room: his dining-
room: and so forth. Of course, one knows that not
even a King can eat or drink more than a subject:
nor can he take up more room: yet one was perhaps
astonished to observe the simplicity with which their
rooms were furnished.

"You see," Sir George remarked, smiling, "why the
public must not be admitted to these rooms: in their
eyes the King must always appear in robes of State:
if with a crown upon his head, so much the better: if
on horseback in gilded armour, so much the better still.
That he should appear as a good old man, living in
quiet ease without any State except on State occasions,
would perhaps cause the loss, or, at least, the decay of

his magnificence as King. It is the same with other dignities: the Judge does well to confine himself to the society of other Judges: the Bishop must consort with Bishops: the General must not descend to the merchant's company. Authority is kept up by dignity: and dignity cannot admit of familiarity save among equals. The world has not yet learned to separate the office from the man: otherwise, in his moments of leisure, the King might walk about Pall Mall or watch the humours of the Park, seated among his people on a chair."

There certainly was an aspect of homeliness not only in the King's own room but about the whole Palace. The Guard in the Guardroom lounged about: the servants sat about: there was a sleepy look in the courts and in the brick walls. But I was pleased to have seen it all.

" It was different," said our conductor, "while the Queen lived. Then the discipline of the service was sharper: Guards and Yeomen knew their duty, and did it with alacrity. The King is old: the Queen is dead: there are no longer the State balls and card-parties and receptions. When the—the successor arrives, he will have to restore that strictness of outward ceremonial which keeps up the kingly dignity." He sighed heavily. "Little ease hath he who wears a crown. No solitude: no moments to himself: much care and little ease." He sighed again. "And now," he went on, "there is little more to show you. The King's Library has been given to the British Museum, where no doubt it will prove of greater use. Reading

is not at present much cultivated at Courts. What?
I said before that we who make history are not concerned about reading it, save for instruction in youth.
Thus, it is useful for an English King to learn that
Richard the Second was ill advised when he seized on
the savings of the merchants: the Stuarts might have
been reigning still had not Charles the Second shut up
the Exchequer and so robbed the City of a million and a
half, for which they never forgave him. Yet the King
must defend his own prerogative or he would not be
King." He spoke as if to himself. "Come," he said,
"you shall see the Queen's Library."

The Queen's Library stands apart from the Palace
in the gardens in the west: it is a small building with
one or two pictures.

"The Library," said Sir George, "was built for
Queen Caroline. She wanted books of a lighter kind
than the old folios, which have now been sent to the
Museum. Her ladies came here in her lifetime: it
has been of late neglected, but you should see it."

We looked round at the books. Some were on the
table: some were on the floor: some were lying carelessly about the shelves. Sir George turned to my
cousin. "You would like to look at the books,
Madam. Walk round the Library and see for yourself what the late Queen loved to read."

Isabel smiled and left us.

Then Sir George took my hand and led me to a
chair which was in a window looking over the garden.

At that moment the door at the other end of the
room opened and there entered an old man leaning

upon a stick : an old man of singular aspect, had one met him in the street : he was followed by two servants who stood at the door while their master entered the room and looked round.

"It is the King," said my lover. "I must speak with him." He walked down the room and knelt on one knee.

"George!" cried the King, surprised. "You in the Library?"

"Yes, Sir. I trust your Majesty is well this morning."

"Ay—ay—well enough. Come to see me presently, when you have left your friends." So he looked at me curiously : shook his head, as if he could not remember my face, and went out again.

"He comes to look at the Library," said George, " because it was the Queen's. Otherwise he loves not reading. But he loves everything that belongs to the memory of his wife."

And even then I did not guess : I had no suspicion : not the least.

And now I understand it all so well : what was in his mind : the sacrifice that he was ready to make : the meaning of it all : how love had trampled upon interest : and how he was prepared even to give up his inheritance after himself, to his brother. He would give all—all—all—for my sake—mine.

"Be seated, Nancy. Oh, my dear! my dear!" He kissed my hand regardless of Isabel's presence : but I think she was among the books. "I have brought you here, dear, because—because"—he hesitated a little, " I thought to show you what should have been the ending of that story of Lord Burleigh and his country maid. He took her to see his castle—his stately castle. Burleigh House is a very noble place : he showed her all over it : his Rooms of State, his Court-yards, his Halls, his Chapel, his Park : everything. And when she understood who and what he was—how great his State—he took her away again—to her old home and said, ' My dear, it is not in that great gilded place that you can love me : it is in some rustic cottage like your own, whither I can steal when I can from the cares and forms of State.' What say you, Nancy ? "

" Will your State be so very great—as great as that of the Lord Burleigh ? "

" It will be greater. It will be—something—something like this."

And even then I never guessed.

I gave him my hand. " Oh ! " I whispered. " I am all yours. Do with me—dispose of me—as your heart and honour please."

Again he kissed me, but on the forehead.

" My honour bade me show thee these things, Nancy. My heart bids me tie myself to thee for life —so that none but the call of God shall part us."

CHAPTER XVI.

"Invest it in my Business."

ROBERT Storey called again—his last visit it proved. He came the day after our voyage up the river, when the words of my lover were still ringing in my brain, with the accompaniment of sweet music, all in fantasy, as happens when one is happy and hears voices singing and silver bells ringing, and melodies hitherto unknown. The sight of the man jangled the bells, and made discords instead of the music. Not only the prim decorum of his dress, the self-satisfaction in his face —these were things which one expected in the worthy bookseller—there was also visible a certain purpose in his face. Yet I received him with an appearance of graciousness.

"I have left our cousin," he said, "in the shop. She is talking with a traveller lately returned from Siberia, (if his word can be taken : but we have many pretended travellers). He has been telling her of the cannibals who dwell in that unknown country, (but one of my poets swears that the traveller hath been seen of late in Grub Street). He is to issue his 'Description of Siberia' by subscription. I doubt not that he will have our cousin's name and guinea before

he leaves her. A plausible fellow in discourse, and
once at Sidney Sussex College, Cambridge. When I
left them, he was beginning upon the marriage customs of those distant islanders. Apparently they
have never heard of the English Church." He shook
his head sadly, sighed, and asked permission to sit
down. He did so, carefully arranging the correct disposition of his legs, and thrusting, as was his wont,
one hand in his bosom.

"When I came last," he said, " I allowed myself to
fall into some heat of temper because it pained me
to watch the continuance of an acquaintance which
from the incompatibility of rank and station, can
never become more than a passing incident—pray
Heaven not a painful incident!—in the history of a
beautiful though unfortunate young lady."

This was the introduction or preface to what followed. I hope my readers are as well satisfied with it
as the author appeared to be.

"You mean something, Mr. Robert, I daresay."

"I always mean something. One of my satirists
told me yesterday when I gave him three guineas,
that my words are of gold, like the Greek Father
named Socrates, which means, unless my Greek is
rusty, he with the golden mouth. What I say, Miss
Nancy, is received by my friends as well as my de-
pendent poets, as something worth the hearing. The
sayings of Robert Storey, perhaps, will prove here-
after as worthy of record as the 'Table Talk' of
Selden, of which I have a share, with six other booksellers."

"Will you kindly proceed to your meaning then? If Isabel grows tired of her Siberian she may return, and so you may lose your opportunity. For, Mr. Robert, I suppose you wish to speak to me alone."

"With your permission. Ahem! The—the—gentleman who comes here nearly every day, with whom you have been seen at Marylebone Gardens and on the river in a barge, with music, is attracted by a lovely face. Naturally—for a gentleman. We in business do not consider the beauty of our fair customers. Handsome or ugly makes no difference in the buying of books. You may believe me, Miss Nancy, when I assure you that although in business hours I must not have any eye for beauty, yet out of business hours, when I might relax from this severity, respect for my own reputation, on which a tradesman's success greatly depends, would not allow me to run after a pretty face if I wished to do so."

"Indeed, Mr. Robert, I am quite sure that you are incapable of running after a pretty face."

"What respect, indeed, should I receive from my poets if I were thus to betray the amorous propensities which they are constantly singing and praising?"

"Do you think, Mr. Robert, that this subject is the most proper one in the world to discuss with me?"

"I introduced it, believe me, for contrast only. That I do not run after pretty faces is due not only to my principles, which would, I believe, resist Helen of Troy herself, but also to my calling, which necessitates a reputation for virtue. Every bookseller should be christened Joseph, even though his temperament should incline him rather to the character of Solomon."

"Mr. Robert, I do not know you this morning."

"I mean, then, that a tradesman of virtue, like myself, is as capable of the passion of love as the greatest man in the country."

"I hope, Sir, that an honest love for a worthy object—if there be any woman worthy of Mr. Robert Storey—will reward these present privations."

I believe that if you humour a man in accordance with his vanity you may say what you please. He took this remark as a confession of admiration and bowed, smiling.

"There is, then," he continued, "this difference between myself and a gentleman. While I am heedfully employed in making a profit by getting copy from an author (whose necessities make him take what I offer, while his unbridled greed makes him still dissatisfied) a gentleman has nothing to occupy his thoughts, and therefore suffers them to rove at will. If he sees a pretty girl, he instantly follows her: converses with her: makes love to her, regardless of consequences which will not injure him. It is the way with his class—his rank. A woman, he thinks, is a creature made for love, and especially for the love of a gentleman. It is condescension in him to offer love: it is an honour in her to accept love. In my rank—the happier because the more virtuous—we do not speak much of love before we tie the nuptial knot. Then, believe me, no nobleman could be more affectionate, no gentleman so constant."

"I believe that you are come again in order to malign certain friends of mine. Mr. Robert, once for all, you need not continue."

"I come, Miss Nancy, with a more important object than that. I have nothing to say against this gentleman. He comes here in order to enjoy your society. His behaviour, I am informed, by your cousin, is as admirable as your own most honourable principles would demand : can I say more than that I believe this assurance ? "

These words naturally softened me. "Since you admit that he is a man of honour, Mr. Robert, I am satisfied. You can therefore go on."

"I admit, moreover, that he comes here after you. I do not doubt that he greatly admires, and perhaps loves, you. Who can be surprised? Who can for a moment doubt? What I would ask you, most earnestly, Miss Nancy, is this : What is to be the end of it ? "

"In reply, Mr. Robert : What right have you to ask this question ? "

He did not answer this question. "Consider, I beseech you," he said, "the position of this gentleman. Consider only what it means."

"Do you know his position ? "

"Of course I know."

I understand, now, that he could not believe that I did not know ; yet if he had only spoken to Isabel he would have learned, at least, that we did not know.

"Do not, I entreat you," he added, "deceive yourself by the belief that no one else knows. I recognised them at the very first evening, when I ran away, as you said. Captain Sellinger knows; that Corporal of Horse Guards knows; the tall lean man on the ground-floor knows: he is said in my shop to be a Jacobite. Sometimes he looks in to ask after rare books. He was talking to me about other things, and from what he dropped, I am certain that he knows your friends."

Everybody knew, except me. And I was not anxious to know. My lover was a man of exalted rank— an Earl, perhaps : or, indeed, I knew not, never having been taught to respect rank, which is an accident of birth. He would tell me himself, in his own good time.

"So, Miss Nancy, since so many people know; and since we cannot stop their tongues; all the world will soon know."

"Well, Sir?" This kind of talk began to vex me. "If a gentleman is his own master, why should he not visit whom he pleases?"

"His own master? Yes. But for how long? The old man is now getting on for eighty. For how long?"

"I know nothing about any old man."

"Tut-tut!" he said impatiently. "Consider, I say, the position. It is impossible for him to marry you. It is perfectly impossible—it is out of the question— not to be thought of. You must acknowledge that."

"I acknowledge nothing."

"You cannot entertain the thought! It would be madness!"

"Mr. Robert! Pray understand once for all that I cannot speak of these things to you."

" If not marriage, then—what ? "

I rose. " Mr. Robert, your talk on this subject is nauseous. Have done, or you will drive me out of the room."

"Well, I have spoken. Pray sit down again, Miss Nancy. I will sin no more, even for your sake, in this respect. I must now tell you that, being in the City yesterday, I came upon your brother, Mr. Joseph, in a coffee-house. I told him, perhaps incautiously, that you were in good health and staying near the Palace of St. James's with the widow of my cousin, Reuben Storey. That, he said, was with his consent, but he would call here when next his business takes him to London."

" My brother Joseph ? My brother here ? "

" Yes. He will see in these lodgings a great deal " —Robert looked round the room—" which he will dis- approve. He is still stiff, I observe, in his Quaker principles. What will you say ? How will you defend your abandonment of their principles ? "

I was silent. I had quite forgotten the very exist- ence of my brother Joseph.

" Joseph is your guardian. You want, it is true, only a few days of coming of age, when you can do as you please. He is trustee, I understand, for a large fortune, which he will if possible keep in his own hands. Shall you return, may I ask, to Dartford ? "

" Never." I shuddered. At the very thought of Dartford the memory of the old melancholy returned to me. " Never."

" Well. He will be here. You must tell him your-

self that you have changed your religion and that you
intend to become—or have become—a member of the
Church of England. As myself a humble follower of
that Church, I rejoice. Joseph will not rejoice. He
is an austere man. He will be angry."

I looked about the room. If we were to deceive
him again—it was by sheer deception that Isabel got
me into her custody—we should have to go back to
the old pretences : we should change again our dress :
change the fashion of our heads : change our conversation : take down all the pictures from the walls :
banish all the books : send away the harpsichord :
hide the music : put away the china and gewgaws.
Oh! But we would not deceive him. I resolved to
let my brother know the truth. But, alas! a sinking
of the heart followed this disagreeable intelligence. I
felt as if the pleasant time was threatened.

"As yet," Robert went on, "Joseph knows nothing
of your visitors. I did not venture to tell him. I
know not what he will say, or think, if he should learn
the truth."

"Joseph," I said, "may be my brother and even my
guardian. But he is no longer my master. Nor shall
he be, henceforth."

"You are warned, however, that he is about to visit
you. It may be to-day : it may be to-morrow—or
next week. I know not how often his affairs call him
to the City of London."

"Well, Mr. Robert, is that all you had to say? You
are, indeed, a messenger of good tidings."

"One thing more, Miss Nancy. I would in cold

blood renew the proposal which last I made in passion. You are now in a perilous position : your reputation, if certain things were known, would be more than cracked : I offer to take you out of the meshes which surround you. Miss Nancy "—he drew out his hand from his bosom and fell upon his knees—" I offer you —myself. I care nothing for what may be said : I take you as you are. Your fortune will be put into the shop. I offer you a good business, a careful and prudent manager of that business, a loving and tender husband, and a partner who will be respected through life for his manners and for his probity. He is also not without learning."

"Get up, Sir! Mr. Robert," I said, nothing moved by his earnestness—because he must have been very much in earnest to offer thus to repair a reputation which he certainly believed to be cracked. At the time I did not understand in this his insults to my good name, nor his eagerness to get my money. "Get up, Sir ; dismiss this matter from your mind at once."

"Why?" he asked, still on his knees. " Nothing stands in the way, so far as the world and your brother know. It is but cutting a knot. I will marry you at once, by license—to-morrow. You need not pain yourself by saying farewell to your illustrious lover : you will only have to leave the house—and him—for ever. I will make people render an account of thy fortune. Consider, my dear Nancy. I cannot bear to think that things will be said about thee. So lovely —so bewitching. Oh ! " he caught my hand and tried to kiss it. " Oh ! Oh ! Oh !" he mumbled.

"Get up, I say, Mr. Robert. How can the man make such a fool of himself?"

Thus adjured, he rose, and taking his handkerchief, brushed off a little dust from his knees. Thus did prudence govern passion in the excellent man of business.

"You will want a man of business," he added, "to make Joseph disgorge and to invest your fortune prudently. I will become that man of business. In my own calling I can invest with safety as much money as I can lay hands on. Nancy, I know of shares in books to be had cheap : and there is money in them of which no one else knows. Marry me, Nancy. You shall invest your money in my shop. You shall have a chariot. You shall have a country house with a garden—what do I care about a cracked reputation?"

I sprang to my feet. "Sordid wretch!" I cried. "To pretend love when all thy thoughts are of money! Go! Leave me. The man—whose shoe-latchet thou art not worthy to loose—is the noblest, truest, purest heart that beats. Go! Let me never see thee or speak to thee again! Go! Lest I . . . but go—go!"

I sank back into my chair and turned my head from him.

"I obey," he replied hoarsely. "I am a sordid wretch. Your brother Joseph will come here in a day or two. You will have to explain a great deal more— a great deal more, I say—than a change of faith. He shall know all before he comes."

So he left me. His threats concerned me little, because I hardly knew what he meant by a cracked reputation—certainly not all he meant. But I confess I was not anxious to meet Joseph. I was willing to avow that I could no longer remain in the Society of Friends : I could tell him that I now loved and practised all those things which, according to the illiterate Founder, send souls in multitudes to the abode of Devils—namely, music, painting, dancing, dress, poetry, books of the imagination. All that mattered nothing. I had the support—the strong arm—of the man who loved me ; who kissed me and called me his tender sweetheart—his lovely mistress—and other sweet things which I cannot write down even after these long years. I had, I say, the support of this man for whose sake I had been baptised and received into the Church of England.

CHAPTER XVII.

"Let him Tell me Himself."

I⊤ was, however, a week and more before Joseph came. When he did come, he found his sister in no mood to listen to any reproaches or threats. What was the anger of Joseph compared with the troubles and terrors which at that moment filled my heart?

It was, I well remember, the 24th day of October—the day before the End. Outside, from my bedroom window, I looked out upon the Park full of people, and full of sunshine, the warm yellow sunshine of autumn. The autumn sun could not reach our garden on the north side of St. James's Place: the dwellers in the garrets, on the other hand, enjoyed all the sunshine that falls upon London and Westminster. So that if sunshine can compensate, poverty has its compensations.

As was often the case in the morning, I was alone. My cousin was gone by water to the City, whither her affairs often called her. The house was quiet save for the chatter of Mrs. Bates and her children upstairs. The window was open for the sweetness of the air; yet, because the night had been cold, there was a small coal fire burning in the grate. I sat beside the table, leaning my head on my hand, an open book of poetry before me, some needlework in my lap, and my lover in my mind. When a girl is loved and also loves —sad for one of these things to be found without the other !—I suppose her lover is always in her mind : she dreams of him : she thinks of him if she wakes in the dark hours of the night : she puts his name, instead of her own, into her prayers : she dresses to please him : she thinks to please him : she considers all day long what will please him. Only to please him she would be beautiful, she would be good. My sisters ! great and wonderful, nay, miraculous, is the power of Love, since it can even raise the soul from lowest depths to heights of virtue.

I have never been to a theatre, but I have read many plays. Every play has a story, which they call a plot : every play is divided into five acts, in each of which something is done which carries on the plot and advances it and increases the interest and absorption of the reader or the spectator. My life is a play— that is, a small portion of my life. The Prologue or Introduction is the House at Dartford with the gloomy Joseph. Act I. is the First Meeting in St James's Place : Act II. is the Masquerade : Act III. is the River : Act IV. is the Morning of October 24. The last Act is the Morning of October 25.

There was a step on the stairs—a step I knew full well : a step that always announced a cheerful face and an affectionate heart—yet not the step I should have wished to hear.

The door opened, and Edward stood there alone.

" Edward ! " I sprang to my feet with the cold

shiver which heralds coming evil. "But where is George?"

"I have not seen him this morning." His face was very grave—what had happened? "George does not know that I am here. Are you alone, Nancy?"

"My cousin has gone into the City with Molly. I am quite alone."

He entered the room and closed the door. "I am so far fortunate," he said. "May I sit down and talk with you a little?"

He sat down, took my hand, pressed it—and kissed it.

"Nancy," he said, "you know that I love you—I would delight in seeing you happy—in the way that you most desire. Believe this always, dear girl. I have no other wish for you—the way you most desire —I know full well what that way is."

"You have always been kind, Edward. Why should I not believe it? You are my brother—almost —George's brother will be mine, will he not?"

"I am not blind, or deaf, Nancy. On the river, dark as the cabin was, I heard and saw—certain things. Forgive me for reminding you. My dear, it is very certain to me that George loves you to distraction, and that you—may I say it?"

"No, Edward; but you may think it."

"My poor Nancy!" Again he took my hand and held it. "All this has been my fault."

"All your fault? Is it your fault that two people love each other and are happy?"

"It was by accident that we met, that night, for the

first time. George was greatly excited by the adventure. He has been brought up, for certain reasons,
in seclusion, so that he has not been allowed the liberty which other young men enjoy—he has not been
able to enjoy adventures and dangers such as other
young men court——"

"But why?"

"For certain reasons," he replied. "As for me, I
am of very little importance—a younger son does not
count. I could go and come as I pleased. Besides, I
was placed in the Navy, where I have had opportuni-
ties of learning the world. Well . . . the truth is
that I was grieved to find George so ignorant of people: this seemed an opportunity for him to observe
certain gentlewomen of tastes and manners delicate,
yet not belonging to the great world. In other words,
I would introduce him, through you, to the better
class of those who work for their incomes."

"Yes—so you brought him here—not thinking
what else might happen."

"If we were always thinking of that we should do
nothing. I wanted to get him outside the narrow
circle—of course a man in his position is always kept
in a narrow circle—it is his greatest danger. You observed that George talked at first as if he had been
taught everything."

"We could understand that he was wonderfully ignorant of many things—how people live, for instance."

"How should he know everything? Nancy, there
was also another point in which he was profoundly
ignorant—the knowledge of women. Above all things

a young man in his position ought to know something on that important subject.   What have I taught him?"

"You brought him here.   He did the rest himself."

"Yes.   At first it was to be a polite call—just to hope the lady is none the worse.   But George was struck: the simplicity of the conversation—let me say it, Nancy: the absence of flattery, self-interest, effort to please : the refinement of the ladies : the ease, and yet the propriety of their manners : add to which, the beauty of one : these things, which he had never met before, fired him in his way.   George is slow in being moved by anything except by principle.   But when he is moved he is firm—even obstinate.   He would come again and again : I must come with him : presently he would not keep away : he talked about you all the morning: in the evening he talked with you : after returning home he sat among his mother's friends as mute as a mouse, because he was thinking about you."

"Well, Sir—was that a calamity?"

"Nancy, he was slowly, for the first time in his life, falling in love.   Yet he is now already twenty-two years of age.   For my part—I am twenty—but—well —sailors are made of stuff more inflammable.   Yet it would be incredible if it were not true.   For the first time, George is fully possessed with the idea of a woman.   Your image wholly occupies his heart."

"Oh!   Is this what you came to tell me?   Will this knowledge make me unhappy?"

"No, sweet girl, I think not.   In thy society George

hath learned more than love. He has learned to
think of men and women as a man himself: they are
no longer of importance to him in regard only to
their position and their rank; he has learned that
however high may be a man's rank, a simple woman
with no rank at all may surpass him in knowledge—
yes, Nancy, and in breeding and in heart. A dozen
times has my brother spoken to such effect as this.
Whatever happens, Nancy, never will he forget the
lessons that he has learned from thee." And the
tears stood in his eyes.

I was silent—foreboding something terrible. He
went on, his dear kind face so full of trouble that I
trembled and shivered.

"This has been a pleasant time, Nancy, to me, as
well as to George. To me, because I have seen that
noble heart bursting the bonds in which an ill-judged
seclusion has swathed it. No one knows what George
might have become, or may yet become, except myself, his brother and his playmate. He is all truth
and candour; full of religion; full of principle; wanting only in the knowledge of men and women. Dear
Nancy, it has been, believe me, a very pleasant time."
Yet now the tears, already in his eyes, came also into
his voice. "But it must stop. The time has come
when it must stop."

"Why must it stop?"

"It should have been stopped long ago. It is all my
fault. It should have been stopped before—before
George felt the whole force of love and before—before,
Nancy, you yourself——"

"Why must it stop? Oh! Edward, tell me—why must it stop? Oh! do you know what these words mean to me?"

"Nancy, has George told you nothing? Child, do you suspect nothing?"

"George is a gentleman of noble birth. What else is there to tell me?"

"Then he must tell you himself. I cannot. I promised I would not. Nancy, in a word, he cannot marry you. Understand. It is not a question of what he would like or would choose. He has no voice in the matter. He cannot marry you. He must make an alliance fitting his position."

I made no reply at first. "Then," I said, "why does he swear that he loves me?"

"Because it is the truth, Nancy—the real downright truth. How he will get out of it I know not. Nay, for him I care little : many a man has to give up the girl he loves—for this or that reason. It is—oh! Nancy—it is not George that concerns me so much—it is the girl whom he must leave behind."

"Why do you tell me all this then? What do you wish me to do?" I asked, trembling.

"I do not know. I want to put an end to a situation which is full of peril. Nancy—sweetest girl—I would to Heaven you were in love with me—then would I brave the world and show the way! But it is my brother. It will make him miserable to end it. Yet it must be ended. It must be ended." Thus he repeated continually, as not knowing what else to say. "His wife you cannot be. Nancy, you cannot—you

cannot. Believe me, you cannot—you cannot—and
his light o' love you cannot be. Never would George
propose such a thing. He loves you too well, Nancy.
What is to be done? Try to think of some way out."

"I know not—yet—Edward—if that is your name
—perhaps I ought to call you Lord something."

"It is Edward. Call me Edward, Nancy. And
don't think too hardly of me for telling you the dreadful truth."

"Do you come from George?"

"No, I have no message from George."

"Does he know that you are here? Does he know
that the end must come?"

"George is in the Heaven of accepted lovers: he is
drunk with love: he cannot listen to reason: one cannot discourse with George as with a rational being.
No, Nancy, George has not sent me: George would
not allow that there must be an end: George is incapable of acting with prudence. I have come myself,
without authority, to give you a warning, so that
you may be prepared. The forces against you are
overwhelming. There must be an end."

I waited awhile, thinking. Then I rallied my poor
shattered spirits, and presently stood up and spoke
slowly.

"You have been so kind a friend, Edward, that I
cannot believe you would seek to do me injury.
Pray remember, however, that you did not court me
for George; he did his courting for himself. He
asked me to be his. I am his—I belong to him. I
will take my release from none other than George him-

self. I shall do what he commands me, not what you wish. If he desires to marry me and keep me in con. cealment I shall cheerfully obey. I am wholly his— his servant—his slave, Edward——"

"Dear girl, you stab me with a knife. What shall I say? I want you to break it off suddenly—to go away and remain concealed—and so to break it off. Better so—believe me, than to wait—I know not what may happen at any moment—and then there will be the full shock—of discovery"—he went on talking as if with himself—"and no more possibility of going anywhere or doing anything except under the eyes of the whole world. Oh! Nancy—Nancy— if you would only go away and bring it to an end your. self."

"I will not. Nothing shall induce me to run away from George. He shall tell me what to do. I belong to him," I repeated. "I belong to him."

"Then I waste my time. Yet I know that there must be an end, and that before long. There must— well—I have executed my task. You will hate me all your life, Nancy."

"No, Edward—you will all my life be as a brother, whether—oh, my heart! my heart!"

He stayed with me while I sobbed and wept. He wept with me. 'Twas the most tender pitiful soul. He could not bear to see tears rise to any woman's eyes: and I know that he regarded me with a partic- ular esteem and affection. Else would he have brought his brother back day after day?

"Let things go on," he said at last. "Let them

end as George and you shall agree. For me, I neither make nor mend in the matter henceforth. George loves you, Nancy, that is quite certain. How he will find an end, the Lord knows, not I. Rocks are on the lee: and a plaguey surf: well—let her drive."

CHAPTER XVIII.

My Brother Joseph.

HE turned and left me. That is, he would have left me, but he was stopped, because, as he opened the door, he was met by the figure of my brother Joseph—none other—who stood there face to face with him.

Edward stepped back with a bow. "Oh, Sir," he said, "I ask your pardon." And so made way for him and would have passed behind him but Joseph banged the floor with his great gold-headed stick and turned upon him with the fierceness of Joshua rather than the meekness of Moses.

"Friend!" he roared—he meant "Enemy," if the voice has any meaning—"what does thee in this place? What does thee with my sister?"

"The lady, Sir, does me the honour of receiving a visit from me. If she is your sister I would point out that your question might be put more courteously, even from one of your coloured cloth."

"I care nothing, friend, for thy opinion. Tell me what does thee with my sister?"

"I have nothing more, Sir, to tell you. Miss Nancy, your brother—if he is your brother—seems angry. Do you wish me to stay? It seems as if you may need some protection."

"Stay, if you please," I replied.

I remember even now the picture of these two and the contrast they presented standing one on either side of the open door. What could be greater than this contrast? On the one side a gentleman well bred and courteous, easy and assured: on the other my brother, angry and rude. As he stood in the doorway, dressed in his stiff Quaker drab, with neither cuff nor collar, and with metal buttons; on his head he kept his hat without lace; his hair was without powder, and just tied behind. His face was red and threatening, full of wrath, hard as the nether mill-stone: his eyes were angry: his brows knit. With it all, because wrath does not go well with Quaker tranquillity, he was stubborn, self-satisfied, schismatic, still. Never was there seen so great a contrast as that between these two men. It made me ashamed to think that I must call this ungainly monster my brother.

Robert Storey must have given him some garbled account of my life and of my friends. Nay, I am quite sure that he must have decorated the account with circumstances, invented for the occasion, of dishonour. Otherwise, how to understand Joseph's condition of rage?

He came, in fact, straight from Robert's book-shop, and was resolved to drag me, willy-nilly, by the hair of my head, if necessary, out of this Pit of Destruction —this Lake of Unforgiven Sin.

It was unfortunate for his purpose that he arrived at a moment when I was face to face with a danger far more terrible than the wrath of Joseph. His arrival was a thing that annoyed—but there was a greater thing behind it.

Joseph began by pointing about the room: at the pictures: at the books: at the music and the harpsichord.

I repeat that the trouble in which I was plunged by the unexpected disclosure—if disclosure it should prove—of obstacles in our way only hardened my soul against the wrath of my brother. This trouble was so great that the interference of Joseph and his indignation over such a trifle as my defection from the Society irritated me. The moment was certainly most inopportune for any remonstrance from him.

" Sister," he said, " is this my cousin's lodging? Or is it thine? "

" It is Isabel's, Joseph. Do you like it? "

He pointed with his stick to the pictures on the wall. "These Allurements of the Devil"—'twas Diana surprised by Actæon. The picture represents nymphs surrounding the goddess in the water. If the Devil has no stronger Allurements than the sight of bare arms and shoulders the women are comparatively safe. "Allurements, I say, of the Devil. Are these the property of Reuben Storey's widow? Or are they thine? "

" They are Isabel's, Joseph. I wish they were my own."

" Nancy," said Edward, " I will with your permission sit down."

" If you please, Edward. My brother will be more angry, I fear, before he leaves me."

Joseph looked at him with displeasure in his face, but said nothing.

"Had these pictures been thine, sister, I should have destroyed them. This tinkling cymbal"—he pointed to the harpsichord—"which drives sinners to the Pit by its foolish jingle, is this also my cousin's? Or is it thine?"

"It is Isabel's. Everything in this room is hers—pictures, harpsichord, books, music, Prayer-books of the Church of England."

"What does all this mean? There is treachery—villainy—the Devil hath broken loose."

"It means that Isabel has returned to the Church of England, of which she was a member before her marriage."

"Robert Storey told me something. She has left us. And as for thee, sister . . . What means this—this man of the world alone with thee?"

"You have to learn many things, Joseph. In the first place, I too have left the Society of Friends."

He banged his stick upon the table.

"Come out from this place," he bawled. "Come out from this accursed den——" He added a great deal more, which I refrain from setting upon paper. Suffice it to say that he accused poor Isabel with all imaginable wickedness, and myself with quite as much. Never could I believe that Joseph could possess an imagination capable of conceiving such things.

"I say, Joseph, that I no longer belong to the Society of Friends——"

"Come out, I say, lest I drag thee from the place

by the hair of thy head—sister of mine? Shame and
disgrace to thy name!"

"Friend Broadbrim," said Edward, stepping forward,
"I am here for the protection of your sister. Understand me: another word of abuse and you shall descend
the stairs head first." He sat down again quietly, but
his face looked ready for mischief.

"Go, sister," said Joseph more quietly, "put on
again the garb of the Friends and come with me out
of the Pit of Hell."

"Joseph," I stood up before him and close to him,
face to face, not afraid. "Look at me well. Behold
your sister, transformed. Look at this dress"—'twas
in pink and blue—"look at the dressing of my head;
listen to the language which I speak——"

"No more," he said; "put off these gauds."

"This very day, Joseph"—why, I had actually forgotten the fact till then, and remembered it oppor-
tunely—"I am twenty-one years of age. I am therefore my own mistress."

"Thine own mistress? Oh! That shall be seen.
And while I live? Go, I say. No more mutinous
words. Obey your guardian, and come. What!
Must I drag thee?"

"No," said Edward. "That must thee not, while I
am here."

"Moreover," I went on, "I have been baptised,
and received into the Church of England."

"Go, child of the Devil. Put off, I say, these vanities."

"Joseph, I shall never go back to the old house.
Henceforth, your ways and mine are separate."

" Sir." It was Edward who stepped forward once
more. " It behoves not a man to interfere between
brother and sister or between husband and wife. Yet
suffer me to remind you that if this young lady is of
age you can have no more authority over her."

" Thee knoweth nothing."

" If any authority, then claim it by law. I am no
lawyer, thank Heaven ; but this I believe, that the
Courts would think twice before they suffered a Quaker
to take forcible possession of a girl belonging to the
Established Church."

" Is this the friend of whom Robert Storey spoke to
me—two young men—great men about the Court—
the godless Court—men who come here constantly to
ensnare and corrupt the heart of women. Sister, thy
position is perilous indeed—I knew not how perilous
until I came here. Well—I threaten nothing—I call
no names--I declare no more of my mind. Choose
between the bottomless Pit and the joys of Heaven.
Choose between your brother and your--what?—your
friend?—your lover?"

" Miss Nancy is of age," said Edward, " and will do
as she pleases."

" Nancy ! Her name is Hannah. She will do, Sir,
as I please. Or she will have no money. Thee can
understand, Hannah, that thee will have no money."

" I gather, Sir," Edward replied, "that this lady,
your sister, has been your ward. Your father--and
hers—either left a will or he did not. If he did, you
can have no control over her fortune after she is of
age. If he left none, the inheritance must be divided.

Let me tell you, that Sir, this affectation of authority
is foolish : and this pretence of power is ridiculous.
Understand also, Sir, that this lady's friends are fully
prepared to set the law in motion on her behalf.
Therefore set your papers in order."

"Law or no law," said Joseph, "she shall have no
money unless she comes with me."

"Law or no law, Joseph, I will not come with you."

Joseph turned to Edward. "Friend," he said, "will
thee listen? This obstinate girl, some time ago, fell
into a kind of melancholy which happens often with
the younger women of our Society from serious contemplation of their soul and its dangers. It is a
wholesome rod administered to young blood, which
might else be presumptuous and headstrong, as a correction."

"As a correction," Edward repeated. "Pray go on,
Sir. Nancy, poor child, was corrected in a wholesome
manner peculiar to your Society. It consists of per-
suading innocent souls that the good God has created
them for torments. No doubt most wholesome."

"My cousin, herself a widow and, I believed, a
godly member of the Society of Friends, offered to
take her away for a change of air. I let her go."

"You did wisely, Sir. The end has fully justified
your judgment in letting her go."

"I now learn the deceit that has been practised
upon me. She has been allured into the vanities of
the world. She is a woman of the world : her com-
panions belong to the world : her thoughts"—he
groaned deeply—"are of the world. She is rebellious :

she has thrown away her religion. Friend, blame not the righteous wrath of one who hath been tricked—tricked—duped—wickedly tricked—even out of his sister's immortal soul." He groaned bitterly, and for the moment I felt almost sorry for him.

"Forgive me if I think that you exaggerate the mischief."

"What! To leave her one of the Elect—to find her a companion of the Devil?"

"Nay, Sir, by your leave. Console yourself, Sir. The Devil, if Nancy is his companion, cannot fail to be speedily converted. He will then, perhaps, join your Society."

"Joseph," I said, "let me speak. Oh! nothing that I can say will move your heart or your reason. You are too far apart from me. I cannot reach to you. But I want this gentleman whom you have insulted to understand what all this means."

Joseph grunted, but made no reply.

"I was driven mad by your cruel doctrines: my cousin pretended to be still a Quakeress in order to get me away. I should have been a poor raving mad woman but for her deception. Oh! my mind was sick with terror. Edward! You could never understand how sick and miserable I had become. I hated even the name of my God, whom I feared with a terror not to be told in words."

"Poor Nancy! I have heard of these things among enthusiasts."

"Then my cousin came, and changed me within and without: she gave me music and taught me to

love painting and singing and dancing. Then, Edward, your brother led me into the fold of the Church
where we are all sheep of one pasture, with one Shepherd who will lead us all—all—all——'' But here I
broke into tears.

" Calm yourself, Nancy," said Edward. " Make an
end of it. You had better go, Sir."

Then I recovered, and finished what I had to say.
" I owe all this to the kindest and best woman of the
world—to Isabel Storey. As for returning with you,
Joseph, learn that, rather than do so, I would become
a scullery-maid in this house. Understand me clearly,
Joseph. I will never go back to the house. Only to
think of that sepulchre makes me tremble and shake.
Now go, brother."

He growled something which I did not understand.

"Come, Joseph. Your authority is finished. Leave
me."

" If I go, it is for ever. I cast thee off. None of
my money shalt thee have ; not one farthing."

" She shall have her own, though," said Edward.

" One more chance—Wilt thee come, sister?"

" One more reply—No, brother! "

Joseph turned and walked slowly down stairs.

I have never seen him since ; and now, I suppose, I
never shall see him. I have heard that he married—I
know not the name of his wife. She was, of course, a
member of the Society of Friends.

As regards Joseph's threat of keeping all the money
in his own hands, Edward was as good as his word :
for he sent a person learned in the law who asked me

a good many questions, and then went to Dartford, where he spoke at length with Joseph. It appeared that no will had been found on the death of my father, and that Joseph had quietly stepped into possession, intending to keep everything as his by right: that, being undisturbed so long, he had come to regard himself as the rightful owner of everything. When, therefore, he learned that there was no quibble or pretence that would save him, but that he would be compelled to pay over to his sister nothing less than one half of the whole estate, including the great house and gardens: the furniture: the paper mills, worth I know not how much every year: many houses and cottages in Dartford and elsewhere: certain farms in Kent: and certain shares and stocks in London: when, I say, he understood that there was no help for it but that he must pay all this money, he became like a madman, falling into a kind of fit, in which his face grew purple and his neck swelled. They blooded him, taking a great quantity. Presently he recovered a little, and moaned and cried like a child. "The half!" he lamented. "The half! I cannot and I will not. The half! I am a ruined man! The half! I will die first!" And so forth, showing very plainly that, in spite of his doctrine, wherein he fancied himself another Gamaliel, or even a Daniel, his mind dwelt continually upon riches as the one thing needful.

In this way, some months afterwards, I learned that I was a great heiress indeed. Robert Storey would have called it a plum, and would have liked to embark the whole in his bookselling business.

No one, I suppose, would refuse unexpected wealth, but I wanted little, as you shall presently learn, and the rest I have endeavoured to use for the assistance of those less favoured than myself.

To return. Joseph gone, Edward went back to the discourse which his arrival interrupted.

" Edward," I said, "do not forget what I said. Suffer George to tell me himself. Whatever he bids me to do—that will I do. But he—and he alone— must tell me that we must part. Not from your lips will I have it—though I think you love me too."

"God knows, Nancy!" he murmured.

"Let George tell me himself. He will come this evening. I will ask my cousin to stay in her own room. Leave us alone. George shall tell me what he pleases: and I will do—whatever he commands."

CHAPTER XIX.

The "Tower of Brill."

LEAVE the love-sick girl. She is best alone. Come now to things of greater importance—to traitors and the clash of arms.

When Edward left me he did not go down the stairs but climbed up as far as Captain Sellinger's room.

The Captain, who was in his shirt-sleeves, sprang to his feet in some confusion when he recognised his visitor.

"Sir," he cried. "This surprise—this honour." He offered a chair, but his visitor remained standing.

"I have been paying a morning call upon your fair neighbours," he said. "Do not disturb yourself, Sir. Nay, I entreat: shirt-sleeves will not hinder discourse. Now, Sir," he sat down on the table. "Let us talk."

"At your convenience, Sir."

"Well, then, I came here, Captain Sellinger, to confer with you about this plaguey business—of which you know."

The Captain bowed.

"Night after night the coach waits in the court, and I hear the voices of the fellows below. Where is it going to end?"

"Indeed, Sir, I know not."

"Will they never grow tired of watching for the opportunity that never comes?"

"We are not tired of defeating their intentions, Sir."

"I believe you are not. Some time or other it will be my duty to acquaint my brother with the whole business. But it is I who am tired of it. Let me tell you, Captain Sellinger, that I am heartily sick of the whole business. Let me tell you that to sneak down-stairs and out of St. James's Place under convoy—even the convoy of the Horse Guards—sticks. It sticks in the gullet. And all for half-a-dozen damned Jacobites!"

"And yet, Sir, with submission——"

"Oh, I know—I know," he replied impatiently. "My brother's person must not be exposed to any danger. And his reputation must be kept clear from calumny. Concerning the young lady below, there should be no scandal—no scandal at all, I repeat, Sir." He fixed his eyes earnestly on Captain Sellinger.

"There is none, I believe, Sir."

"Well, Sir. I have considered the case, and I think I have found a way by which my brother will be safe-guarded—name and fame and life and limb. But I shall want your help, and that of your fellow the Cor-poral."

"You shall have both, Sir."

"And your silence, drunk or sober, until the thing is done."

"Sir, I am never drunk till your illustrious brother is safe."

"Ay—ay. We don't drink on board as you drink ashore, otherwise we should be on the rocks or among the breakers very speedily. But of course there are some . . . Captain Sellinger, there is a kind of man who, when the drink is in him, babbles like a running brook, the louder and the more foolish the more he drinks. And there is another kind of man whose lips are sealed like wax, the tighter with every glass. To which kind, Captain——" He did not finish the question.

"To the latter kind, Sir. But, indeed, if you doubt, I will undertake to drink nothing—a bottle or so, no more—at a sitting until this business is despatched. As for being tired, Sir, let me entreat you not to think of it. They must grow weary of the nightly watching with the nightly baffling : they must understand, by this time, that their designs are suspected ; they will get tired of bribing the Dutch skipper ; besides, the nights grow cold ; we shall soon have frost and snow."

"It is not certain that they will grow tired."

"The ladies might change their lodging for some place unknown."

"Yes : but I want to give the fellows a lesson, and as sharp as you please."

"I am pleased, Sir, with what pleases you."

"As for the termination of the business, that, Captain Sellinger, I frankly tell you, lies with my brother, not with me."

Captain Sellinger bowed.

"But the termination of this watching and waiting

I will end as soon as I can—and I say that I have found a way in which we may end it without my brother's name being so much as mentioned or suspected."

" If, Sir, I might be trusted——"

" You shall be trusted.   Hang it, Captain, I have climbed this steep stair of yours with no other object than to trust you.   There will, perhaps, be a little fighting.   There are six of them, you say."

" One for the coach : five for the seizure, without counting the old man, the Doctor."

" Good! We are three.   Well, this is my plan. The Corporal will get into hiding on the evening of action : under the stairs : in the kitchen : there will be a light on the wall in the passage—there is a sconce, I believe.   You will remain quiet upstairs in your own room.   At half-past nine o'clock you will come down and knock at Mrs. Storey's door.   I will come out : we two will descend the stairs as noisily as we can : this will be a signal for the Corporal to hold himself in readiness.   Your Jacobites will think it is my brother coming downstairs with me.   Out they come : out flies the steel, and to it hammer and tongs. What do you think of that, Captain Sellinger?"

" Why, Sir, except for the danger to yourself——"

" Never fear, man ; the danger to me is nothing : my brother's name must not be mentioned, and those fellows must be scattered.   Do you agree to this plan ? Can you think of a better ? "

" Sir, I believe it is excellent.   I will answer for the Corporal when you choose to give the word."

" Why, Captain, I love not to think of your suffering privation in our cause. We will strike the blow to-night—this very night—and you shall go back to your bottle released from your self-imposed penance."

" To-night, Sir. By all means."

So it was decided. The Captain looked after the simple arrangements : one candle on the landing : another in the passage : the Corporal in the kitchen with the door locked : they allowed Molly to sit there as well, on the condition that she was not to be told before the evening what was intended. At half-past nine, when the two gentlemen came downstairs, the Corporal was to step out quickly, armed and ready for the fray.

At half-past eight our friends arrived. Isabel remained in her room, at my request, pretending a headache. I received the two brothers. George was agitated : he sat down to play, but rose again : he sat beside me and talked about things indifferent. Edward, anxious for the time to pass, walked about the room and looked at the clock. We were all three full of disquiet.

Upstairs, the Captain sat at his window watching. In the court below the coach was standing : two men stood at the horses' heads : that was satisfactory. The Captain shut his window and waited in the dark.

Downstairs the Corporal, in his hiding-place, removed the bricks and listened to the conversation in the Doctor's room. They were talking about desisting from the attempt : it was disheartening to find them-

selves baffled every evening : their purpose must have
been discovered and guarded against, and so forth.
The Doctor, on the other hand, earnestly entreated
them to persevere a few nights more ; this nightly
guard simply showed that Captain Sellinger had re-
cognized the visitors, and that he made it his business
sometimes to let them understand the fact : accident
any night might place in their hands these two gentlemen, unarmed, without the power of resistance : then,
what a splendid prize to carry across the Channel !

He then went out to look about him, to reconnoitre,
as the soldiers call it. He walked up and down St.
James's Place ; neither Captain nor Corporal was there :
he went out into St. James's Street, but could see
neither of them : he looked in the back garden : no
one was there, and the door was bolted : he tried the
kitchen door ; it was locked.

"Who's there?" cried Molly. "I'm not going to
have no one in my kitchen."

" Where's the Corporal, Molly ? "

" I don't know.   He's gone out."

" I would speak with the Captain, Molly.   Have
you seen him ? "

" He's gone out too," said Molly, the shameless.

So the Doctor returned to his own room and reported with great contentment of mind what he had
seen and heard.   Both guards—if they were guards—
gone out : the job was easy : before their prisoners had
found room or time to draw their swords, they would
be seized and pinioned and gagged.   A dark and
cloudy night, too ; a threatening of rain : nothing

could be more convenient for this great and holy purpose of theirs.

With the Doctor this evening were four men. One of them, a great fat fellow of six feet or more, the Corporal took to be the Skipper of the ship engaged to carry the prisoners—namely, the *Tower of Brill*—because he was dressed somewhat like a sailor and because he talked execrable French.

"You have hired me, gentlemen," he said, "and I will fight for you and carry off your prisoners for you. But I think we shall come badly out of this business. Every night we have been watched and baffled. Do you think that knowing we are here and the object of our attempt is there"—he pointed up stairs—"that they will ever suffer those two persons to be without a guard?"

"There is no sign of any guard," said the Doctor.

"There must be a guard. Gentlemen, you are, no doubt, prepared for the worst. After dangling for a minute or two, they will cut us down and strip us and prick out the place where the knife is to go. We shall look very pretty, all of us. However, you have hired me—I am your servant."

The others sat in patience and silence: they were gentlemen of English descent, born in France. Mostly they were pale of countenance, for the audacity of the enterprise was such that it moved the heart even of a Jacobite.

At a quarter past nine the Corporal left off listening and watching and replaced his bricks.

"A few minutes more, Molly," he said, "and I am

"I COULD PROTECT THEM AGAINST FIFTY."— *Page 251.*

at last Fortune's Favourite. I may now speak openly, because there is no fear of your tongue."

"I am no talker, Corporal."

"Thou art as discreet a woman as lives, Molly. In a few minutes, therefore, let me tell thee that I shall win my commission in the noblest way possible, or I shall have left my wife—poor disconsolate wretch!—to the gratitude of my country, while I myself shall be sitting on a golden stool or throne playing the harp."

"God forbid, Corporal!"

"God forbid, indeed, Molly! I confess, that at present, at the early age of twenty-eight, I prefer the King's commission if I could get it, even to the celestial harp. A single jug of small ale, Molly. Thank you. Learn, my girl, that the object of the bloody villains in the other room is to secure the persons of the two gentlemen now sitting with Madam and Miss Nancy overhead—to secure their persons, Molly, and to take them prisoners across the seas. To their own poor beggarly country."

"What for?" asked Molly.

"That I will tell thee on another occasion. I must now make ready for the fray. Ha! my time has come." He loosed his sword in its scabbard. "Ha! my wrist is firm: my eye is steady. 'Tis the day of Fortune—wish me luck, Molly. It is my happy chance to protect those two gentlemen. I could protect them against fifty. Ha!" he made as if he was thrusting. "Ha! I had you there. Come on! Come on! Come all!"

So he vaunted, in his braggart way; yet it was a

brave heart and ready to face death in the cause of loyalty. And the moments passed all too slowly for his impatient spirit. "Not half-past nine yet?" looking at his watch. "Molly, time crawls for the hero who would still stand sword in hand. Ha! I had you there!"

At last the expected steps were heard upon the stairs, and the welcome signal—the three knocks. The Corporal drew his sword and stepped out into the passage dimly lit by the candle in the sconces.

The two coming down on the stairs were close to the bottom: there was a little more light upon the stairs from a candle higher up at the landing: the Corporal saw the glimmer of their swords, which were drawn. He stood waiting for one moment only. Then the Doctor's door was thrown open and the four men rushed out. They were unarmed: they trusted to the suddenness of the attack.

"Ha!" cried the Corporal. "Have at you!" and sprang upon them. It was the big sailor who led the party, I suppose on account of his weight. He threw himself forward but met, I know not in what part of him, the Corporal's sword. Whether he was killed or whether it was but a blood-letting will never be known, for he fell with a deep groan and moved no more. All this that takes time to relate passed in a moment. The other three recoiled and drew their swords. Captain Sellinger pushed aside his companion, and stood astride the fallen man sword in hand. Beside him stood the Corporal, lunging and parrying and crying all the time like a fencing-master. "Ha! ha! ha!"

We heard it upstairs, and could not understand what had happened, the last thing in our minds being a fight. Yet these were the words: "Ha! Come on then! Ha! Take your bellyful, then. Ha! ha!" stamping with heel as if at a fencing-school.

"It is your friend the Corporal," said George upstairs. "He is giving somebody a lesson. A strange time and a strange place! By candle-light, in a narrow passage!"

He was, indeed, giving a lesson, but not the kind of lesson that we thought.

Then the old Doctor snatched up two candles that stood upon the table and brought them to the door, throwing their light upon the scene of battle. I say that these things, as told to me by the Captain, lasted not a moment. And I say, further, that the end would have been the death of some besides the fat Dutch skipper, who perhaps was only wounded, had it not been for an unexpected blow, quite contrary to the recognised principles of polite warfare. One must admit that the decisive blow in this battle was delivered by a woman—none other than Molly.

When she saw the Corporal rush out of the kitchen, sword in hand, she ran after him : she saw him with that swift lunge despatch one of the assailants—the biggest and the strongest. She neither shrieked nor swooned nor wrung her hands : she acted much more sensibly : she ran back to her kitchen : you think, to weep and wring her hands? Not at all. Molly was a quick woman : quick to see and to act : she was also as strong a woman as you will meet on a summer's

day: strong and strapping and brave. She remembered—'twas a kind of inspiration if we may venture
to think so—yet why not, considering the magnitude
of the danger and the audacity of the assailants? Yes,
I needs must think it was by a kind of inspiration—
she remembered the great black pot hanging over the
fire, and filled with boiling beef broth: she quickly
lifted it off the chain: she carried it out in her strong
arms, which were burned and scarred for life, of which
she took no heed: and she threw the contents—the
bubbling, boiling broth—full in the faces of the three
men at the moment when their swords were drawn,
and the battle was beginning.

They shrieked: they dropped their swords: they
leaped in the air, cursing and shrieking: they were
scalded: they were blinded.

"What sort of a lesson is this?" asked George,
above. "Some one must be hurt." He rose to go
downstairs, but I stopped him.

"They are laughing," I said. "It is some horse-
play of the Captain and his friends."

The Corporal seized their swords. "Surrender,
gentlemen," he said. Alas! They could neither surrender nor fight, such was the agony of their faces
from the boiling broth.

Captain Sellinger put up his sword. "I think,
Sir," he said to his chief, "that Molly, the maid, carries
off the honours of the field. What shall we do
next?"

"When these gentlemen have arrived at a lower
pitch of pain, which will enable them to speak— Do

you surrender, gentlemen, or shall Corporal Bates finish this encounter for you ? "

" We surrender," one of them replied.

" We surrender, Sir," said Dr. Mynsterchamber, sitting down and replacing the candles on the table.

"Gentlemen, I am sorry that we did not proceed to a more legitimate conclusion. Let us hope that when your designs are more complete, you will allow me to meet you in the open field. For the moment, I have but one thing to say. If we take you prisoners, there is no doubt that you will end your days on Tower Hill or at Newgate. As your attempt has proved futile, I am disposed to think that the less said about it the better. You will therefore get into the coach you designed for my brother and myself: you will make your way to the *Tower of Brill*, your ship ; and if that vessel is found in the Pool to-morrow morning you shall all be arrested, tried, and hanged as traitors."

No one replied. The pain of the scalding forbade any reply.

" Here is a man either dead or wounded. Carry your man away."

Thus, in grievous plight, in the agony of scalded cheeks and blinded eyes, they lifted their great fat skipper and bore him into the coach.

Captain Sellinger followed after. He declared afterwards that the wounded man groaned audibly ; so that, perhaps, he was not killed. When they were all in the coach he stood at the window and addressed the discomfited conspirators.

"Gentlemen," he said, "I congratulate you. The attempt was gallant : but you were ill advised in trying to fight in so narrow a space, which exposed you to the sword of the first comer—and in the flank. Moreover, you did not take into account the devotion of the women to our cause. Believe me, the Roman Catholic Pretender, should he land, will go home with a dishclout to his tail. Remember, that the evidence against you is full and complete. You are allowed to escape, but you are known : if any one of you should venture to show his face again on this soil of Great Britain, he will have himself to blame for his own trial and subsequent hanging with its usual trimmings. Corporal, is the coachman ready? Good. Coachman, you will get your fare embarked as soon as you can at Whitehall Stairs. You are also known after your long attendance in St. James's Place. You had better get into the boat as well. What has been said to the gentlemen inside, is also said to you. 'Ware prison ! 'ware gallows! Gentlemen, bon voyage! Some kinds of soft soap or goose-grease are recommended for scalds and burns. No doubt, on board, you will find all that the ' Pharmacopœia ' itself could recommend."

The Captain returned to the house when the coach had rumbled out of St. James's Place.

He found his chief sitting at the table in the Doctor's room, his sword lying across the table.

" So," he said, "they are gone, Captain? Thus is broken up a nest of traitors and rebels. Let them go. Is the man dead ? "

" I believe he groaned as they carried him. Another is pricked, but I believe not seriously: the hot broth did the job, Sir."

" Here is the contriver and leader in the whole business. I have kept him for a little conversation."

The Doctor was dressed in a long travelling roque-laure: his neck was muffled up: he wore his hat. The box in which he kept his papers was open and empty: his cupboard door stood open: it was evident that as soon as the attempt was resolved upon he had made hasty arrangements for immediate flight ; and that, whether the attempt was successful or not. He stood leaning against the wall, his wrinkled old face showing no sign of any emotion whatever : at the door stood the Corporal as guard, carrying his naked sword, on the blade of which he observed with infinite grati-fication signs of the recent conflict. On the table lay a packet of papers, tied up.

" These papers, Captain Sellinger, were taken from the pocket of our prisoner—this man whom they call Dr. Mynsterchamber. He was preparing for depar-ture and had tied them up in readiness. I have looked at them. I find sufficient proof in them that he is a double-dyed traitor. Tell me, Sir, what should I do with him ? "

" Hang him ! " said the Captain, " unless some other and slower form of death can be found."

The Doctor neither spoke nor moved.

" It is now some weeks since I made it my business to ascertain who and what this Dr. Mynsterchamber professed to be. The creature "—he spoke and looked as if the man was not present—" is by profession a

spy. He is a spy, say. He is in the service of his
Majesty's Government to act as a spy in France. He
is in the household of the Elder Pretender. As a spy
in our service he can come here and live here when he
pleases : as a Jacobite he is free to go all over France
as he pleases. It is a most honourable occupation.
First, he deceives his friends in France and reports
their doings. Then he comes over here and takes the
King's pay, and spies out our doings."

" Hang him ! Hang him ! " said the Captain.

(" They are quite quiet again," said George, upstairs. " I wonder what all the noise meant.")

" What shall we do with this villain, Captain ? "

" Hang him ! "

" As for this conspiracy, it was audacious enough to
be successful. Had it not been for the accidental discovery of Corporal Bates it would have been successful. The kingdom, for some time afterwards, would
have been thrown into confusion. But no great harm
would have followed. We've got to fight out the
quarrel with France, whether my brother and I are
prisoners or not. Still, the attempt, made by one in
English pay, was, as I said, audacious." He turned
suddenly to the prisoner, " Now, Sir, have you anything to say ? "

The Doctor lifted his head, took off his hat, and
cried in a strong resolute voice—

" God save King James ! "

" The Pretender ! " said Captain Sellinger.

" And God save Prince Charles Edward ! "

" Very good. What else have you to say before
you go into Newgate Jail ? "

" Learn, Sir," the Doctor replied with dignity, "that my friends are loyal men. With us loyalty means an attachment to the Throne, which you could hardly be expected to understand. The loyalty of the Jacobites survives everything: the stupidity of one King: the profligacy of another: the obstinacy of a third. If a King is a weak or a bad King, he is still King by Divine appointment: we wait for a better King. James the Second threw away the Crown: but he could not throw away the loyalty of the faithful. Our loyalty means not only loyalty to death, but more: it means loyalty to dishonour if necessary. I am a gentleman: my father was ennobled by James the Second when in exile: yet I am a spy. I pretend to betray my King's secrets in order to obtain the secrets of your Court. I take money from you: in return I supply you with false information as to the strength and the destination of the French fleets——"

" The villain!" said Captain Sellinger.

" And I am permitted to come over here; to go about where I please; to converse with Ministers; to learn your plans. All that I learn and discover I most faithfully report by means of secret messengers, who are English on this side and French on the other. These things—this treachery which would be dishonouring in any other cause, are accounted among loyalists as honourable and commendable. If, Sir, I have the approbation of my King and my friends, what do I care for any opinion of yours?"

" You confess that you lie, degrade, and debase your

soul every day. Yet it is in the cause of righteousness. Then we may break all the Commandments daily in support of the Christian Faith."

"I am loyal. That is the sum of all. Now, Sir, I am ready to go to your prison. I am an old man, seventy-five years of age. Not too old to die for my King, but too old to fear death."

"Perhaps there will be no prison. I think, Master Loyalist, that if you are once out of the country you can do us very little further harm. Therefore, while we keep the papers, we will not keep the writer. Corporal, search the prisoner for more papers."

There were no more. All the papers were in the packet lying on the table.

"Now, Sir, you can go. There will be time for you to get on board the *Tower of Brill* before she weighs anchor. Should the ship be taken to-morrow morning, I fear that you, too, will be hanged with the rest. The Corporal here, who understands French, will give sufficient evidence for hanging purposes."

"Oh!" The Doctor looked astonished. "You understand French—you? Perhaps you, too, are a loyalist."

"I am. To the House of Brunswick," said the Corporal stiffly.

"And you listened, I suppose: and reported what you heard. Villain!" Indignation choked him. "A spy! Faugh! A spy!"

"Come," said the Captain roughly. "What the devil are you yourself? Pack! March! Get thee to thine own friends, double-dyed traitor!"

The Doctor walked away with dignity, tall and erect as a lance, although so old. It degrades a man to be a spy: but loyalty covers all.

"Corporal Bates." The Chief turned to his defender.

The Corporal stood at attention.

"It is not likely that I shall ever forget the events of this evening. Had it not been for your zeal in discovering this horrid plot; and for your discretion in keeping the thing a secret; and for your bravery this evening, which at the very outset despatched one of the villains, my brother and I might now have been occupants of a French prison with a dismal outlook as regards liberty. Or we might have fought for our liberty and fallen. Be assured that as opportunity offers I shall inform my brother as to these particulars. Meantime, here is my purse, which contains, I believe, fifty guineas. Take it, Corporal Bates, as an earnest of future favours."

The Corporal received the purse with a salute and in silence. He hadn't expected a gift of money, which he could not refuse. Yet it was not what he wanted.

"I understand further, Corporal Bates, that you are a person of many accomplishments; speaking other languages, skilled in the art of fence, able to instruct in fortifications and the mathematics; and that you are, in addition, a sober man, well mannered, creditably married, and in no way likely to bring discredit upon epaulettes not of wool." The Corporal made no sign save that his cheek turned pale. He was now on the point of achieving his fondest and most constant dream. "I understand, further, from Captain Sellinger, that you are desirous, above all things of obtaining his Majesty's Commisson."

"Sir, I have no other ambition," the poor Corporal murmured.

"It is a highly laudable ambition. Well, Sir, I take it upon myself to speak for your valour. As to the rest of your accomplishments I take the word of Captain Sellinger. I shall venture, Sir, to recommend you to his Majesty."

The Corporal's face fell. Other patrons had made him the same promise, but he remained a Corporal.

Then Captain Sellinger whispered something.

"Corporal Bates," said the Chief, "would you exchange your woolen epaulettes for the gold lace of a Royal Marine?"

"Sir, you make me the proudest man in the whole world."

"Then it is as good as done. Captain Sellinger, present to me Lieutenant Bates, of his Majesty's Regiment of Royal Marines."

The Lieutenant fell on his knees while the tears of joy ran down his cheek. "Sir," he said, "my only prayer is that I may be sent in command of a company to take the enemy's forts, and that under your very eyes, to justify this promotion!"

"We will dispense with your convoy to-night, Captain Sellinger." So he went upstairs, nodding his head good humouredly to the Corporal.

"Lieutenant Bates," said the Captain. "We are now brothers-in-arms. We can drink together. There are—ah!—arrears to pull up and new toasts to drink. 'Confusion to all Traitors and Rebels!' 'Success to the Youngest Officer in his Majesty's Service!' 'The Health of the Divine Nancy!' Come, Lieutenant. This night, if ever, thou shalt have a skinful."

CHAPTER XX.

"There shall be no Obstacle."

ALL that afternoon my cousin and I talked over the position of things. I had no secrets from her: I told her exactly what Edward had said: how at the end he melted: how I had resolved to leave everything to George himself.

"Not able to marry you? What does the man mean?" my cousin asked. "Why, Nancy, to be sure, he is a great lord: I am certain of that: the star which he sometimes wears betrays his rank: and as for us, we belong only to the trading class: but Love levels all: and Sir George has over and over again assured me that he has never found, among the greatest ladies, any whose manners are more polite than your own; nor any whose mind is purer and whose face and form are more bewitching. Not marry you?"

"Edward was all kindness, Isabel: he shed tears while he spoke to me."

"Not able to marry? Then the creature must be married already."

"Nay; I am certain that he is not. I am, he has told me, the first. His brother assures me that no other woman has ever yet attracted his eyes."

"Then—what can he mean? He is of age; his father is dead; he can please himself. Perhaps they promised him when he was of tender years to some girl of his own rank. Why can he not please himself? If he would please himself, it would be with thee, my Nancy. Of that be well assured."

"Indeed," I confessed, "I am well assured of that. Never was any woman more assured of her lover's truth."

"So we all think; yet . . . not that my Reuben ever gave me any cause to think otherwise. But, Nancy, the question is, what are the reasons? Why cannot Sir George marry you?"

"The reasons he must tell me himself."

"Shall I ask him, child? Stay in your own room this evening and I will ask him."

"Nay, but I would not have any one—not even thee, cousin, between him and me. Let him tell me what he pleases. If we are to part, it must come from his own lips . . . ." And again tears came to my relief.

"Part—part—why?" My cousin bent over me and kissed me. "Has the man eyes? Has the man a heart? Part with the sweetest girl in the world? He cannot, my dear. He cannot, except he were the King of Great Britain and Ireland. Heart up, Nancy! Heart up! Thy sweetheart shall carry thee off to church—he shall—with a laugh on his lips and a shake in his leg, and ring thee before all the world. Why else did he wish thee to be baptised? Why else did he take us on the river and to the Gardens? My

dear, it were else a most monstrous thing thus to play
with a girl's affections. It were worse with such a
girl as my Nancy, than to betray the blowsy innocence of some milkmaid. No—no—Sir George could
not. His face and his discourse : his heart and his
mind : are too full of truth and of religion. He could
not, I say. Oh, he could not."

"Then there is another thing, cousin. If to marry
me would bring trouble upon him, it were better that
I should die."

"Trouble? What trouble, I pray?" she replied
quickly. "Out of honest love no trouble ever sprang.
Say he is above thee in rank, Nancy. Call him Earl
or Duke—he is master of himself and his own actions.
What can his friends do when they find it out?
Nothing. They may be disappointed. Those fine
Court ladies of whom Robert speaks so kindly will
tear their hair for spite. But, since the thing is
done——"

"It is not yet done, cousin."

"It will be done—and that very soon—if I have
studied that young gentleman to any purpose. My
dear, men are like chips and matches, some of which
catch fire quickly and burn out in no time, while
others are slow to light but burn on steadily and
gradually. Sir George is one who is slow to light.
But once he burns he is all pure flame."

Thus we talked, and though my cousin assured me
of her perfect confidence there lay upon me the
weight of foreboding—a sense of coming evil.

In the evening, about half-past eight, our friends

came as usual. Isabel begged to be excused, because she must go to see a poor woman in the garrets who had children to clothe. So she went away, promising to return shortly.

What happened next, you know. At a certain signal Edward went out, also promising to return shortly.

Then we heard the noise below: the trampling and the shouting.

"One would think it a fencing-bout," said Sir George. "A strange place and a strange time for a fencing-bout!"

Then he sat down beside me.

For the first time we were alone. He sat down, I say, beside me : then he sank on one knee and caught my hand and began to kiss it fondly.

"Oh, Nancy!" he said, "sweet maid—heart of my heart!" I cannot write down all that he said. Sure, never did fond lover express his love more passionately, or with greater extravagance. Women do not love in the same way. Their sweethearts are not gods to them—yet they desire no other gods: they love the man: they see him as he might be: as he was intended to be : as the Lord meant him to be : they see, though in a glass darkly, because their eyes are not strong enough to gaze upon the glory, nor can their minds imagine or figure to themselves the splendour of the truth—but they see imperfectly the man as he will be, glorified and made perfect : they understand his shortcomings and his faults, which are to them only like so many excrescences that can be shaken off. Never did I worship George as he worshipped me: why, the fact itself that he should find in me so much perfection when I was conscious of so many faults, made me feel his weakness. Yet every woman likes it. Oh! how happy did it make me to be told that I was a goddess! Oh! how did my poor heart beat and the colour fly to my face when that dearest and best of men—that man in whom were united all the virtues of honour, truth, and purity—knelt at my feet to tell me with such extravagances as moved me well-nigh to tears of joy and happiness that he loved me—he loved me—he loved me.

" My dearest Nancy," he said, calming himself after a while. " We are so seldom alone. This is the rarest chance. It is only on such a chance that we can speak. Nancy: when wilt thou be mine, altogether —my bride? "

"Oh! When my Lord shall command. I will obey in anything."

"Yes—yes—I will think. I will consult Edward. I can do nothing without Edward."

" He was here this morning. He told me . . . he said plainly . . . that there were reasons which would stand between you and me."

" What reasons are those? I know of none that I cannot meet, if I choose."

" I know not. He would not tell me. Nor, indeed, did I press him, because I would know nothing except from your own lips. If there are reasons, let us part at once."

Part at once! Why he was sitting beside me: my head was on his heart: he was kissing me fondly: one arm was round my waist : one hand was holding my hand. Part at once!

He laughed. " Part at once?" he cried. "We will part, my Nancy, when the span of life is finished and I am called away. Then you shall remain to pray a little for me (if it is allowed to pray for the dead)."

"Child !" he said, after these transports, or in the midst of them. "I cannot live without thee. Edward has been telling me this, and that, and the other. They are obstacles, he says. I will admit no obstacles. I care not what they say. If I cannot please my own heart, I will step down and suffer Edward to take my place."

"Nay," I said, not understanding what he meant, " but I love thee too well, George, to stand in thy way. It is enough for me to be loved. Let me go and re-member that."

"Go? Never! I will not leave thee, Nancy. Now listen. There are reasons why I cannot place thee be-side me : we must love in secret, and thou must live in obscurity. But I would not wrong thee. Oh! to wrong this pure angel—to bring sorrow and shame upon thee—I could not, Nancy, were I the deepest profligate in all this wicked town. I could not, I say. Believe me, dearest girl. I were not worthy to love so much goodness if I were capable of such a thought."

There needed no assurance on this point. I told him so.

" Edward and I have talked it over. Edward is the best brother that ever lived. Of all creatures I love him best—next to you. I told him, this very day,

that I would hear of no obstacles. He gave way.
He will help us in everything. Now, Nancy, listen to
what we have arranged. We will be married to-
morrow morning—I know not in what Church—Edward knows: I know not by what clergyman—Edward
knows: in some name or other—perhaps that of Le
Breton—Edward knows. The coach shall come for
thee in the morning about eight. After the ceremony
we shall go to some place—it is a small house close by
in Catherine Wheel Alley, looking over the Park. He
found it, bought it, furniture and all, this afternoon:
he has also put a few servants in it : it shall be thy nest,
my love, thy bower, where thou shalt sit and dream of
love and of thy lover. Nancy, never did I know what
happiness meant until I learned to love thee. I am
not like one of the town gallants who catch fire at the
rustle of a furbelow : I cannot, I think, love a woman
unless I am truly persuaded that she is as beautiful
within as without. I would lay my whole heart open
to the woman I love. I would make her the casket to
contain all my secret thoughts, my ambitions, and
everything. With such a woman for a partner a man
might become indeed a king." He raised his head :
his eyes became fixed : he was one who saw in a vision
noble deeds and kingly thoughts.

"But thou must be effaced from view—an invisible
bride—canst thou do so much for me, Nancy, without
repining ? "

" I can do more than that, George, for such a lover—
I could die for him—oh ! so gladly, if it would help
him."

With that he kissed me again, and so we continued our discourse till Edward came back, this business of his happily accomplished.

" You have had your fencing-bout?" said George.

"Ay, ay! We have had the fencing-bout," he replied. " Now, George, have you told this sweet girl what to-morrow brings with it?"

" I have told her. She agrees."

Oh! But he never asked me if I agreed.

" Then, Nancy, to-morrow we shall be brother and sister—as dear to me, believe it, as any other sister could be. George is not worthy of thee, I begin to think. Yet a moderately fond lover; and I dare swear, as constant as any of his rank in Europe. Well, Nancy, I hope the house will be to thy liking. The rooms are small; the house belonged to old Lady Harlow who died some months ago. There is a window in the first floor overlooking the park, with a Venetian balcony."

"And we have never yet told her our real names," said George.

" Tell me at your own leisure. Not to-night, George. Let me not be dazzled with greatness. I am too happy to-night. To-morrow, be Baron, Earl, or Duke —what you will."

" I shall use your permission—I will be what I am. I remember what you told me, about the Lord Burleigh who married the country girl : that he should not have taken her to his grand house. Have you got a grand house ?"

"I have two or three. In due course I shall have more."

"Then, my dear, do not take me to them : leave me in that modest cottage of which you speak, near at hand, so that I may see you often. Let me remain in obscurity : believe me, I shall never desire to take my place before the world : it will be happiness enough for me to be so in reality and enjoy your affection."

"Nancy !" So he fell into a transport again, swearing—but you know what he would swear at such a moment.

At this moment my cousin returned. "Sir George," she said, "I pray you to forgive me. That poor woman, with her six children——"

"Let me minister, through you, dear lady, to their wants." So he lugged out his purse, filled with guineas, and laid it in her hands. "It is a thank-offering," he said. "I give thee this money in memory. This fair cousin of yours, Madam, has this morning come to an understanding with me. We have, in a word, arranged things for our own satisfaction first ; and for the consideration of other people—who must also be considered—next. I am blessed indeed, for my own part, because she hath promised to become my own whenever those arrangements can be made." He spoke now with the greatest dignity. "I trust, Madam, that you will believe me when I assure you that whatever arrangements I may be compelled to make—always subject to my Nancy's approval—I shall be guided only by the resolution to make her happiness the first consideration, and her interest the chief study of my life."

" Oh, Sir ! oh, Nancy ! . . . I have, of course, looked for this. I could not choose but be aware of what was going on. Else why should you and your brother so often visit two simple ladies who have none of the arts and accomplishments of the Great? "

He laughed.

" My Nancy has arts and accomplishments which the people you call the Great cannot have. She has taught me, dear Madam, some of the dangers and temptations which beset great people. By your leave I will tell you what these are. We—may I say *we* and not *they* ? We, I say, have not to work for what we enjoy: therefore we enjoy nothing: we have not to long for something and save up for it, and deprive ourselves of this and of that in order to get it : if we want a thing we have it. Therefore, we value nothing. No one contradicts us ; therefore, we think we know everything, and are vain accordingly. We have no uncertainty about fortune : it is true that history is full of the sad ends of prince and noble : but in this polite age such deaths by violence or by Civil War do not happen. There will be no more murder of princes in the Tower : no more beheading of Kings at Whitehall. Again, we know nothing of the struggle for a livelihood and of the patience of women in poverty and their contrivance to keep the children. We are raised, as they call it, above these things. Therefore we grow selfish. Now, my dear Nancy has contradicted me times out of number. She has taught me that I know nothing : she has shown me what they are like—the people of whom I used to speak ignorantly.

I am lowered in my own conceit, and therefore I am raised in reality. She has herself most unconsciously made me more worthy—yet still most unworthy—to be her lover. Believe me, Madam "—again he took my hand and kissed it—" there is no rank so lofty which would not be graced by Nancy. There is no title so grand as that of Nancy's lover."

" Oh ! Sir," cried my cousin, quite overcome and unable to say more. " Oh ! Sir ; it is too much, indeed," and so fell back into a chair, where she lay, half in tears and half laughing, fanning herself violently. She said afterwards that the reason of this emotion was the first discovery of the authority—not to say the majesty—with which this young man spoke. In a Bishop, she said, or in a Judge, such authority might be looked for: but in so young a man 'twas wonderful. However, the events of the next day might possibly have coloured her imagination. All I know is that the dear woman was profoundly affected when she heard this gracious speech. I may say it here, and once for all, that whatever my cousin did for me ; whether she took me away from my sepulchral home: whether she took off the Quaker habits and made me drop the Quaker speech : whether she showed me the wicked world : whether she allowed these young men to visit us : whether she suffered them to offer entertainments : all she did was done out of pure love for me and consideration for me. First, she would drag me out of the melancholy which oppressed my soul, and next she would encourage the passion of which she watched and knew the first beginnings. If my cousin's conduct brought upon me my greatest misfortunes, it gave me my greatest happiness. But for her, Robert Storey might have been in my estimation a man of the finest manners. Nay, more: but for her, Robert Storey might have been my husband.

CHAPTER XXI.

To Dress the Bride.

It was late when they went away, for there was much to say, and Edward was full of spirits, all the more because of the victory won down below, of which we heard from Molly you may be sure.

When they were gone, my cousin fell to kissing me again. "Thou art born for love, Nancy. Oh! not the common kind. He who once loves thee will never forget thee! What have I read? There is a love, even between man and woman, which is heavenly love: there is also the love which is earthly love. Thine is the heavenly love! So long as thy lover is filled with thy image he will never go wrong: he will be guided always by the principles of honour and religion."

"My lover wants not that guidance, cousin."

"Women," she went on, "may pretend what they please, but there is no solid happiness in life unless it be accompanied by love. Oh, yes! here one and here another, cold and unfit for love. I talk of the sex, my dear. 'Tis love, 'tis love—'tis love they still desire. Love protects them from the rubs and knocks of the world: love provides them with all the good things for which their husbands, work: love fills the heart. I am a widow, and I think I shall not marry again because love has filled my heart and fills it still, though my Reuben has been called away. Now to bed, my dear. Wake in the morning with rosy cheeks and bright eyes. Go not to the altar with pale cheek and dull looks. Go like one who greets the day with a thankful heart."

So I went to bed : but not to sleep.

In the morning, at seven o'clock, a letter came to me : brought, Molly told me, by a footman in splendid livery. It is the only love-letter I ever received.

"Dearest Nancy! Dearest Nancy! Dearest Nancy!" Thus the letter began. How tender and sweet were the words! "All night long have I been awake with thy loving idea in my mind, so that I had no desire to sleep, but would fain lie awake for ever. It is now six of the clock, and I am sending thee this note for a Valentine to greet thee on thy pillow. In an hour or two thou wilt be mine. Edward has arranged everything. We have only to do as he tells us. It is pleasant to obey for one's own happiness. Well, I enter this day upon a life of obedience. This world may obey me, but I shall obey my Nancy. It is like taking the vow of a monk. I take the vow of poverty, for all my wealth is thine, to the uttermost farthing : and of constancy to thee : and of celibacy, except to thee : and of obedience. You shall hear me take those vows at the altar.

"A pretty story Edward had to tell me about that fencing-bout. My dear, it was no fencing-bout, but a battle with Edward, Captain Sellinger, of the Horse

Guards, and a Corporal on one side, and half-a-dozen traitors and would-be kidnappers on the other. They were peppered. I must thank Captain Sellinger at the first opportunity. Edward will procure for the Corporal a commission in the Royal Marines. It is a pretty story, and it must be kept private for the sake of certain ladies of whom we know something. If Edward was endeared to me before, by a thousand acts of friendship, think what I must feel for him now when he has risked his life to save my liberty. Everything was arranged: a coach in readiness: a ship in waiting. Well—Providence has interfered, for which I am, I hope, properly grateful.

"Thou wilt be in bed, my dearest, when you get this note. Rise, Nancy, and in thy morning prayers remember me. This day shall see us to the altar, and ever after shall we be happy as the day is long in each other's arms. My dearest—my dearest—my dearest. Thy fond lover, GEORGE."

Did ever a girl receive so peremptory an order to get up and dress in order to be married? Yet did ever girl kiss the bridegroom's letter with greater fondness? Did ever girl obey so readily and so joyfully, as thinking to make her lover happy if she could?

I dressed: I took my letter to my cousin's room and showed it to her. She, too, made haste to rise. I called Molly: I told her that it was my wedding day: that I was to be taken away, but not far, by my husband: but that I should expect to keep her in my service.

While she dressed my head, she told me about the

terrible battle and the boiling broth. I rejoiced over the bravery of our side, and congratulated her upon her contribution. One man, she said, was carried off wounded, and perhaps dead : there was a red pool of blood only just dried up on the floor to show that his wound was desperate. I shuddered. Was a fight, with a death, of good omen to a wedding-day ? But then the fight was in a good cause and the right side won.

"Corporal Bates," she said, "is well-nigh off his head. He struts about this morning like one possessed. The gentlemen gave him fifty guineas : the other gentle-man—yours, Miss Nancy—sent his wife fifty more : they are rich : the children are to have new frocks : Mrs. Bates is buying a new frock : and the Corporal is to be called henceforth Lieutenant."

I was pleased, indeed, to hear of his good fortune.

"The Doctor is gone," she continued. "They took away his papers and they let him go. If he returns, he will be hanged and drawn and quartered for a French spy."

That, too, was a pleasant thing to hear.

"Well, Molly," I said. "We shall all, I hope, prove fortunate over this event. Meantime, wait for your share, till I go to my new home which I have not seen in St. Catherine Wheel Court."

"Miss Nancy, may I go to the church, too?"

"Surely, Molly. I could not be happy unless thou wert present. The church is—we shall find out where it is presently. It may be St. James's ; or St. Martin's-in-the-Fields : or even St. Margaret's, Westminster : but we shall find out."

"The bridegroom would like a dish of chocolate and some buttered toast before starting," she said. "The mornings are cold and raw. You, too, Miss Nancy, must take something before you go out."

"Everything," said my cousin, always ready to welcome a cheerful aspect of Fate, "has turned out for the best. You suffered from melancholia at Dartford: you repined at that affliction: but for that you would not have come to me. You gave up the Society: but for that you would not have met your lover. You were ignorant of the world: but for that artless ignorance he would not have loved you. It was necessary to tell your brother Joseph something of your change. He came and stormed like a madman, yet learned all that it was proper for you to tell him. You need not keep him informed, for the future, of your doings. You have explained to him the things which concern him : a lawyer will make him disgorge what I verily believe he intended to keep altogether: it matters not how rich George may be— a few more thousands are always a pleasant addition to one's fortune. Thy George, dear Nancy, will be a pattern to all husbands: sober, religious, virtuous, of kindly temper : he is everything that a husband should be. Add to this that he is young, strong, and well formed. What matter if he expects obedience? A wife should obey her husband cheerfully. I always did, the more readily because Reuben would never command anything unless he knew that it was in accordance with my wishes. What was the result, my dear? How was I rewarded? The whole of his fortune devolved upon me: not a life interest, or a moiety, or a third part, on which some poor widows have to scratch along. Obedience? 'Tis the first mark of a good wife that she obeys cheerfully and readily. An obedient wife makes an obedient husband. Obedience ensures for a wife her own way : it gives the responsibility of work to the man and the enjoyment of the harvest to the woman. Never, my dear, was apostolic injunction more misunderstood than that in which is enjoined obedience in women."

So she went on chattering while we busied about the bridal dress, giving me such hints and advice as to the management of a husband as wedded women like to bestow out of their experience. The sum of it all is, I believe, that if two people love each other they will give way to each other, study each other, take care not to insist too strongly on their own wishes, and never think obedience a duty, but a pleasure. Alas! It was love's labour lost, this advice, as you shall presently see.

I put on my white satin frock over a hoop : Isabel trimmed it with laces and with white ribbons : my hat she also trimmed with white ribbons, very fine ; and she gave me a pair of white silk gloves.

"It is said," she said, "that thou wilt be married with so few spectators. I could wish all the Society of Friends to be in the church : thy brother Joseph at the head of them. And Robert Storey to stand like a play-actor: and the fine Court ladies in a row: all to see thy beauty, and to burst with envy at the spectacle of thy great fortune."

"Oh, dear cousin! There will be enough—with thee and Molly and Edward."

"My dear," she stepped back and looked at me from top to toe, "thou art, indeed, a charming bride! Some women at the altar make charming corpses : as for thee, thy colour so comes and goes ; thine eyes are so bright, thy cheeks so soft! Oh, Nancy, Nancy!" she caught me in her arms— "How shall I live without thee? Oh, what a happy three months have I spent! and now, though everything ends as it should, I am loth, I am loth, my dear, to let thee go."

I turned over my drawers to see what things Molly should bring me. I had not much to fit out a bride. But for Isabel I could not have made a decent appearance. Among the things which I turned out, one was the miniature of Mademoiselle de la Vallière, first love of King Louis XIV. of France. Her sweet sad face looked upon me as if with pity. Yet why should she pity me, the happiest and most fortunate girl in the world? I put it down again, somewhat dashed. Such little things suffice to jar upon one. We are full of joy and happiness : then we remember something ; we hear something ; we see something ; and lo ! it is like cold water poured upon the boiling pot : the water sings no more, the bubbles die : it is like an ice-cold wind blowing over the meadows on a warm spring day : our joy is suddenly sobered.

CHAPTER XXII.

God Save the King!

By half-past seven I was out of Molly's hands, dressed and ready for my wedding. I sat down to wait. The clock ticked slowly, slowly: the hands seemed unable to move. My cousin sat down beside me—I remember all she said—I remember all that was said and done by everybody till the end. My cousin talked. Her voice was like the voice of a person afar off: yet I heard it, and I remember all she said. It was the shadow of coming calamity that weighed down my heart. Molly brought some chocolate. My cousin took a dish, talking the while.

" My dear," she said, " what shall I do without thee? How shall I live? What shall I do in the long winter evenings for a companion? The house will be empty. The Corporal, now that he is a Lieutenant, will go abroad. The Lieutenant's lady—poor Mrs. Bates!—will give up her garret. Molly will go to cook for thee: the old Doctor, the long lean Don Quixote, the Knight of the Sorrowful Countenance—he, too, has gone: to his own place—villain! Pity the wretch was not pinked, as the men say, last night. The only person left at night will be the Captain with six bottles inside his belt. What shall I do?

" I will go and stay with you, my dear, whenever thy husband is away at his country seat. Sometimes when he is at home he will ask me. I think he must love me. I am sure he does. But for me, he would never have met his Nancy. I was the instrument of Providence: the poets would call me Love's Messenger—Venus's handmaid. He has always spoken kindly of what he calls my kindness to thee, my dear, as if any one with a heart could help being kind to the sweetest and fondest of her sex.

"Some day, my dear, in spite of what has been said, thou wilt be a great Lady. Oh! it will be impossible for him to avoid that end. He will grow only more affectionate as the time goes on: such a man as this is always constant: thine image will be carven so deeply on his heart that he will never be able to tear it out. I know that look. I know that slow, deliberate mind, which gradually grasps a thing and never lets it go. Then nothing will do but he must publicly place thee beside him in the full light of day. Well, there is no position which thou wilt not grace. And to think that Robert Storey dared to aspire to thine hand! Well! Fools rush in where angels fear to tread, as the poets say.

" Strange, that he has never told us his name and family. He reserves it to be a surprise at the wedding. Captain Sellinger knows, and he will not believe that we do not know. Corporal Bates—now Lieutenant —knows, and pretends that we know as well. The old French spy and traitor knew. All the world knows, it seems, except the person most concerned.

Patience, my dear. It is now a quarter to eight. In half an hour thou shalt know.

" That was a pretty piece of business downstairs last night. To carry off two young men of rank and fortune : to design them for a French prison : I suppose to have them held to ransom. It is like an old story of Moorish pirates. I am sorry they let the wretch go in peace. My dear, our friends might have been killed. Now we understand what was meant by his talk about loyalty. Fine loyalty, truly! Wretch!"

At eight o'clock the rumbling of wheels told us that our bridegroom had arrived. He jumped out and ran up the stairs with the eagerness of a bridegroom, threw himself into my arms, regardless of my head, which he nearly ruined, and regardless of Isabel's presence. "My dear!" he cried. "My dear!" and kissed me again and again. All the weight and fear left my heart at sight and touch of my bridegroom. I was perfectly happy again.

Then he perceived Isabel. "Madam," he said, bowing low. In the presence of his bride a man may well have eyes for none other—even for Mrs. Reuben Storey. "Pray forgive me."

"Dear Sir, there is nothing to forgive, and most heartily do I wish you joy."

He kissed her hand and laughed. "Joy!" he cried. "I am the most joyful man in the whole world. I would exchange places with no one."

"Not even with the King?" said Isabel.

He changed colour in a moment. Something touched him. "Indeed," he said, "I do not wish to take the place of the King." Then he recovered. "Where is Edward?" he asked, looking round him.

" He has not yet come."

" Not come? Edward is generally most punctual. Well, it is but just eight. We can afford to wait a little. I shall give him ten minutes more. If he does not arrive by that time, he shall be punished by not being present at his brother's wedding. That would indeed be a punishment for my loyal and affectionate brother."

" Where is the church?"

"I don't know. Edward knows. Oh, he will come! He will come!"

But his face showed a little anxiety.

" May we offer a dish of chocolate against the morning air?" my cousin asked.

" Dear Madam, who can think of food—even of your chocolate, which is the best I ever tasted—on such a day as this? I wonder what makes Edward so late."

The chocolate was brought up, and he took some with a little bread-and-butter cut thin and rolled as Molly knew how to make it.

" Edward," he went on, " is the best of brothers. Some men are jealous of their elder brother: not so Edward. I have heard cases where the younger wished the death of the elder. Not so Edward. There is nothing he would not do for me. He has arranged this business for us, Nancy, all by himself. I believe he loves thee as much as I do—yet without envy. The other day he began to remonstrate, all in thy interests, dear girl. There must be some kind of end, he said. Thy name would suffer if we continued night after night to enjoy the heaven of thy society. He wanted me for thy happiness, dear Nancy, to give up coming here: he tried to persuade me that I could never hope to marry thee—could not hope—those were his very words. In remonstrating Edward is the very devil: these sailors know not round-about methods: they steer straight as a line. Could not hope—he said: his very words. I wonder why Edward is so late." He looked out of the window and then resumed his discourse, talking rapidly as one who is naturally agitated by the occasion. There were other reasons for agitation of mind he knew not. In a word, he was about to take a step the consequences of which no one could foresee. He would not sit down, therefore he kept walking up and down the room, looking continually out of the window for his brother. He continued, therefore, talking. " Well, Edward declared that there were insuperable obsta-cles. What were they? I asked him. They were this: they were that. I must marry into my own class and rank. Everybody would demand it. There would be jealousies: the English nobles love not a *mésalliance*. He instanced cases where jealousies amounting to civil wars have followed such *mésalliances*. I speak freely and frankly, because we have agreed, dear girl, on what we shall do. There will be no jealousies aroused because you will live retired and unknown. The world will not know that I am married. Dear Nancy, think not that I am ashamed of thee. Far from it. Thou art my chiefest pride. The world will

presently discover that I am not inclined to marry—
in my own rank. Then Edward will become of greater
importance. That will not harm thee, my dear, nor
myself. So when he talked to me of obstacles, I
brushed them all aside. 'Obstacle or no obstacle,'
I said, 'I will marry my Nancy to-morrow morning. I
must and I will.' 'Well, George,' he said, 'if you
will you must: if you must you will. As for what will
happen when it is discovered I know not. They cannot order you off for execution on Tower Hill. Yet
there will be mighty indignation in certain quarters.'
He said a great deal more, but I made an end. 'Come
what may,' I swore, 'I will marry my Nancy.''

"And now," said my cousin, "we shall learn your
true name."

"I am afraid you must. Is it true that you do not
know it? Yes—yes—it is true. The sweet and simple friendliness would have been impossible else. It
was because you did not, either of you, know my
name that you were able."

He laughed gently. "To me," he said, "one of
the chief charms of our friendship has been the fact
that you accepted our incognito with no apparent desire to penetrate to the truth."

"Indeed, no!" my cousin replied. "It was enough
for us that we were receiving two gentlemen who
were perhaps of rank, but certainly of good breeding
and honour. Our Quaker experience teaches us to
set no value on rank alone."

"At first we doubted whether you really were
ignorant of our names. The people who live about

St. James's Street for the most part know us. You
were from the country, it is true, or from a part of
London which does not know the faces which are here
familiar. The liveries, the arms, I thought would
proclaim aloud——''

"The Quakers do not know liveries and have no
knowledge of arms."

"So I learned. Well, dear ladies, what happened?
I found myself, for the first time, among people who
were not in the least afraid of contradicting me. If
you only knew the happiness of being contradicted.
You paid me no respect on account of rank—'twas
like stepping out of a prison into the open air: you
sought no favour from me—neither place nor pension
nor office—for yourselves or your friends—how charming to meet such people !"

"Why, Sir," said Isabel, "what could we ask?"

"And you—you offered no favours," he added,
with a blush. "In a word, dear ladies, I learned to
love you because you did not know me. Oh, the
happiness of equality! You never flattered me:
when I spoke in ignorance you corrected me: you
told me things that I had never learned before: you
talked to me about the people—the working people—
you told me what the Quakers mean, but the Church
above all! Dear Nancy, you have learned to love me
wholly for myself as a private gentleman, happy in the
duties and in the blessings of the position." He had
been walking about during this long speech—agitated
in his mind, but full of sweetness and full of dignity.
Then he took my hand and kissed it again. "Well,"

he added, "if you really wish to know—if you cannot wait until we leave the church, I will tell you now."

"George," I murmured when he took my hand.
"No—no—no. Let me be all yours before you tell
me. Then, if you must, tell me when you please.
But oh! believe me. I do not wish to know. I
would that I could never know except that I am
loved by a gallant and noble gentleman, and that his
love is the greatest honour and the greatest happiness of my life."

"Have it your own way, dear—all shall be your
own way. Ah!" he looked out of window again.
"Here comes Edward running."

I sprang to my feet and looked out, beside him.
Why—Edward's face was pale and anxious. He ran
across the court as fast as he could run. He ran up
the stairs—again I felt the dreadful presentiment of
misfortune. He threw open the door. His face was
white: his eyes were wild—

"George!" he cried, gasping in a harsh and broken
voice.

"Well, brother, you are late. But there is plenty
of time. Now, Nancy dear, we will go downstairs."

"Come with me, come, I say," Edward cried.

"With you? No—you are coming with me. This
is my wedding-day. Are you in your senses, brother?"

"Come with me, George. Oh! come without asking why!"

"Leave my bride? Edward, are you mad?"

"I wish I was. Come, George—Nancy, my poor
child, send him away—Mrs. Storey, take her away.

"GEORGE STOOD SILENT, HUSHED, AWED, HIS BROTHER KNEELING
BEFORE HIM."—*Page 291.*

For God's sake, take her into her own room—take off
that dress!"

George stepped forward. "What is it? What has
happened?"

"Everybody is looking for you. Come, you must
come. Oh, Nancy! Nancy! Poor girl! Come,
George!"

"What is it, man?"

Edward threw out his arms. "Then if you must be
told before her—THE KING IS DEAD!"

Then he knelt on one knee, placed George's hand
on his left arm and kissed it, saying solemnly and
slowly—"GOD SAVE THE KING!"

No one spoke for a moment—a long moment. I
know not how long. George stood silent, hushed,
awed, his brother kneeling before him.

Then the whole truth burst upon me. I reeled and
fell and was caught by my cousin. But I was not
fainting. No—I was not in a swoon. I saw and was
conscious of everything.

My lover, my bridegroom who was never to be my
husband, stood with his face turned upwards—alas!
away from his bride. And his face was changed.
There was in it a new authority—a new majesty—
that of the Sovereign: a new expression, that of kingship.

Love had gone out of that face. It was filled with
a new emotion. The young King saw, suddenly, before him, the vastness of his responsibilities: the burden of empire: the great duties. What was the simple
girl beside him, in presence of these things? War

and peace: prosperity and adversity: the happiness
of millions or their misery: the sovereignty of a great,
proud, and free people: their love and loyalty: or
their hate. How could love survive that sudden
shock? In a moment the passion died out in his
heart, though the memory of it might afterwards return. He was the King. Needs must that he marry
in his own class.

How could love remain when the new kingship
filled the soul? Love was gone. I knew—alas! I
knew—alas!—I saw—Love had gone for ever: our
simple, artless Love could not live beneath the shadow
of the Crown.

"Dei Gratia," he murmured. "By the Grace of
God!"

Then he turned to me and his brother rose.

"Nancy," he said solemnly, "Fate calls me. I am
now the King—unworthy. Pray for me. My brother
will see thee. What has passed I pray thee to forget.
Thou art all goodness, Nancy. Farewell. Be happy."
He stooped and kissed my head—and I fell back.

When I recovered they were gone, and my cousin
was weeping beside me.

Sometimes I think it would have been better for me
if I had died that day. But yet . . . no—I have still
these tender memories which I have tried to set down.
I can think of my gallant Prince. I can remember
how he loved me. Surely no woman was ever loved
so well. This short chapter makes all my life. And
I was the first—yes—the first. I was the first. When
I meet him in the world to come, I shall go up to him

fearlessly. I shall say: "George, you loved me first.
I was the first : you loved me before the Other came
across the sea. A man's first love is his best. You
loved me first, and since I have never ceased to love
you, I think that my image must be in your heart
still."

CHAPTER XXIII.

Conclusion.

I SAW my death warrant in his face. When the sudden shock had passed away—when he understood, indeed, that he was King—then the light of love, I say, went out of his eyes. He kissed my forehead, indeed, but it was no longer the kiss of a bridegroom. I knew that it was all over. I knew that I had looked upon his face for the last time.

As for the days that followed, let me forget them; or if that may not be granted, let me pass over them.

Prince Edward came often to sit with me and comfort me. Sometimes he wept with me—it was the kindest heart in the world. "Consider," he said, over and over again, "that a King cannot marry whom he pleases, or where he pleases: he must marry among the sovereign houses of Europe: he must make an alliance that will advance the country either for safety or for policy, or for the good of trade. His sons who will succeed him must be of kingly rank on both sides: his daughters must marry Princes for the good of their own country. Why, if the King were to marry one of his own nobility, there would be such jealousies that his throne would be in danger or succession disputed. Nothing is more certain than that the King must belong to a Royal House and be married into a Royal House."

I do not know that these words comforted me: but they brought the Hand of Fate into the business. It grew to appear inevitable.

" I consented," he said, " to a secret marriage because George was headstrong and determined. But it was with a heavy heart, believe me. Now, consider what would have been your lot. A secret marriage : a wife put away in a cupboard : not allowed at Court. Then the House of Parliament would petition the King to marry—if they knew the truth they would urge him to divorce you. The Archbishop would show that the case was excusable and laudable. If he resisted these importunities, I believe he would have to abdicate. As for your children, what would be their lot ? Born in wedlock, yet not the heirs ; born in the highest rank, yet possessing no rank at all."

Still I was not consoled.

" As for me," he said, " I declare that I have had no happy moment since the time when I perceived that George was in love with you, Nancy—and you with him. For George is in everything serious and sincere. It was in no light mood that he fell in love with you, but seriously and sincerely. If George loved you yesterday he loves you to-day. Yet I do not think that he will speak much about it to me, not even to me. His sorrows he will lock up in his own heart. His memory he will keep under lock and key."

A great deal more he said, but to little purpose.

Time alone could heal that gaping wound, which would leave a horrid scar for the rest of my days.

I heard nothing from the object, or the Cause, of these troubles. At first I thought he would send me a letter : but the days went on : no letter came. Then I thought he would send me a message or a token : but the days went on : there was no token nor any message. No letter, token, or message has ever come to me. And now I am glad to think that he chose to sever the bond as he did, at one stroke.

Edward spoke about it. " At that fatal moment," he told me, " George said ' Farewell.' He meant you, and me, and your cousin to understand, then, that it was ' Farewell.' He has since talked to me, but only once, and with few words. He said, ' What must be done had best be done as quickly as possible. I have said ' Farewell.' "

Wonderful it was how the thought that one might be cast away but not forgotten comforted me. Since I was led to suspect that he was suffering on my account it seemed a duty plainly laid upon me to strive after such resignation as I might attain to.

I told Edward this, and began to put on some measure of cheerfulness. When one is young, it is not difficult, even in the worst kind of bereavement, when the object of one's affection is not dead, but carried away out of reach and beyond the power of speech.

He was patient with me : he saw that I took some small pleasure in his coming. He came, therefore, every day. But everything, as you know, was

changed. The whole house was changed. To begin
with, Captain Sellinger's elder brother had died un-
expectedly, the day after King George the Second,
and left him the title of Viscount De Lys and an
estate, so that he resigned his commission in the
Guards and went to live upon his country estates.
Corporal Bates had become Lieutenant Bates of the
Royal Marines, and was off to sea. He called to say
farewell, looking very gallant in his new uniform and
the gold lace instead of the woollen epaulettes.

"Ladies," he said, "I have come to ask your good
wishes. I am now on the lowest step of the ladder.
A soldier has no chance until he has the King's commission. I start for Portsmouth to-night—I join my
corps on arrival. If I am lucky in action I may be
gazetted to my company in a few weeks. Then,
ladies, to victory or death! It may be the gallant
death of a simple Lieutenant: it may be the funeral
of a hero in Westminster Abbey. Fortune of war!
Fortune of war!"

We asked him what would become of his wife and
children. They were to stay on in the house, but had
come down from the garrets to the second floor. So
he went off, to meet his death, poor man. Yet one
would not pity him, because I am sure that his last
breath must have been one of satisfaction that he had
been permitted to fall on the field. The Doctor was
gone: no one ever set eyes upon that man again: he
and his treacheries and villainies are now, I suppose,
all dead and forgotten.

One day about the end of November Prince Edward

spoke to me seriously about my future. What did I wish to do? Where would I live? I had been reflecting on the subject for some time, and my mind was made up, as you shall see.

I told you that by my father's death without a will I was entitled to half the fortune which he left behind him. My brother had in his keeping the whole, as you have seen.

" I have been wishing," I said, " to converse with you upon this subject. My cousin would have me live on with her. But I am a kind of wife—a woman that was to have been a wife—and I must live as an independent woman."

" Quite so."

" I do not wish to live in London. I desire to find a cottage in the country, where with a garden and a few books, and Molly to wait upon me, I can meditate."

" Nancy, you are but young. This is but a passing storm."

" Nay, it is what you sailors call a *hurricano.* My ship is wrecked well-nigh to sinking."

" Say that you find the cottage, how long before you will pine after London again? "

" Edward, do you know me so little ? "

" Well . . . first, there is this inheritance of yours. Let me at least instruct some of my people to get that out of your brother's hand."

" Yes, if you will be so kind. At first I was set against interfering with my brother at all. Let him keep everything, I thought. It is all he cares about.

But afterwards I reflected that it would be best to have the means of retrieving a little distress in the world. There is so much poverty and unhappiness. I also **am** myself so unhappy that I can feel for all. It is the consolation which the Lord gives to the unhappy." Here Edward turned away his head. "So, if you will be so kind, get for me what is mine. It may be little, or it may be much. And now let me open all my mind."

He took my hand, but said nothing.

"Remember, Edward, I was promised to him—to your brother. I am his, as much as any nun is vowed to Christ. But one short half-hour more, and you would have been my brother."

"Nancy," he said, "I am your brother. I am always your brother. Tell me all—all—that weighs down your poor soul."

"Let me feel, then, that I am in reality your sister. Send me not adrift in the world. Let me feel that I owe something of my life to you, besides the memories. That cottage in the country of which we spoke—give it to me, Edward, yourself, for the sake of your brother. Let it be your gift—your wedding gift—for the wedding which will never be celebrated. Oh! my brother—let me live in a house that I may call my brother's gift. And come to see me sometimes. It will be a consolation to me only to call you brother."

I have done. The house in which I live was given to me by Prince Edward, Duke of York. It hath been rumoured abroad, I believe, that it was given to me by the King himself. The house, with all the furniture, was bought for me, and given to me, I say by Prince Edward, in remembrance of that happy time when the royal brothers came night after night to talk with two simple gentlewomen.

My story is told. Many a Prince has loved a maiden beneath his rank. Love cares not for rank and station. Yet never before, I think, was a poor woman so suddenly dashed to the ground as I myself. I hear people speaking of his happiness, his domestic happiness, with the Royal Lady his consort. Oh! think not I grudge his happiness: he cannot be too happy for me: my prayers go up for him both day and night: but still I feel—yes—I cannot choose but feel—I was the first—I was the first. Before the Other came across the sea, I was the first.

THE END.